HIS CURVY GENIUS

A SMALL TOWN CURVY GIRL ROMANCE

BOOK BOYFRIENDS WANTED
BOOK 10

MARY E THOMPSON

BOOK BOYFRIENDS WANTED

It's summer time in MacKellar Cove and things are getting hot! Someone else is falling in love and we're here for it every step of the way. Never miss a thing when you sign up for Mary's newsletter.

Romancing the Curves comes with subscriber exclusive freebies, sneak peeks, and a first look at everything Mary has to offer. Be the first to know about new releases and sales and all the curves ahead!

SUBSCRIBE NOW AT MARYETHOMPSON.COM

Happy reading!

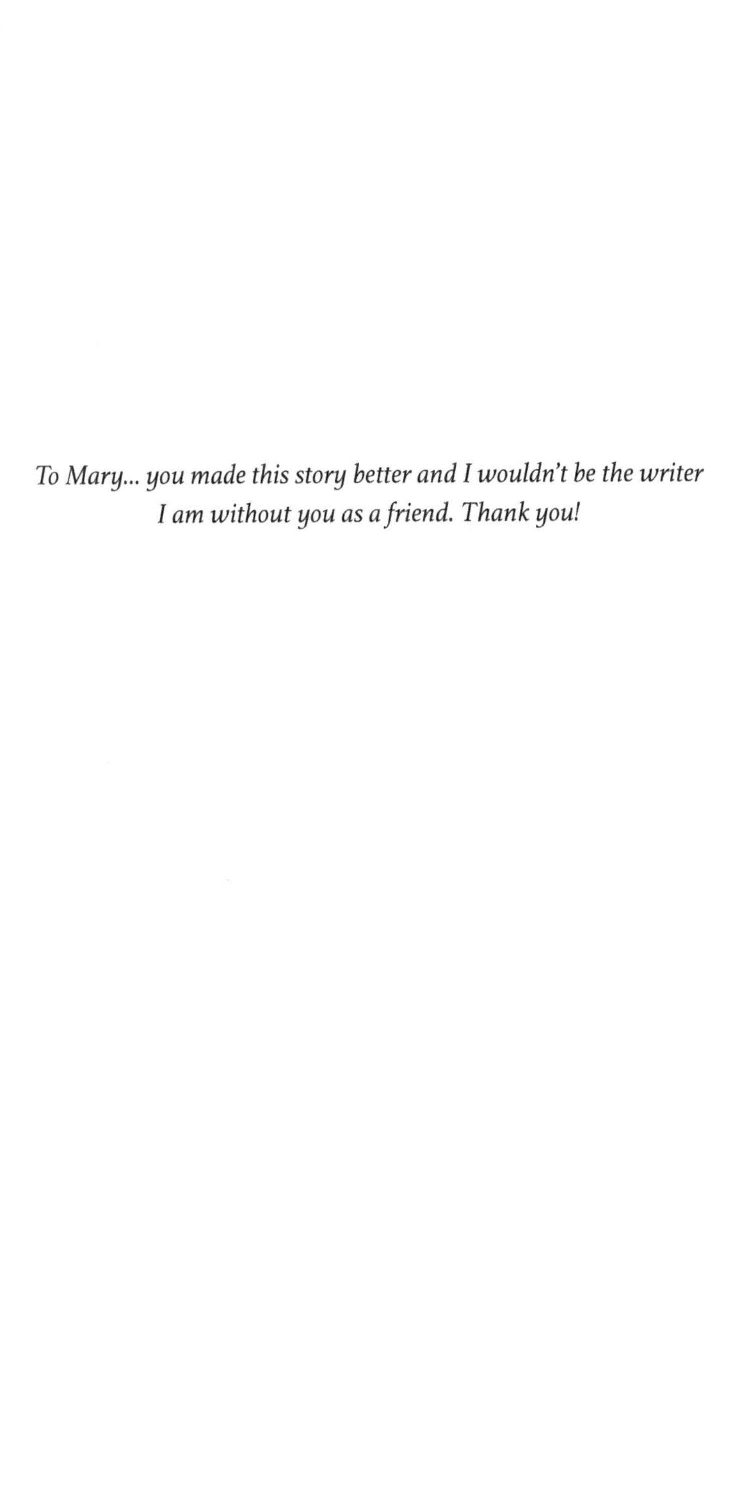

To Mary... you made this story better and I wouldn't be the writer I am without you as a friend. Thank you!

1

KARISSA

Spending the evening with my friends was the absolute last thing I wanted to do. It wasn't fair. I should be able to enjoy time with them. And I would if Xavier Hogan wasn't there, too.

He made everything harder for me. Like my skin was on too tight. I was always tense, especially when I knew I'd have to face him. We'd only spoken a handful of times since he moved to town five weeks ago. No, I wasn't counting how long he'd been in my town. My space. My life. Ugh.

I couldn't see my closest friend and roommate, Finley, or her three-month-old son without seeing Xavier anymore. She was only home one or two nights a week, spending the others with her boyfriend, Trent, and baby George at MacKellar Estate. Not that I blamed her. Their little family was new, and she adored them, and she and Trent were getting married. I got it, but I missed my friend.

So, I sucked it up and went to their house whenever they called and invited me over. Like tonight. For Finley.

I parked next to Finley's car in the driveway and turned

off the engine. I needed a minute before I faced them. Another minute. Just to make sure I was okay.

It really wasn't fair how great Xavier was doing. Between his adorable, sassy teenage daughter and the job Trent created for him, his life was easy. I didn't know the full story about his ex, but I could do the math and didn't want to know.

McJenna was fifteen. Which meant Xavier got together with her mom a few months after we broke up. Maybe. Assuming he wasn't cheating on me when we were together. How the hell did I know? I didn't know the man at all, apparently. If I had, I wouldn't have been blindsided by him.

I blew out a frustrated breath and reminded myself I wasn't there for him. I was there for Finley. And George.

I finally forced myself out of my car and went to the door. I rang the bell and waited for someone to let me in. It was a beautiful day out, sunny and gorgeous and the kind of day that made MacKellar Cove perfect in the summer. A part of me wanted to stay outside all afternoon, but then the door opened and I was beckoned inside.

"How are you?" Trent asked as he pulled me in for a hug. Trent MacKellar was a hugger. He was affectionate and friendly and seemed to think of me as family. It was weird after thinking of him as royalty most of my life, but why the hell not?

"Good. How are you guys?" I asked.

I never asked just about Trent. It felt weird. If Finley wasn't there, I wouldn't be either. They were a package deal in my mind because she'd still be living with me if he hadn't pulled his head out of his ass and realized how lucky he was to have knocked Finley up out of all the women he could have accidentally gotten pregnant and been tied to forever.

"Good. Really good. Fin's starting to talk about a normal work schedule again."

"Really?" I asked, laughing. Finley was determined to go right back to work after George was born. She insisted she wasn't going to be one of those women who altered their life completely when their baby came. Then George arrived. She hadn't worked a full week since. I couldn't blame her, but for her to talk about going back full time was definitely laughable.

"That's what she says."

"I'm sure her parents will be thrilled with that idea."

Trent nodded. "Yeah, I think they've been working on her. But Anna's been amazing. Finley is really grateful she's been willing to help so much."

"That's what Fin told me, too. I haven't gotten to know Anna as much, but I'm glad she was available." Anna was a friend of a friend and started working for Finley before George arrived. She was a God-send and had definitely saved Finley's romance only bookstore from shutting down.

"Me, too." We walked into the kitchen, which was wide open with the back doors thrown wide to let the fresh air in. "Can I get you a drink?"

"Just a water would be great. Thanks."

"Bottled or tap?"

"Either."

"We have that sparkling water Finley said you like. Want one of those?"

"Sure. That would be great." I smiled at Trent as he lit up. He was trying, and I appreciated that. We'd only just been getting to know each other when Xavier moved in, which put the brakes on Trent and I becoming better friends. I felt bad, but I couldn't just put aside seventeen years of regret and act like nothing happened between

Xavier and me. He broke me, and a part of me hadn't recovered.

"Hi, Ms. Karissa," McJenna said from the staircase.

I turned and smiled at the teenager. She was the only reason I tolerated Xavier besides Fin. McJenna was funny and smart and curious, and she made the times I came over much more tolerable. She liked computers and asked me a lot of questions about designing apps and expressed an interest in computers herself.

My mom was a server at a restaurant, and my dad worked at the hardware store. Neither of them knew anything about computers, so when I wanted to learn more, I had to teach myself or find the answers online. If I'd had a mentor, I think my career would have been different. I knew that wasn't who I'd ever be for Xavier's daughter, but I also wanted to encourage her as much as possible.

"Hi, J. How are you doing?"

She shrugged and slid onto a stool at the breakfast bar. "It's so boring here."

"It's summer. It should be fun right now. Just wait until it snows and you can't get off the property."

"Does that really happen?" she asked, her brown eyes wide.

Trent opened and closed his mouth, then handed over my water. "It can, but it won't happen much."

"I don't think I can handle that. I need to move."

McJenna walked away, her feet dragging with each step. I snickered as I watched her go, then I caught Trent's expression.

"Why did you tell her that?" he asked, a smile tugged at the corner of his mouth.

"It's true, isn't it?"

"That happened once in high school."

I chuckled. "It's possible."

"She's already been complaining because she doesn't have friends. I know if she lived in town she'd be able to wander and meet people, but being all the way out here, she's the weird Estate kid."

"Like you were?"

Trent rolled his eyes. "You know how it is."

I nodded. I did. There weren't a lot of Black families in MacKellar Cove. Trent's family was wealthy, and people respected money, so growing up there wasn't as hard as it would have been in other places, but we were still the minority. And for McJenna, being new to town and living on the Estate where other kids didn't just wander by and ask her to hang out, it would be harder to meet new people and make friends.

"Why is McJenna talking about needing to move before it snows?" Finley asked, walking inside with George in her arms.

"I need my godson," I told her, reaching out for him with grabby hands.

Finley handed him over and raised an eyebrow at me.

I carefully avoided her gaze.

"Rissa told J summer is more fun and to enjoy it because when winter comes, we might get stuck out here."

"You did not!" Finley gasped.

"I was joking. Sort of. She needs to go meet some kids. What about Anna's son? Are they the same age?"

Finley shook her head. "Joey's a year older."

"Do we know anyone with a fifteen-year-old? How old is Goldie's son?" Karissa asked.

"I think Paul's fourteen," Finley said.

"Does Valentina have a fifteen-year-old?" I asked.

Finley's brows drew together. "I'm not sure. I know her girls are older, teenagers, but I don't know how old they are."

I made a mental note to stop into Cove Bakery sometime and talk to Valentina about her daughters.

"I'm going to start cooking," Trent said. "Are you okay with that?"

Finley nodded and tilted her chin up for a kiss from him as he walked by. She smiled and watched him walk outside. He said something to McJenna we couldn't hear, then went to the grill.

"How are you?" Finley asked me.

I smiled and focused on George. "I'm good. Busy. You know how I am."

"I do, which is why I asked."

I opened my mouth to tell her the truth when the reason for my hesitation cleared his throat from behind me. I clammed up, nuzzling against George's neck and inhaling the baby smell that calmed me.

"Hello, Karissa," Xavier said.

"Xavier." I couldn't bring myself to look at him, so I didn't. I just waited until he walked outside, letting all of my attention stay on my godson.

"Are you sure you're okay?" Finley asked.

I forced a smile neither of us believed and nodded. "Of course. Why wouldn't I be?"

SITTING across the table from the only man, besides my father and step-father, that I ever loved was downright painful. I never thought I'd see him again when I moved back home, when he said small town life wasn't for him and refused to come with me.

And now, he's living a small town life. Complete with a kid of his own. Guess the joke was on me.

But I wasn't there for him, good or bad. I was there for my best friend to celebrate the first time her newborn baby slept through the night. I didn't know anything about kids, but apparently it was a big deal.

"I was so scared. I went in and checked three times overnight. I was sure something was wrong," Finley said with a laugh.

"Me, too," Trent said. He looked between Finley and the baby with so much love in his eyes it actually ached inside me.

I was happy for them. Really, truly, I was. I was there through all of their ups and downs, and I wanted Finley to have the kind of love she deserved. The kind that made everyone around them believe that love was real and it was out there for all of us.

I would have believed in it if it weren't for the walking heartbreak across the table.

"The first night McJenna slept through the night, I did the same thing. It was a hard adjustment," Xavier said.

"Dad," McJenna said, drawing out the word like only a teenager could.

I forced a smile for the table. The one and only non-parent in the group. The only one who had no idea what it was like to wake up at night and wonder about the safety of another person. I'd always assumed I'd have kids one day, but one day turned into one year, and I was staring down thirty-nine on the other side of a preventative double mastectomy that left me feeling even less like a desirable woman than I ever felt before the surgery.

I didn't regret the choice I made, but seeing my friend

coo and fuss over her tiny little bundle made me think about all the things I never did.

Like find someone who wanted to live in a small town. Someone I could build a life and a family and a future with. Instead, I helped countless other people find love.

Regrets were a funny thing. My mom talked about regrets when she was close to the end of her life. Her regrets were different, but maybe that was a few extra decades and the love of not one but two amazing men that changed her. As for me, I regretted all the things I promised myself I'd do one day but didn't.

"What are you working on these days, Karissa?" Trent asked. He was trying to be nice and bring me into the conversation, but I wasn't really sure I wanted to be included.

"I've been developing something new for a client. I was approached a few months ago about it," I told him.

"A few months? That must be a big project." Trent understood a little about how app design worked, but not much from what I could tell. It wasn't the most exciting topic for people who didn't get all hot and bothered about computers.

"It is, but the pay is really good and it's given me a place to focus my energy lately."

"That's always a good thing. Maybe I should have you design an app for the theater. Something to help with buying tickets or choosing seats or something."

I pressed my lips together and nodded. I hated working with clients who thought they wanted an app but didn't really know what they wanted. It was easier to deal with the ones who knew exactly what they were looking for. Trent hired me to design an app for Finley's store before George was born, but I knew exactly what

Finley wanted and needed. A *maybe I should* was never helpful.

"Can I be done?" McJenna asked. She pushed her plate away from the table and looked at her dad. Her soulful brown eyes tugged at me. I'd never be able to say no to her. Good thing I didn't have to worry about that.

"Put your plate in the dishwasher. We don't need to create more work for Ms. Emily."

She nodded as she stood. Her phone was in her hand before she made it to the dishwasher in the next room, texting someone.

"I don't know how we're going to deal with all that," Trent said to Finley. "I don't think I'm ready for a teenager."

Finley snorted. "I think that's why they start out small. By the time we have a teenager, we'll be able to handle it."

"I hope so. It does not look like a lot of fun to me."

"Especially when you drag your kid across the state to a place she doesn't know and people she doesn't know. I'm pretty sure she hates me," Xavier said. He leaned back in his chair and sighed.

"She agreed to it. She'll be fine. I hated growing up here, but it's a good place for families. And she can't get into as much trouble here," Trent said.

His tone was light, but his words were loaded. I wanted to ask what kind of trouble she got into before they moved, but I didn't have the right.

"Maybe not, but she'll try."

"Are you guys ready for dessert?" Finley asked loudly. "Karissa brought cake."

"I could definitely go for some cake," Trent said. "Thanks. We're glad you could be here tonight. I know we're boring and only talk about baby stuff, but we want you to be comfortable coming over here whenever you want to."

"Thanks," I told him. I would never feel comfortable going to his house, but I would try. For Finley, I would try.

"I also really hope you two can get along again. I know you were friends in college, but—"

"Friends?" I asked, turning to look at Xavier. "You told him we were friends?"

He shrugged like that was the best descriptor for what we'd been to each other.

"Did I say something wrong?" Trent asked.

I huffed a laugh. "No. No, you didn't say anything wrong. But I think us being 'friends' again is going to be a high bar. I mean, maybe I'm wrong, but a prefer to be friends with people I can trust. People I can count on. People who don't spend three years planning a future with me only to decide, out of the blue, that all the times we talked about getting married and building a life together was just fiction."

"That's not fair, and you know it. I told you I didn't want to live in a small town. That there weren't a lot of job opportunities there."

"Yeah, and then you said we could try it."

"I said maybe we could try it. Maybe. In the end, it wasn't for me."

"But it is now?"

Xavier glared across the table at me. "My life has changed a lot in the last seventeen years."

"Well, I hope you're happy with all the changes in your life. Funny enough, my life hasn't changed all that much. But this is my small town. This is where I live. This is my home. And I'll be damned if you're going to make me feel like I don't belong here."

"I never—"

I stood and turned away from him. "I apologize for

running out, Trent, but I seem to have lost my appetite. Fin, I'll catch ya!"

"Rissa," Finley tried.

"Nope. I'm good. Love you."

"Love you," she said.

I let myself out and drove home alone to my condo on the other side of the cove. A year ago, I never would have thought I'd be living alone or living in the same town as Xavier Hogan. Life definitely didn't go the way we planned. Ever.

2

XAVIER

I watched Karissa run toward the door and sighed. Dammit. It had been weeks, and I hadn't made any headway with her. And now...

"Sorry, man. I didn't know she'd take offense to that word," Trent said.

I nodded. I knew. Friends was not even close to what Karissa and I were to each other. But when Trent asked me about her, McJenna was there and there was only so much I could say.

Judging by the look on Finley's face, she got it, but she was on Karissa's side, which meant I was even deeper in the doghouse.

I sipped my wine and let dessert happen around me. I ate the cake Karissa left behind, groaning in ecstasy and wishing I could tell her how much I enjoyed it. She was creative with her baking in college, but nothing came close to the delectable cake in front of me.

"Can I go into town tomorrow?" McJenna asked, drawing my attention back to the table. She'd joined us again when she heard there was dessert to be had.

"Sure. What do you want to do? I can take you after work." I pushed my plate away and leaned back to look at my daughter.

She scrunched up her face and, for an instant, reminded me of her mother. Denise was quick-witted and funny, but she knew her tongue was sharp and would hold back. Not always, but when she did, she made the same face.

"What is it?" I asked, knowing J wanted to say something I wasn't going to like.

"I kind of want to go by myself," she mumbled.

"By yourself?" I arched a brow at my one and only child and wondered if she'd lost her damn mind. Nope, I didn't need to wonder. She clearly had.

"Yeah. You keep telling me this is a safe town and that it's a good place and all these things, but you hover around me like we're in the worst parts of the city in the middle of the night."

I stared at my daughter, my mouth opening and closing like a dying fish. She was right. I didn't like it, but she was right. I had been hovering, and I didn't trust her. I didn't trust anyone. Not with my kid. She was mine, and the only other person on the planet who was supposed to love her as much as I did deserted both of us. How could I trust someone else?

"Why don't you come to my store?" Finley suggested. "Maybe you can ride with me in the morning? There are a few shops close by. Cracked is down the street, and Blake's working. You can wander but have places to go if you get bored or need a backup plan."

I glared at Finley, but there was no heat behind it. She was helping, and I appreciated it, but I wasn't ready for my baby to leave the nest. Even if the nest wasn't mine.

"Please, Dad?" McJenna said. She smiled up at me, her

baby features no longer visible as the young woman she'd become when I was too busy to notice pleaded with me.

"Fine," I said, not liking the whole thing but knowing I had to accept it. She was right. I chose to move to MacKellar Cove for her. To get her away from the less than stellar life she was living in Niagara Falls. She didn't have friends there, not good ones, and leaving meant a fresh start. It was good.

Moving to the town where Karissa lived was just a bonus. A pretty big bonus but still.

Finley and J made plans for when they would leave the next morning. I had a full day at the theater, which meant I wasn't going to be around or available if J needed something.

My circle was getting bigger. I didn't like it.

I cleaned up the dishes from dessert and started the dishwasher. I covered what was left of Karissa's cake and put it in the fridge. Then I went to the patio to tell everyone I was heading upstairs.

"It's not that late yet. You're already going to bed?" Trent asked.

I nodded. "I have to be in early tomorrow. I want to walk through a few things before the contractors show up. They're coming at six."

"That is early. I didn't realize. We could have planned this for another night." Trent looked at Finley for confirmation.

Finley lifted George over her shoulder and patted his back. "Yeah, we definitely could have. I'm sorry."

"It's no big deal. Thanks for taking J tomorrow." I leaned down and kissed the top of my daughter's head. "Be good for Finley. And get some sleep tonight."

"I will," she said as she dodged any further attention. "I'm going to go to my room."

I stood and nodded to my best friend and soon-to-be bride and followed my daughter up the stairs just as George started to fuss.

I said good night to J again and continued past her to my room. She waved without looking up, her nose in her phone.

I closed my bedroom door and groaned. My room was supposed to be an oasis, but it felt more like a prison. I owed everything to Trent, but that reliance on him was starting to feel like I was taking advantage of him. For years, our relationship felt unbalanced, but whenever I brought it up, he insisted he thought of us as family and wanted us around. It would destroy McJenna to move out of Trent's estate, but it was time for me to stand on my own two feet. Nothing reminded me of that more than walking into a newly decorated room that I had zero attachment to.

THE HOUSE WAS quiet when I got up. I showered in my private bathroom and snuck out, making sure I reset the alarm after I disarmed it.

The sleepy town of MacKellar Cove was dead so early. No one was out. I had to admit it was peaceful, even if the quiet gave me too much time to think sometimes.

The old theater was right in the center of town. Trent said it was a popular hangout when he was in high school, but it was definitely not maintained. Which was why we were doing a complete remodel. I wasn't so sure about running it, but I didn't have anything else to do, so I was jumping in with both feet and hoping I could pull it off.

The crew was nowhere to be seen when I arrived, but a silver sedan told me my assistant was already there.

I let myself into the front door, the door we all used for safety reasons, and found Genevieve sitting behind the counter with her computer open, typing away. She didn't bother to look up, just pointed toward the coffeepot and baked goods. Neither of us were fans of the morning and had learned over the last few weeks to coexist but not interact unless absolutely necessary.

I started to feel awake after my breakfast. I took my time walking through the site and getting a feel for the progress we'd made so far. Trent didn't give me a budget to work off of, but I was determined not to go overboard, especially once Genevieve laid out the income projections for the theater. With two screens and the reality of a small town, sticking to a budget was not optional. It was required.

The projection rooms were at the top of the list for renovation. Technology had changed so much that having a projector was no longer necessary. Movies were digital, which meant new equipment and a room that was clean and secure. Thankfully, it was cheap to do. The theaters themselves were going to be a different story.

The screens left hanging in the theaters were useless without a projector. They were also uneven and dirty. Getting rid of them was an easy decision. Finding replacements was not so easy. Neither was finding replacements for the seating.

A knock on the door had me returning to the front of the theater just in time to see Genevieve let the crew in. She tilted her chin back to accept a kiss from Teddy, one of the men on the crew and her husband.

"Are you awake yet?" Teddy asked her.

Genevieve shook her head and shuffled back to her seat behind the counter.

Teddy chuckled and followed the rest of the crew into the first theater.

"Today's the day," David said.

I nodded.

"And you're sure about this?"

I looked over the sea of seats and nodded. We couldn't leave them in. Even though I hadn't found replacements that were anywhere close to the budget I'd set, I couldn't leave the old seats in place. They were worn out and dirty. They squeaked every time they were moved. And they would ruin the entire experience of going to the theater if they were still there once everything else was finished.

"Okay," David said. "We'll yank them all out."

I stood back and watched as he addressed his crew. He paired them into teams to work on the rows of seats. Each section was four seats together as one piece. Getting them out was not going to be an easy process.

"Have you thought about tables?" Genevieve asked. I didn't hear her walk over, but she was standing next to me.

"Tables? In a movie theater?"

"Yep. I haven't been in one like that, but I've heard about them."

"I thought people wanted to relax. All the big theaters have those huge reclining chairs and wide aisles."

"I know, but why do we have to do the same thing?"

I looked at her and tried to make sense of it. We were doing the same thing. We were showing movies. Why would someone want to watch a movie from an uncomfortable chair? Especially when they could go twenty minutes away and find a theater with the expensive recliners.

"It's okay," Genevieve said. "I was just thinking out loud. I thought it seemed like a fun idea. Especially if you themed the two theaters. One for families and one for adults only."

"What does that mean?" I asked. "Adults only? We're not showing porn."

Genevieve laughed. "I didn't suggest that, but glad to know that's where your mind goes, boss. I meant you could serve alcohol and offer food and make it more of a dinner and a show kind of thing. Instead of just candy and popcorn."

I stared at the open space. There were no steps that would limit how we set up the theater. The ground was sloped, but we could work with that. It was definitely an option.

"Dinner and a show? I think I like that. Let's look at photos of other theaters and we'll talk. Tables and chairs should be easier to find than theater seats. And cheaper."

"I agree."

I walked away as the idea rolled around in my head. It would definitely make the theater unique. And would create an appeal other local theaters didn't have. It could be a great selling point.

David's crew worked through the day, removing the seats from one theater until it was all bare floor. Once they left, I walked around, checking for holes and marks that would need to be repaired, marking them all with spray paint so nothing was missed later. The sticky floor was worse where seats had covered the mess left behind by years of neglect and not enough cleaning.

"Do you need me to stick around any longer?" Genevieve asked long past time for her to have gone home.

"Nope. We'll start to make a plan tomorrow and source some seating. Thanks for your help today."

"You're welcome. I'm excited to see this place open again. It's been too long. Make sure you get out of here tonight. Your kid needs to see your face."

I smiled and thanked her. She was right, but I wanted to finish just a few more things.

I went through the websites Genevieve sent me earlier of theaters set up for a show instead of just a movie. One of them had live performances in addition to movies, but I didn't think that would be a huge draw in a place like MacKellar Cove. I couldn't fathom very many people willing to perform for a small town audience.

The fourth place I looked at made me sit up and really pay attention to the design. It was eclectic with mismatched seating. Each table was different and none of the chairs matched. I loved it on sight, but I wasn't sure if Trent would go for something so outside the box. Getting him to agree to tables and chairs was going to be a big enough leap, to have them all different might make his head pop off.

But I saw the quaint quirkiness of it and knew it was the right move. Getting a liquor license might not be easy, but Trent should have some pull. And if we couldn't get a liquor license, we could allow people to bring in their own alcohol.

I never would have thought of any of it without Genevieve, but she was right. It was definitely going to make a difference.

After making a few more notes, I finally packed up and left the theater. The sun was sinking, telling me I'd worked too many hours yet again. I didn't intend to work twelve-hour days, but I couldn't let the work drag on. I needed the theater to open so it could start bringing in money so I would know I was contributing. Not that Trent needed the money, but I needed to know I wasn't being a drain on him. Not anymore.

The house was lit up and loud when I got home. George was screaming at the top of his lungs, and Finley was crying.

I stopped at the edge of the kitchen, wondering what in the hell happened, and caught Trent's gaze.

"Everything okay?"

Trent shook his head. "George has been crying most of the day. Finley didn't even go to work today because he woke up screaming, and we couldn't get him to calm down."

"Gas? Colic? New food?" I asked, pulling the things that upset McJenna from deep in my memory. Those years were a blur at the time, but now, I hated that they were gone. I would have loved to have had more kids. Especially with Karissa, but that wasn't in the cards. Not then.

"We don't know. It's been a long damn day."

"Why didn't you call me?"

"You were working."

"You still could have called." I reached for George. Finley handed him over without hesitation. I flipped him onto my forearm and patted his back gently. He kept screaming.

"I need a minute," Finley said. "I'm sorry. I just need a minute."

I nodded and walked the baby out to the patio. He kept screaming, but I kept patting his back and moving around. I supported his head in my hand and rocked and bounced him.

"This has been the worst day yet," Trent said, following me onto the patio. "He's just been screaming. He hasn't been like this before. I thought Finley was going to walk out."

"She wouldn't. She's not the same."

Trent didn't reply, but he didn't have to. McJenna's mom walked out after a day like the one they were having. She couldn't handle being a mom at all, but she definitely couldn't handle a crying baby. Finley was not like that. Finley always looked at George with love in her eyes. Denise never looked at McJenna that way.

As I rocked and bounced, George started to quiet down. I felt his belly roll, like gas was working its way somewhere. He let out a loud fart, then whimpered and farted again.

"Damn, dude," Trent said, staring at his son. "No wonder he was upset. We tried that, but it didn't help."

"He just wanted to share it with me. But now it's time for Daddy to take over." The stench was filling the air and making me choke.

"Oh, man. Are you sure you don't want to finish the job?"

I laughed as Trent took his son. "You know I would if you needed me to."

"Yeah, I know," Trent said as he cradled his son against his chest. "I got it."

I watched them walk away and missed those moments. I missed my kid. She was growing up far too fast and it wouldn't be long before she was moving out.

Damn.

I took the stairs and knocked on the closed door to McJenna's room. I let myself in when she called out. "How was your day?"

"I didn't do anything. Finley didn't go to work, so I sat in here all day. This place sucks, Dad."

"J," I warned.

"Sorry, but Dad, what am I supposed to do? I don't know anyone. And if I can't go out, I'm not going to meet anyone. Maybe we shouldn't have left."

"You hated it there."

She grunted.

I got it. Nothing was good. And watching Finley and Trent create their own family was making my kid feel like she was a burden. An afterthought.

"It'll get better, J. I promise."

"You said that before, Dad."

She was right. I did. One day I would be right.

3

KARISSA

I READ THROUGH THE LATEST EMAIL FROM MAXWELL Robertson and put the finishing touches on my proposal. I checked the clock on my computer and switched over to the meeting request he sent me. When it was one minute to the meeting time, I clicked the link to join and waited.

I pasted a smile on my face and stared straight at the screen, waiting for him to appear. When he did, I waved. "Hello, Mr. Robertson. How are you?"

"Good morning, Ms. Thomas. I'm well. How are you?"

"Good, thank you."

"Good, good. I know we were supposed to talk about your proposal today, but we have decided to go with another designer." His dark gaze avoided the screen for a moment, like he was looking at someone on the other side of the computer.

I flinched, my smile slipping. My eyes narrowed, and I tilted my head. "Excuse me?" We were having a meeting to discuss my proposal. The proposal he hadn't even heard yet.

"We've been doing our due diligence on all the designers we've spoken to, and your name came up with a colleague."

His beard twitched when he spoke. It was peppered with gray in the dark brown, and his dark skin was weathered and loose around his eyes. I thought he looked kind when we spoke the first time, but now I saw him in a very different way.

"Um, okay?"

"We understand this is a competitive business, but the colleague was unable to give us a positive recommendation for you."

I wracked my brain to think of who might have given me a bad recommendation and only one name came to mind. It had been years since we worked together, but I'd heard a rumor lately that he was in danger of closing his business because of trouble with the app I designed for him. An app he refused to hire me to maintain.

"So, you're not willing to hear my proposal based on the word of one colleague? I would assume any reasonable business person would want to hear from more than one colleague. I would be happy to give you the names of some of my clients who've agreed to be references for me."

"That won't be necessary. We have already awarded the contract to someone else."

My brows shot up. I wanted to tell him exactly what I thought of his business practices, but instead I said, "Well, thank you for letting me know. I wish you the best of luck."

I hung up before he was able to reply.

Fuck.

I lowered my head into my hands and groaned. The project I was working on was almost finished, and I needed something else when it was done if I was going to pay my bills. I was counting on the money from Mr. Robertson's project. I thought it was as good as mine. When we spoke the first time, he sounded like I was the only designer they were seriously considering. The proposal felt like a formality more than anything else. I spent hours creating it, and now it was junk.

I deleted the email from him about the call, then went through and filed all the emails from Mr. Robertson into my closed folder. I wasn't excited about the project, but I was excited about the money. And about the work.

I'd been stuck since Xavier arrive in MacKellar Cove. Trapped inside my own mind. Why was he really there? And what did he want? He talked to me like he still knew me, but he didn't. We hadn't spoken in a lifetime. His daughter's lifetime.

Bitterness welled up inside me. He went out and lived his life. He did the things he wanted to do. And he did them without me. I didn't hate him for it, but I regretted that I hadn't done more. I didn't have a family or a significant other or anything beyond my career. And if I couldn't come up with some new ideas or secure some work, I wouldn't even have that.

Why did he have to walk back into my life?

Xavier was a dream I let go of a long time ago. He was someone from my past, not my present or my future, and I needed to forget about him. I needed to push him from my mind and make my world my own once again.

The apartment door opened, and I listened to Finley's shuffling feet as she moved closer to me. I left my bedroom door open since she was rarely home anymore. She quietly peeked in my room and waved when she saw me looking at her.

"How did your meeting go?" she asked.

"I didn't get the job."

"What? I thought you were almost guaranteed it."

I shrugged. "Me, too. Guess I was wrong."

"Well, crap. I'm sorry."

"It's okay. I'll figure something out. How are things going with you? How was yesterday with McJenna?"

"We didn't go. Or, I didn't go. It was a rough night. After celebrating George sleeping through the night, he didn't sleep at all. The irony."

I snorted. "Sucks, doesn't it?"

"Yep. I felt bad for ditching McJenna. She really needs to get out of the estate."

"It'll get easier when she's in school."

Finley nodded. "I know, but I feel bad for her. I wanted to help."

"I'm sure she gets it. Having a baby is hard."

Finley nodded again and looked around. She was avoiding something.

"Just say it, Fin."

She looked at me like she was surprised I was able to read her. We'd lived together for years. I knew her as well as I knew myself.

"We finally set a date," she said softly.

"What? That's amazing! Congratulations. When is it? Why don't you seem happier?"

She fiddled with the massive ring on her finger and chewed on her lower lip. "It means moving out."

"Um, yeah. Of course. We always knew we wouldn't live together forever."

"Yeah, but it's been years. And I feel like I'm just ditching you. And you didn't get this job, and—"

"Finley, stop. You're getting married. It's exciting and fun and amazing. You found the person you're going to spend forever with. You should be thrilled, not worried about me. I promise, I'll be okay."

"Yeah, but—"

"Finley, no. No buts. You love Trent, and he loves you, and you have George. It'll be easier when you live together, and you're a unit. You need to be together."

"I just... It's going to be hard to live anywhere but here." She sat on the edge of my bed and looked around the room. "God, we've done so much here. It's been home forever."

"And you'll create a new home with Trent and George. When are you planning to move out? When's the wedding?"

"We decided on September twenty-fourth. Blake's due in December, so we want to make sure not to go too close to that. September felt right since that's the month we met."

"And are you moving in before then, or after?"

She shrugged. Her gaze slid to the floor.

"Finley, you're allowed to be happy."

"Am I? Because I feel like my happiness has done nothing but hurt you."

"It hasn't been on purpose," I said. When Xavier moved and we realized who he was, I was angry. I wanted to blame anyone and everyone, but the only person who was really to blame was Xavier. He knew where I lived, and he knew Finley and I were friends. He wasn't surprised the day he moved in when he found me on the patio.

But it still hurt. Even though I didn't blame Finley or Trent, it was hard to be around them and be happy for them and know their happiness brought heartache to me.

"It still hurt you. And that's not fair. I don't want you to not want to be around us. And if I move out, I'm afraid I won't see you again."

"You'll still see me. We'll get together. We have Book Club every week, and we'll do things. It'll be different, but that's okay."

"I still can't believe he never said anything to Trent about knowing you. All those years."

I shrugged. "It doesn't matter even if he did. It's all in the past. He's in the past."

"Is he?"

"Yes. In fact, I was thinking about checking to see if I had any matches. I need to move on with my life. I took care of my health last year with the mastectomy, and now it's time for me to take care of my happiness. To find someone to share my life with."

Finley didn't say anything, which spoke volumes more than any words. I ignored her silence and clicked through to my app, the one that had brought not only Finley and Trent together, but many of my other friends. The app I created out of my heart with my mother in mind the entire time because she was the matchmaker. She was the one who could see two people who needed each other.

I just wish she'd found someone for me before she passed.

"You know you don't have to be strong for me. Or pretend it doesn't bother you."

"I know, but I can't live my life wondering what he's doing. I spent the last seventeen years trying to forget him. And now that he's back, I'm not going down that path again. I can't. I don't trust that he's here for good."

"He says he is."

"It doesn't matter. Nothing has changed as far as I'm concerned. He has a life, and I have a life, and they don't have anything to do with each other."

Finley didn't reply as I opened the app and looked through possible matches that had come up. The first guy was clever and funny. His profile pic was a hammer, which made me laugh. When I set that up as an option, I wondered if it would actually come up for anyone. Guess it did.

My profile pic was a crown because I was the queen.

I accepted that match and moved to the next one. He checked the boxes, but he wasn't entertaining in his post. He came across as stiff and unbending. I didn't think I could handle that, even in a first meeting. I denied that one.

The third match actually made me laugh out loud. He was sarcastic and self-deprecating, which I loved. If someone couldn't laugh at themselves, I didn't have time for them. I accepted that one, then set my phone back on my desk.

"Are you going to be able to pay for this place alone?" Finley asked.

I'd been wondering the same thing, and I honestly wasn't sure if I was willing to. "I can, but I'm not sure I want to. It would mean having very little extra income."

"Again, I feel like I'm deserting you."

"You're not. I'll figure things out. If I stay for a few months and then go, it'll be fine. If I decide to leave sooner, that's okay, too." I had plenty of savings and had considered buying a small house, but I didn't know what I wanted to do. I had a lot of choices to make in the next few months.

"Are you sure?"

"Of course. It's okay. Hey, I need to get back to work. Do you need anything else?"

"No, sorry. I'm going to grab some clothes and head back to Trent's."

"That's your place, too. You can call it home."

Her lips turned up in a ghost of a smile. "Maybe one day it'll feel like that."

Finley waved and went to her room. Not long later, the front door closed behind her and I was alone again.

I GOT messages from the two guys I matched with and talked to them a little over the next few days. I was determined to put Xavier out of my mind, but he was taking up more of a residence the harder I resisted.

Sunday night was Book Club. I hadn't seen Finley since she picked up things a few days earlier. She was smiling and looked more rested when she let me into Book Boyfriends Unlimited.

"Did George sleep again?"

She groaned. "Yes, thankfully. It's been a good weekend."

"That's great news. How's everything else going?"

"Good. My mom is driving me a little nuts. She's anxious to start planning."

I laughed. "Of course she is. She's going to enjoy this."

Finley nodded, laughing as she led the way to the back where we all sat. "I'm almost dreading it. I love my mom, but it's going to be a little crazy."

"You'll survive. It's nice she wants to be involved."

Finley hesitated, then nodded. When Blake and Ian got married, Blake's mom was barely involved. Melody and Willow's mom was difficult at best, and my mom was already gone. Finley was lucky.

"I need to remember it could be very different." Finley's voice was softer, regretful.

Before I had a chance to say anything else, someone knocked on the door. Finley left to answer it while I pulled out my phone to look at the book we'd all read. I finished it the night before, and even though we didn't always talk about the book, I wanted to refresh my memory of the story.

A wounded soldier returned home to help his father after a stroke left him unable to care for himself, and he met the home health assistant who was hired to take care of his father. The two of them developed a friendship that turned into more as the father told them the story of falling in love with his mother.

It was two stories in one, following both men as they found themselves and love in someone unexpected.

I enjoyed the book more than I thought I would. It reminded me that love was possible even when we doubted it.

"Hey, Rissa," Blake said, joining me on the couch. Her newly expanded belly led the way into the room. She was four-and-a-half months pregnant, but her belly was making sure the entire world knew.

"How are you feeling?" I asked her.

"Really good. I have energy for now. Julie keeps saying it won't last and to enjoy it while I have it."

"Finley was that way, too. But you should be good for a few more months."

"I hope so. Right now, I'm eating everything in sight. The little one is growing."

"Are you going to find out the gender?" I asked.

"We haven't decided yet. Ian wants to be surprised, but I'm leaning toward finding out. In a way, it doesn't matter because we're going to have a neutral nursery and all the big items will be neutral. But I struggle to not know." Blake scrunched up her nose.

"I wanted to know," Finley said. "I needed to have some feeling of control over the shitshow that my life was at the time."

"I get that," Blake said thoughtfully. "I think I just don't like being in the dark about anything. If someone knows, I want to know."

"That's how I am, too," I admitted. "I don't think I would have waited if I'd ever had kids."

"You could still have kids," Blake said.

I shook my head. "I gave up on that dream. A long time ago. And I'm okay with it."

"She's back in the app," Finley provided as she walked away to let more people in.

"You are?" asked Blake. "What made you decide to start dating again?"

Melody, Willow, and Elise heard the end of Blake's question.

"Are you dating Xavier?" Elise asked.

"No. Definitely not," I said.

"Why not? I thought he was your one and only," Willow said.

I shook my head. "Once upon a time, I thought so. But that was a lifetime ago. A lifetime I let go of."

"Did you, though? Did you really let go of it?" Melody asked.

"I had to. We wanted different things. And neither of us were willing to give up what we wanted for the other. I second guessed that choice for a long time, but when Mom got sick, I knew it was the right decision. I got to spend her last few years with her. To be with her at the end. If I'd followed Xavier and built a life with him, I would have resented him when I missed out on being with my mom. And now, it's too late for us."

I shrugged like it was no big deal, even though it was. All the major things in my life made me think about Xavier. When my mom died and when I had my mastectomy, I thought about him the most. It would have been nice to have him, or someone, there with me, but it wasn't meant to be. I survived those things alone. I survived them with my friends. Never with Xavier. I didn't need him in my life.

"Why is it too late?" Melody asked. "If you're dating, why can't you date him?"

"We were kids when we dated. It was special and magical and amazing, but it wasn't real life. We got to be young and crazy together, to enjoy our early twenties together, but the challenges of life, we tackled alone. Too much has happened. He's a stranger to me."

"He doesn't have to be," Blake said.

I forced a smile and shook my head. They didn't get it. They were all in relationships and happy. They saw love as something real that was right there every day. For me, it was a fantasy. One I desperately wanted to believe in but struggled to grasp. It had always been that way.

"If Karissa doesn't want to date X, she doesn't have to," Finley said. "He lied to everyone and ambushed her. She deserves better than that."

"Thanks, Fin," I said.

She smiled at me, but her gaze was worried instead of sure. "I just want you to be happy. And you haven't been since he got here."

"I'm fine. I'm happy. Xavier Hogan has zero effect on me. I promise."

I grabbed a slice of cake and smiled broadly. Maybe if I pretended, we'd all believe it one day. Even me.

4

XAVIER

I LOOKED AT THE LONG LIST OF THINGS I NEEDED TO accomplish and groaned. I wasn't sure it was ever going to get done. I was already working six or seven days a week, and it felt like zero progress was being made.

I needed to take a step back. I hadn't done that since we arrived. Six weeks working sixty plus hours was taking a toll on me. Life had been nothing but work and think about Karissa. Since I wasn't making progress on either front, it was time to regroup.

David and his crew were already gone for the day, so the theater was quiet. Genevieve was finishing up, and she wouldn't be far behind them. If I was going to take a day off, I needed to talk to her before she left.

"Hey," I said when I found her packing up her computer behind the old snack counter.

"Hey. I was going to come find you in a sec. Anything else you need from me today?"

I nodded and hated that her smile slipped. "I'm sorry. I know. I need a day off. And this is shitty for me to say because I know you do, too. Neither of us can work like we have been. There are a lot of decisions that need to be made, and I need to take a step back for a day and get a separation from here. Can you handle things tomorrow?"

"Of course," she said, her voice and face tight.

"From here on out, you are taking all your weekends off entirely. And I want you to schedule one weekday off every other week. We'll alternate weeks."

She tilted her head and narrowed her eyes at me. "I don't have a lot of vacation."

"Let me worry about that. You will not lose pay. All the hours you've already worked are enough that you should be taking time off. That's another thing. I want you to start working eight-hour days."

"Are you almost out of money?"

"No. This has nothing to do with the money and every-thing to do with us needing to function. I know I'm useless to my kid when I get home. She's not adjusting to life here. I need to spend some time with her, and I need to get away from here for a little while. And if I'm feeling that, I'm guessing you are, too. I'm going to talk to Trent about paying you a salary for the rest of the project and creating a job description that works for both of us once this place is up and running."

"Salaried? That means I won't get paid for my overtime." Genevieve didn't look too thrilled with that idea.

"Yes, but I don't want you working so much overtime."

"I need the money to pay my bills. Teddy doesn't have insurance with his job, so we have our own. It's not cheap, and we're saving up so one of us can be off work when we start having kids."

I took in the panicked tone of her voice and nodded. "I

get it. I promise, I do. I'm not going to have this hurt you. Let me talk to Trent, since he's the one with the money, and we'll come back to this on Friday. If what we come up with isn't going to work for you, we'll keep things how they are. Okay?"

She hesitated, then nodded. Her brown eyes were leery of me, but she didn't argue.

"Is there anything else you need tonight?"

"Nope. All set. Have a good night. And let me know if you need me tomorrow. I will still be available, if necessary."

"I will. Thanks, boss. Night."

Genevieve walked away with a tightness to her shoulders that wasn't usually there. I really did understand her concerns. I was learning a lot about living in a small town with Finley around all the time. She had her own health insurance, too. She paid all her own medical expenses out of pocket. And she paid her own taxes and everything else. She worked hard, but she made it clear she'd been worried about how she was going to pay for George before Trent stopped being an ass and stepped up to help.

When McJenna was born, I had a job with health benefits. It wasn't cheap, but it wasn't impossible. Taking care of her was so much easier without that one thing to worry about. And if I'd had to worry about it, or worry about my hours or my pay getting cut, it wouldn't have been possible to care for my kid.

I would do everything in my power to make sure Trent knew how invaluable Genevieve was to the theater, and to me. I wanted to bring her on as a full time, permanent, salaried employee with full benefits. Hopefully, he would go for it.

I walked through the theater one more time, starting to see it coming together even as I wondered how it would. I turned off all the lights and locked up, heading home for the night to see how McJenna's day was.

The house was unusually quiet. After a minute, I heard the soft murmur of voices on the patio. Finley loved it out there. I couldn't blame her. The view was spectacular, and the overall feel of it made everything else melt away. It was the only place in the estate I felt comfortable.

The four of them were sitting around the table with McJenna holding George. She was smiling at him, cooing at the baby. Fuck, it hit me hard. McJenna was the reason I never looked Karissa up. Wishing my past with Karissa had turned out differently felt like I was saying I wish I hadn't had my daughter. I loved McJenna. She was my world. I wouldn't trade our life for anything.

But I would be lying if I said there weren't times I wished Karissa was her mother instead of Denise. That Karissa and I had built a life together. A life with more kids and the two of us.

For whatever reason, that wasn't meant to be. When I met Trent and found out who he was, I couldn't tell him about Karissa. I wasn't sure if they knew each other, and if they did, I wasn't sure I wanted him to invade those memories of her. I didn't want to know who she was before we met, or who she was after. She was frozen in time for me, forever twenty-one and happy and mine.

Watching my kid with her 'cousin' broke my heart a little. J would have been a great big sister. She would have loved any kids I had after her. She still would, but she was going to college soon. She was going to find her own path, and I could only watch as she walked down it, away from me.

I wanted to give her the world and be there as she

claimed all of it, but she was going to have to find her own way. And it hurt.

"Hey, you're home," Finley said, noticing me in the doorway.

I moved outside, my gaze locked on McJenna and George. "Yeah, long day."

"They all seem to be long," Trent said. "How are things going?"

"We're making progress," I lied. No, it wasn't a lie. It just felt like it because the plan I put together was unreasonable to begin with, but I wasn't willing to let the construction go longer than necessary. Not when I was only a drain on Trent's bank account until the theater started bringing in something.

"That's great news. Are we going to be able to open as planned?"

"Of course. I won't let you down. But I need to talk to you about something else."

Trent glanced at Finley and McJenna and nodded toward the house. Finley owned her own business and McJenna had been a part of enough of our conversations about money over the years that it didn't bother me to talk in front of them, but I wasn't going to argue.

Trent walked behind the island in the kitchen and pulled out a bottle of water from the fridge. He offered me one, then nodded for me to say what I needed to say.

"I want to bring Genevieve on full time. I know it's going to change things, but I can see that she's feeling the same way I am."

Trent tilted his head. "And how is that?"

I drew a deep breath and let it out slowly. Admitting I couldn't do everything wasn't easy. Especially when I saw myself as someone who could do anything. But I had to be honest with Trent. He was my boss. And I wasn't going to hide everything from him.

"I'm burned out. I need a break. Not a long one, just a day, but I can't keep working like I have been."

"Thank God. Why have you been killing yourself?"

I shook my head and ran a hand through my hair. I really needed to get it cut. One day. "I want to get it all done. I'm just syphoning money from you, and it's not okay."

"This is my business. I decided to buy the old theater. You're not syphoning anything. You're making it possible to earn money from it."

"But my salary—"

"Is probably not even close to what you deserve for the work you're taking on. Listen, I get that it's different. And it's going to be hard to transition from what you were doing to this. But I always loved that theater. My mom took me there when I was a kid, and I hung out there in high school. When I moved back, I wanted to take Finley there, but she told me it was closed. It's one of those things I always thought about when I thought about MacKellar Cove. Pushing you to take on the project—"

"You didn't push me."

Trent breathed a laugh and shook his head. "We both know I did. I should have gotten my hands dirty and managed it, but with George…"

"I needed something to do. You created a job for me. And I appreciate it, but—"

"Whoa, is that really what you think? That I created that job? That I didn't really need you?"

I shrugged. "I mean, yeah. I know you trust me, so I was an easy choice, but I also know I didn't have an income when we moved here. I have my savings, which I only have because you let us live with you forever, but it wouldn't last that long, even though I'm still living off of you."

"Shit," Trent breathed. He shook his head and closed his eyes. "I never meant to make you feel like you had to do this. Or that you were anything other than family to me. If I had a brother, I'd be doing the same for him. You're my family. You and J. Yes, I have Finley and George now, too, but that doesn't mean you and J are any less important to me."

"But—"

"No. Listen, I need to know if you want to be doing that job. You're working yourself to death, and if you want me to hire someone else, I will. I asked you to do it because I knew you could and I knew you'd make it amazing, but you don't owe me anything. Ever."

Trent stared at me for a long moment, waiting for me to answer. His gaze didn't drift, not even when George whimpered outside, then started crying.

"I don't know if I can meet the original deadline," I confessed.

"I never thought it was reasonable."

"I wanted to get everything done ASAP so it would start making money."

"The theater is going to be something for locals more than tourists. It's not going to be a big draw. I don't care if it's done before summer is over. As long as it's done right."

"It will be," I assured him.

"Does that mean you want to stay on and finish it?"

I nodded slowly. "I do. I'm enjoying it. And Genevieve is amazing. She's smart and creative and her ideas are going to make it even better than I ever thought it could be."

"Good. What will it take to bring her on full time?"

"Money. She works a lot of overtime to earn the money. Her time is always well spent, but if we're going to rework the timeline and slow down a little so we can breathe, I'd like to move her to salaried so she doesn't have to worry about the overtime."

"Do you have a number in mind?"

I nodded and told him what I wanted to pay her. It was more than she was making weekly with her overtime, not by much, though.

"How does that compare to what she's making?"

"A slight increase."

"Offer her fifty percent more than her highest week. As a salary with full benefits. When the theater is up and running, is she going to stay on?"

"I hope so. I want to come up with a job for her."

"She sounds like someone we should have on the team. I'm okay with that. Get an idea of what schedule she'd like to work. If you want her as an assistant still, that's fine, but if you think there's something else she should do, get her input and let me know. I want to be involved with this project, but I know I'm still going to be traveling and managing the hotels. I won't be able to handle the day-to-day stuff. That's why I wanted you there."

I nodded, finally feeling like my place wasn't destroying him. "I appreciate it. Really."

"If that changes, let me know. We've always been honest with each other. At least, mostly." He leveled me with a look that said he wished I'd told him about Karissa.

"You know why I couldn't."

He nodded. He said he understood, but I wasn't sure he really did. I wasn't sure I really did sometimes.

"Are you okay with me taking tomorrow off?"

"I'm not your keeper. You are salaried and you make your own hours. You don't have to answer to me."

I nodded. "Thanks."

He clapped me on the shoulder and nodded to the patio. "Let's eat. We waited for you, and we're all hungry. Maybe Finley has some ideas of things you and J can do tomorrow on your day off. Unless you're planning to spend it with someone else?"

I shook my head. "My one and only girl."

Trent grinned. "For now."

I pressed my lips up into a smile. Karissa was never going to give me another chance.

Finley handed George over to Trent when we walked outside. He snuggled the baby against his chest and took his seat next to her. I took the seat next to McJenna.

"Want to do something tomorrow?" I asked her.

"Go to work with you? No thanks," McJenna grumbled.

"Actually, I'm taking the day off. See the town a little and have some fun."

"Is there anything fun to do around here?"

"There's a lot to do," Finley said. "My brother makes wooden boats and has a few he lets family and friends borrow if you want to go out on the water. My friend is a tour boat guide. There are restaurants and places to eat. We have Catherine Park. MacKellar Cove Inn has a lot of events. And another friend of mine is the director of tourism in the area. I can check with her and see if anything is happening."

"All that in this tiny little place?" McJenna asked skeptically.

"Yep. There are kids your age, too. I know you don't know any of them, but they wander around town during the summer. I usually have to chase them out of my shop a few times because they want to find the good stuff."

"Can I read the good stuff?" McJenna asked.

"No," Trent and I said together.

"You're not dating until you're my age," Trent added.

"If then."

McJenna sighed and rolled her eyes at us.

"I'd recommend going to Cove Bakery for breakfast tomorrow. After that, get on a tour to see some of the stuff around here, especially the castle, then go through the shops around Catherine Park. You can grab lunch from Cracked and eat in the park. That's fun to do. Oh, and you have to go on the Riverwalk. O'Kelley's is right there. They have food for lunch if you want to eat there instead. But it's fun to eat outside. Then again, we do almost every night."

"Breathe, babe," Trent said, putting his hand on Finley's arm. "They don't have to do everything in one day."

"I know, but Xavier's been working so many hours that he really hasn't seen the town, and McJenna hasn't done much either, and I—"

"We'll have more days. I'm not going to work as many hours as I have been. I need downtime, too. We moved here to slow down, and I've been running around a little crazy." I caught McJenna's gaze, hoping she was willing to trust me that things would get better.

"We'll see," McJenna said instead.

"J," Trent warned.

"She's right," I said. "We agreed things would be better, and I haven't let them be. You haven't met anyone, and I haven't been around. But I'm going to change that. Tomorrow, we'll get breakfast and go on a tour, and whatever else you want to do. Maybe we'll meet some kids your age."

"Ooh, yay, just what I want. To meet new kids with my daddy hanging around."

"Well, you're going to have to get over that one because tomorrow is for us." I cocked my head with the same attitude she was giving me.

She fought her smile, but I pursed my lips and bobbed

my head at her until she lost the battle and laughed. "You're so crazy."

"Yes, I am. And you're stuck with me, kid."

She shook her head and smiled. The first one I'd seen in far too long. It was definitely time for a day off. And time for some fun with my kid. We were going to make our new life a good one.

5

McJenna came down the stairs a little after eight the next morning. When she saw me sitting at the island, she stopped.

"You're here."

I nodded, wondering why she was confused. "We talked about this last night. I said I was taking today off. Do you not remember?"

She shook her head. "I do. I just didn't think you were actually going to take the day off."

"Wow," I breathed. That one hurt.

"I'm sorry, but lately all you've done is work."

I stood and went to her, taking her hand and pulling her to the island where I had my cup of coffee and was ready to make anything she wanted for breakfast. "You don't need to apologize. It's true. That's part of why I wanted to take today off. I'm working too many hours and I'm not myself right now."

She nodded slowly, like she didn't believe me. I couldn't really blame her. My actions the last few months, years really, said the only thing that mattered was my job. It was going to take more than one day of showing up for my kid to prove I meant what I said.

"How about breakfast? French toast? Pancakes? Eggs and bacon? Omelet? What sounds good? Or we can go out."

"French toast?" Her voice lifted at the end like she was asking.

"Got it." I grabbed the items I needed and started working on my infamous French toast while she watched me like I was going to run away at any moment.

I mixed the ingredients together and put the first piece of thickly sliced fresh bread into the frying pan before McJenna said anything else.

"Your phone's ringing."

Fuck me. I just wanted a day off.

I ignored the phone for a minute, focusing on food instead. If it was work, and I was sure it was, Genevieve could handle anything. I wasn't going to leave her hanging for long, but I was going to get my kid breakfast before answering the call.

"Are you okay?" McJenna asked.

"Of course. Why?" I turned to face her and found her smirking at me.

"You just ignored a phone call. I think your head might explode." She snickered, her face lighting up with humor.

"Ha ha, smart ass. Last I checked, you're just as glued to your phone as I am."

Her smirk turned to a scowl, and she rolled her eyes. "Not anymore. I don't have anyone to talk to. All my friends, the few I did have, blew me off when we moved. They said if I wasn't coming back next year, there was no reason to keep in touch over the summer."

"Seriously?" I blurted before I could stop myself. What assholes.

She shrugged like it was no big deal, but I saw the hurt on her face. Everyone had abandoned her. She was alone in MacKellar Cove. Something I ignored for far too long.

"It's no big deal."

I deposited the first slice of French toast on a plate and slid it across the counter to McJenna. I got butter and syrup from the fridge and set them in front of her with a fork and knife.

While I calmed my raging emotions, the prominent one being guilt, I added another slice into the frying pan. Then I faced my kid.

"I'm sorry about your friends. And I'm sorry I haven't been around much. I'm going to start taking more time off and working a better schedule. I wanted to get the theater up and running as quickly as possible so it was bringing in money. That's what Uncle Trent is paying me to do."

"And you think we're taking advantage of him."

I shook my head even as I knew it was a lie. I did feel that way, but I didn't want her to feel that way. "He's always said we're his family. He thinks of you as his own."

"But I'm not. I won't get this house or the hotels or anything else."

"None of that really matters, J."

"No, it doesn't. Not really, but it means I'm not his. George is. And I love him, and I don't feel like I should have something, but what am I supposed to tell people about where we live? You know they're going to ask."

"I didn't know that was bothering you. Do you think people are going to judge you?"

She shrugged and put a bite of French toast in her mouth to avoid answering me right away. I knew that trick and waited her out as I finished cooking the second piece. I slid it onto her plate and started a slice for me.

"Finley was teasing Uncle Trent about how things were when they were growing up. About him being the rich kid everyone wanted to be friends with."

"And you think people are only going to want to be friends with you because you live here?"

"I'm not a rich kid. I live here, but I feel like I'm the help instead of supposed to be here."

My brows shot up, and I rocked back on my heels. Damn. "You are not the help. Neither of us are."

"Aren't we? You work for Uncle Trent. That makes you the help."

"Yes, technically, but it's different."

"Dad, it isn't."

I scowled at her and grabbed my French toast off the frying pan. I added a second piece even though I wasn't sure I could eat it.

Yes, I'd been feeling like McJenna and I needed to find our own place, but I didn't want her to feel like we should. Trent adored her, and he always treated her like she was his. Over the years, more than a few people thought we were a couple because of the way we were with McJenna. Trent may not have contributed DNA, but he was her family.

"I thought you were excited about living here. What changed?" I asked.

She focused on her plate instead of meeting my gaze across the island. "I guess being here instead of the hotel made me realize it's not normal. Finley and Karissa live together, but they both pay half. Finley is worried about Karissa not being able to afford their condo with Finley moving out. I just realized our life is very different. It's not normal."

I sighed and tried to find the words to tell her she was right without telling her she should feel bad.

"When your mom left… I struggled. Trent was working for me then and knew what happened. He invited us to move in with him so I wasn't raising you alone. We were friends, and he was already spending a ton of time with us, and it made sense at the time. As you got older, he and I talked more than once about us finding our own place, but Trent refused to hear of it. He kept telling me we were his family and that he wanted us there. I paid for as much as I could, as much as he would let me, but he pushed back most of the time. Trent's stupid rich, and people always wanted to be friends with him because of his money instead of him."

"That's dumb. He's awesome."

"I agree. And that's why he kept us close. Because to us, he's Trent. He's not some rich guy, he's family. It was the first time he was more than a bank account to someone."

"That sucks."

I nodded. "It does. But after all these years, and George and Finley in his life, there is a part of me that feels like things have changed."

"Do you want to leave?"

"Only if you do. But I've been thinking about it and looking for options. There are some decent homes not far from here, so we would still see Trent, George, and Finley all the time, but we'd have our own home."

"Can we drive by some of them today?"

I smiled at her and nodded. "Of course."

"Good. We'll start with that."

Damn, I had an amazing kid.

AFTER BREAKFAST, we both showered, and I returned Genevieve's call, then we headed out. I didn't have an appointment with a realtor, so we just drove by the houses and looked at them from the road.

McJenna didn't love any of them and said we should keep looking. She was on the hunt now, too, but I wasn't sure if that was good or bad.

Our first stop of the day was Catherine Park. Since we had breakfast at home, we decided to start with a walk along the Riverwalk and go from there.

"It's pretty here," McJenna said after a few minutes of walking.

I nodded. The morning sun was bouncing off the water in the cove and on the river, making everything sparkle. It was peaceful with the sound of the waves slapping against the wall the walkway was built on. A breeze danced around us, cooling off the already warm morning.

"Do you really think things will be better here?"

"I do, J. The way Trent talked about this place, I think it's going to be good for you."

"And Karissa?"

"What about her?" I asked, trying not to sound defensive.

"What about the way she talked about this place?"

I exhaled quietly, hoping J didn't pick up on the fact that I was holding my breath. "I wasn't willing to hear what Karissa had to say about MacKellar Cove when we knew each other."

"Why not?"

"It wasn't what I wanted for my life. I wanted cities and excitement and a big career. I wanted to run a news program and tell important stories. I never wanted to play small."

"But now you do?"

"When did you become so grown?"

"When you were at work."

"Damn. Okay. Again, I deserve it. To answer your question, I've realized that the things I wanted back then aren't the things that gave me a full life."

"What do you mean?"

I looked out at the water and waved my hand at it. "When we lived in Niagara Falls, I never stopped to take in the beauty of where we lived."

"We went to the Falls every year."

"Yes, but it was something we did. We planned it and spent the day there and played tourist, then we went home and nothing had really changed."

"Are you saying walking along the water right now is changing you?" Her voice dripped with skepticism and sarcasm.

"No, but stopping to enjoy it might. Like you said, normally, I'd be at work. Even you were surprised I actually took the day off. I don't want you to not care what happens with my remains when I die."

"Ew, gross."

I chuckled. "I just mean, I don't want to be forgotten. I don't want my only impact in life to be the broadcasts I produced. I want there to be more."

"And moving here is going to make that happen? Because people will remember you as the movie theater guy?"

I shook my head. "The opinion that matters the most to me is yours, J. I want to leave a mark on you. And being here... we moved here because I wanted to be able to spend the last few years you're at home with you. I don't want you moving out the day you turn eighteen and never looking back."

"I won't."

I shrugged. "I hope not, but I don't know. The way things were going in Niagara Falls, I felt like that was going to happen. Trent made it sound like we could create a different life here. One that was slower and better in a lot of ways. That's what I want."

"One that includes Karissa?"

My heart squeezed at the sound of her name, and I couldn't deny, to myself, that I wanted that, too. But if it didn't happen, if she didn't give me another chance, I still moved to MacKellar Cove for McJenna. "We'll see."

We walked silently for a few minutes, passing all the shops until the pathway narrowed and pushed us to a sidewalk at the end. We kept walking, not worrying about where we were. It was impossible to get lost.

"I like her, you know. Karissa. She seems great."

"She is," I said instantly. "She's always been kind and smart and funny. You remind me a lot of her."

"Too bad she isn't my mom." McJenna kicked a rock on the sidewalk and clenched her fists.

I'd been honest with her since she was little about her mom. I didn't want someone to say something and make her question the truth. But growing up knowing your mom didn't want you wasn't easy. We've had more than our share of blow-ups as a result. But that was the first time J ever said she wished she had a different mom.

"I wish things were different. And I hate that your mom didn't stick around. But that's on her, not you. You aren't to blame."

"If she didn't have me, she might not have left."

"We weren't right for each other. And she wasn't ready to be a mom. None of that is on you, though. We are the ones who made the choices that got her pregnant. And I made the choice to be your father because I loved you from the moment she came to me with tears in her eyes and said she was pregnant."

"Did you know she was going to walk away when she told you?"

I shook my head. "No. I thought things would be okay. She never mentioned abortion or acted like she was anything but happy."

McJenna nodded slowly, kicking stones and staring at the ground.

"Want to head back toward town? Maybe we can check out that bakery Finley mentioned before we go on our tour."

"Ooh, yeah. I forgot about that. Let's go."

I smiled at her excitement and turned back to MacKellar Cove. Our conversation was lighter, McJenna guessing what options they would have at Cove Bakery.

"Is that it?" she asked, spotting the pink and white awning out front of the store.

I nodded. "It looks like it."

There was a line out the door of people waiting to get their sweet treats. We stepped in behind a young couple with their arms around each other.

"I wonder what today's special is?" the woman asked. "I hope it's something with chocolate."

"You love your chocolate," the man said.

"There's a special?" McJenna whispered.

The woman turned, her hand on her very pregnant belly. "There is. Valentina makes something different every day. There's always the regular stuff on the menu, but she adds something different."

"Valentina?" McJenna asked.

"The baking mastermind behind this place. Harriett works the register now since she can't really do the baking anymore. She's the one who opened Cove Bakery before I was even born. Valentina started working for her years ago, and now she does all the baking. Harriett lets her experiment and have fun, trying out new things and offering limited exclusives."

"Is that why there's a line?" I asked.

The woman nodded. "It is. Usually the daily special is sold out by lunch, so people get in line so they can try it. Where are you two visiting from?"

McJenna looked up at me like a deer caught in headlights.

I smiled and shook my head. "We're not. We moved here at the beginning of summer."

"Oh, well, welcome. Where do you live? We're over on Peach Street. There are a lot of high school students on our street. It's a great family area. I'm Jill, by the way."

She offered her hand, and I shook it. "Hi, Jill. I'm Xavier. And this is McJenna."

"So nice to meet you both. This is my husband, Anthony."

Anthony smiled and shook my hand, a man of few words as he let Jill do all the talking.

"Have you met a lot of kids since you moved here?" Jill asked McJenna.

"No, not really. My dad's been working a lot. I haven't had a chance to really get out and see the town," McJenna said.

"Are you in a neighborhood?" Jill asked.

"Honey, they might not want to tell complete strangers where they live," Anthony said gently.

Jill gasped. "Oh, my God, I'm so sorry. I didn't even think. Everyone knows everyone here so it never dawned on me you would think that's weird. I apologize."

"It's fine. It's not a big deal. We're actually living at MacKellar Estate right now."

"MacKellar Estate? Like the mansion on the other side of the cove?" Jill asked.

I hesitated and nodded, unsure how the rest of the conversation was going to go.

"Well, no wonder you haven't met anyone. It's isolated out there. Beautiful, but I imagine hard for a kid. You should get out and see the town more. Meet some people before school starts," Jill said.

"That's part of what we're doing today."

We all moved forward as people in front of us took their treats and found tables.

"That's good. It's hard to move, but to move somewhere so isolated isn't good. You—"

"Jill, honey. Give them a break," Anthony said. "I'm sure Xavier and McJenna are going to figure it out. And the soon-to-be mom they randomly met in town is not going to fix everything for them."

Jill's cheeks reddened, and she looked up at me with an apology in her eyes. "I overstepped. I'm so sorry. I tend to do that a lot."

I shook my head. "It's fine. I promise. It's an adjustment for us to be here, and then to be at the Estate, it's been more of a challenge than we expected."

"Where are you working?" Jill asked.

"Honey, seriously?" Anthony gasped.

"Sorry," Jill said. "I need to just stop talking."

"You're fine. I'm working on the theater. Getting it ready to open back up again," I told her.

"Oh, yay! I have been dying to see what's going on in there. I haven't been since I was a kid, but I'm really excited it's going to open up again."

"We're thinking fall. I think it's going to be great. We're really looking forward to it." I smiled at McJenna, who really couldn't care less, but she smiled at me, anyway.

"That's smart. After the summer guests head home and some places get quieter. It'll be a nice new attraction for the locals," Jill said.

"That's good to hear."

"Next!" the woman behind the counter called out.

"That's us, honey," Anthony said, tugging on Jill's arm.

"Ooh, I need my chocolate. Enjoy! And nice meeting you both," Jill said, smiling and waving.

We waited until Jill and Anthony got their order, then stepped up to the counter for our turn. McJenna asked what the special was and got a chocolate eclair. I ordered a peanut butter cup brownie. We both asked for bottles of water and decided we'd go back after our tour to get some desserts to bring home.

I paid and turned from the counter to find a seat. We were almost to a table when McJenna stopped.

"Karissa! Hi! You have to sit with us," she gushed. Loudly. For the entire place to hear. Leaving Karissa no room to say no.

God, I loved my kid.

6

KARISSA

I PRESSED MY LIPS INTO A SMILE AND TRIED TO FIGURE OUT how I could get out of agreeing. I could say I was working, but then why was I standing in line for twenty minutes to get dessert? Yeah, I had nothing.

I nodded, avoiding looking at Xavier. "Of course," I told McJenna.

She smiled and turned back to her dad, who'd already found a table in the crowded space. One with three chairs. Like it was already predetermined. Dammit.

McJenna waved at me to make sure I saw them. I waved back, hating myself for going in there when I did. I should have gone earlier. But I was working. Or later. But then I'd miss out on the special. Crap-tastic. I was spending the morning with my ex and his daughter.

Kill me now.

I checked messages on my phone while I waited for the line to move forward. When it was my turn, I ordered the special and debated getting the chocolate croissant I really wanted.

Screw that. Xavier didn't get to judge me if I ate two

things. I was not a small woman, and I was not trying to change who I was for anyone. If he didn't love every single one of my curves, then forget him.

No. Forget him anyway. He didn't need to love my curves. I loved my curves. And he wasn't getting his hands on them ever again.

I handed my card over to Harriett and made small talk while she put my eclair and croissant on a plate. She handed me my water and plate, then told me to enjoy.

I hoped Xavier and McJenna would be done by the time I made it to them, but nope. Neither of them had touched their food. Not one bite.

"You got the special, too?" McJenna asked when I sat down.

"I did. It's why I'm here. Valentina has only been doing it for a few months, but it's a huge hit. Everything she makes is so good," I said.

"Is this new?" McJenna asked.

I nodded. "It is. She's never made eclairs before. Yesterday was salted caramel dark chocolate brownies. Delicious."

"Do you come here every day?" Xavier asked.

I took my time looking up at him, steeling my resolve against him. He was sitting right next to me, too close for my sanity. His voice was the same one I heard in my dreams, the voices I played in my head forever. Especially when my mom was dying. He got me through it as much as my friends did, even if he didn't know it at the time. And never would. I imagined him there with me, holding me on the nights when the loss was too much for me to bear.

But now he was there. Sitting next to me in my hometown bakery acting like it was totally normal for him to be there.

"I do. Is that a problem?" I said, my tone cold. He had no right to judge me.

"Absolutely not. Just good information to have."

I wasn't sure what he meant by that, so I ignored him again and turned to McJenna. "Want to try it together?"

She nodded, her dark brown eyes bright with excitement. "Yeah." She picked up her eclair and leaned forward. It hovered over her plate, like mine over my plate. We opened our mouths together and leaned forward, closing the distance between the eclair and our mouths. We bit down, and my eyes closed on a groan.

Oh, God, it was better than sex. Or at least, better than my memories of sex. Actual sex hadn't happened in far too long. But damn, that eclair made up for it.

"That's so good," McJenna said with her mouth full.

"Mm hm," I agreed, nodding. I set my eclair on my plate and wiped my mouth on my napkin. I twisted off the top of my water as I chewed, then took a sip. "Amazing."

"How does Valentina decide what to add to the menu?" McJenna asked. "Because she should totally add this."

"She takes suggestions. If you really like this, you need to let Valentina or Ms. Harriett know. If something gets a lot of unofficial votes, they'll add it."

"This gets my vote," McJenna said, going in for another bite.

Xavier watched us closely, not saying a thing as we devoured our eclairs. When I reached for my croissant, McJenna looked up at the counter.

"What is that?" she asked me.

"It's a chocolate croissant. It's my favorite thing here. I get one whenever I come in. Even if I'm getting something else. They're too good to pass up."

McJenna wrinkled her nose. She pursed her lips. Then

she scowled at her father. "How come I didn't get one of those?"

I coughed to cover my laugh.

"I didn't know you wanted one," Xavier said. "We'll come back. As good as this place is, I have a feeling we'll be here a lot."

"Karissa, will you meet us here again so I have someone who'll tell me what to get?"

I opened and closed my mouth, but found myself nodding. "Of course. Um, do you want to share my croissant?"

"Oh, no, I couldn't. Thank you, but I'm not going to take your food," McJenna said, surprising me with her kindness.

"How about a bite? So you can taste how good it is? You need to try everything Valentina makes, and if you start with this, then you can try something else next time." I pulled off a decent sized piece and waved it toward McJenna.

She looked at her father, but he just lifted his brows, letting her make the choice for herself. She reached out for the croissant and popped it in her mouth, then groaned. "Oh, wow. That's good. It, like, melted."

I nodded. "It does. It's amazing."

"You are my best customer," Valentina said from next to me. "I think we sell more just because you tell everyone how good everything is."

"It's not lies," I told her. Valentina and I didn't know each other well, but after my surgery last year, Finley got me treats for breakfast every day. Valentina asked why I wasn't coming in with Finley, and Finley shared about my preventative double mastectomy. Valentina brought me a care package once a week for the next few months, until I could get out and visit Cove Bakery on my own. We'd been building a friendship since.

"How are you feeling?" Valentina asked. She always did, but with Xavier and McJenna there, the question felt more personal.

"I'm good. Thanks." I glanced at Xavier and McJenna, then smiled up at Valentina.

She widened her eyes at me and clearly got the message. "Good. Awesome. The eclairs are good?"

"So good," McJenna said. "I love them."

"It's their first time here. This is Xavier and McJenna Hogan. They moved here with Trent MacKellar."

"Oh, it's so nice to meet you both! I've heard all about you. I'm sure most of it isn't even close to the truth, but it's nice to meet you." Valentina shook their hands. Her smile was genuine. She was a few years older than me, enough that we weren't in high school together, but I'd heard of her as a kid. She married a man she met in college, but they moved back to MacKellar Cove after college to start a family and be close to her dad.

"I feel like we should be worried," Xavier said tentatively.

Valentina laughed and shook her head. "No, not at all. This town likes to talk. And if they don't know someone's story, they create one."

"That doesn't sound any better," Xavier said.

"It'll be all good. Of course, seeing the three of you together will have people thinking you're a happy family," Valentina said.

I choked on my water, coughing hard to remove it from my lungs. I slammed the bottle on the table and pressed my hand to my chest, like it would help. I covered my mouth with my other hand and coughed until the water cleared and I could take a breath.

"Are you okay?" McJenna asked.

I nodded. "I'm good." My breath stuttered in my lungs, making me cough again. I sucked in a full breath, finally feeling like my lungs were working as designed again.

"You sure?" Valentina asked. "I didn't mean to kill you."

"All good."

The three of them looked at me like I was going to pass out on them. Fair, but still annoying.

"Well," Xavier said, "we should get going. We have a tour boat to catch."

"Oh, are you going on Elise's tour?" I asked.

"We are. You should come with us," McJenna said.

"Oh, um, no, I couldn't," I stammered, reaching for an excuse that didn't exist. I did not want to go on a tour boat, or anywhere else, with Xavier and McJenna, no matter how amazing I thought she was.

"You have to. It'll be so much fun. Please, Karissa," McJenna begged.

"I'm going to leave you to it and head to the back. It was nice to see you, Rissa, and nice to meet you, Xavier and McJenna. I hope to see you all again soon," Valentina said loudly enough that the whole place heard her. She smirked at me. The brat. She knew exactly what that would do to the rumor mill.

Damn small town.

"Please, Karissa. Dad, tell her she should come with us," McJenna said.

"If she has work or something else going on, we can't force her," Xavier said. He avoided my gaze like he was just as uncomfortable with the idea as I was.

Well, that was kind of a reason to go. If Xavier was going to be unhappy I was there, maybe I should tag along.

"Please, Karissa. It'll be fun. And I want to talk to you

about designing apps. I think I might want to go to college for something like that," McJenna said.

"You do? Since when?" Xavier asked her.

McJenna shrugged. "Since I met Karissa and found out it was a job people do."

Xavier closed his eyes and shook his head.

"You know what? It sounds fun," I heard myself say. "It's been a long time since I've been on a tour. Elise will hate it if she's our guide, but I think it'll be fun to go with you guys."

"Awesome. My dad will drive us. We parked by the park," McJenna said, looping her arm through mine.

She and I headed out the door, leaving Xavier to trail behind us after he cleaned up the table. The sun was bright, and the air was warm, and it had nothing to do with the sweet teenager chattering to me or the man walking behind us staring at my ass.

Yeah, I checked. And he did not look away when I did.

I was in so much trouble.

ELISE WAS the guide on our boat, and she was not happy when we sat in the front row where she'd be talking. But she rolled with it and made us part of her act.

"For those of you who wonder what the locals do around here, you get to see three of them in their natural habitat right here," she said, pointing to us. "The locals are just like you, enjoying the tour and soaking in all the history of the area. Although, in defense of two of them, they've only lived here a little while. My friend here has lived in MacKellar Cove almost all of her life and could do this tour for you if she wasn't so busy designing apps."

The crowd murmured their appreciation of my job, and I resisted the urge to flip Elise off. She just smirked at me.

The boat tour took us around the Thousand Islands, giving us a water view of the Thousand Islands Bridge that led drivers to Canada. Elise pointed out the imaginary line that separated the US and Canada in the water. And she showed visitors the houses, each more interesting than the last on our ride through the river.

When we docked at Boldt Castle, Elise thanked everyone for taking the tour and gave them brief instructions for getting up to the Castle. She had to walk out and speak to people but told us to follow her so we could chat before we went exploring.

"I didn't know you were going to be here," Elise said when we had a minute.

"McJenna talked me into it. We ran into each other at Cove Bakery this morning," I explained.

"I'm so jealous. What was the special today?" Elise asked.

"Eclairs," McJenna said. "They were really good."

"And you didn't bring me one?" Elise teased her.

McJenna laughed and shook her head. "I don't think it would have made it here."

"Cruel! You're cruel," Elise said. "Is this your first time visiting the Castle?"

McJenna nodded. "My dad's been working a lot. He took today off so we could spend time together. Finley said we should come here."

"It was a great recommendation. What else are you planning today?" Elise asked.

McJenna looked up at Xavier, and he shook his head. "We haven't decided. Lunch somewhere and we'll go from there."

"O'Kelley's is always good, Cracked I'm sure you've been to. There's also Bob's Burrito Barn and Will Work For Burgers. Rissa's favorite is Rolled Up, which is sushi and other Asian foods. It's really good."

"That sounds good," McJenna said. "I like sushi, too."

I smiled at her. Was she trying to get me and her dad together? I had a hard time imagining a teenager cared, but I was starting to think that was exactly what was going on. She hadn't asked me one question about designing apps, like she said she wanted to talk about. Just personal questions about my life in MacKellar Cove.

The kid was a matchmaker in the making. Just like my mother was.

"We can decide when we get back to shore. I think we need to let Elise go, though. Should we go see the castle?" Xavier asked.

"Yeah, let's go," McJenna said. She waved to Elise and thanked her for the tour. Xavier did the same. I tried to get away with it, too, but Elise shook her head at me.

"You are going to spill on Sunday," she hissed. "You owe us these details."

I rolled my eyes and shook my head. Great. Just what I wanted to do. Explain to all of my friends why I was hanging out with my ex and his daughter when I didn't really know. Could I plead temporary insanity? Crazy for him?

Nope. That would only make it worse. I had to come up with something. Good thing I had three days.

I followed McJenna and Xavier through the castle grounds and up to the main house. McJenna marveled at the house that never held a family and the beauty of it.

We went back outside to tour the rest of the gardens and see the other buildings, and Xavier slowed his steps to match my pace.

"I'm sorry she roped you into spending today with us," he said quietly.

"You didn't want me to join you?" I asked, trying to keep the smile off my face.

"It's not that. I just know I'm the last person in town you want to be spending time with."

I nodded. "Maybe not the last."

He chuckled. "Listen, Karissa, I know we have a lot of history and a lot of hurt. And I'm sorry I came here and sprung it on you the way I did. I knew I should have told you, but I was afraid you'd be angry and Trent would uninvite us, and J needed this."

"Do you really think Trent would have done that?"

He looked at me with his dark brows raised. I'd forgotten how expressive he could be without saying a word. And my guess was right now he was saying Trent would have done exactly that.

"If the choice was me or Finley, there was no choice. He's like a brother to me, but she's the love of his life. I've never known him to fall for a woman. He's dated, but it's either been women who didn't know who he was or women who dated him because of who he was. He's never had someone like her in his life, and even from the first time they met, I could tell she was different for him."

I nodded slowly, staring off over the water at the town across the way. "I can understand that. I still don't think he would have told you guys not to come."

Xavier shrugged. "I don't know. I was too scared he might. And I was too scared I'd lose my nerve once I found out Finley knew you. She mentioned your name once, and I couldn't breathe. I knew you went back home after college, but I never let myself look you up so I didn't know you were still here. Hearing that you and Finley were roommates felt like moving was definitely the right thing to do."

Wow. The nerve.

"Why? Why would you think that? Did you think you could just walk into town and I'd throw myself at you? That I'm so desperate for a man in my life that I'd forget that you made plans with me and then walked away from them?"

"No, it wasn't—"

"You know what, Xavier? I think you were right. I think you are the last person I want to spend the day with. Please tell McJenna I said goodbye."

I didn't wait for him to respond and walked away. Lucky for me, there was a boat just pulling up when I was heading toward the docks. Perfect timing to get away from Xavier.

Asshole.

7

———

It was stupid to let him get to me, but dammit, he did. I was angry and hurt and felt so ridiculous for thinking that maybe we could be friends or something.

I stewed the entire boat ride back to shore, and as soon as it was docked, I was off the boat and searching through my matches. Impulsive? Yes. But I needed to prove to myself as much as Xavier that I could get a date. One that wasn't him.

One of the guys I'd been messaging had asked about getting together sometime, and I'd been brushing him off. I didn't like the idea of meeting someone after only a few conversations, but screw it. I needed to go out and feel good about myself. I needed to remember who I was. I was beautiful and smart and funny and I had a lot to offer a man.

Screw Xavier for making me feel differently. Then and now.

My match agreed to meet me for dinner at O'Kelley's that night at seven. I pushed away the pit in my stomach and told myself it was going to be great. We had good conversations, and he made me laugh. It was going to be a good night.

By the time I was walking into O'Kelley's, I was nervous as hell. It had been a long time since I went out on a date. I created Book Boyfriends Wanted to honor my mom and her ability to match people. It worked well and had matched a lot of locals with someone they really connected with. But not me. Because I resisted the magic.

Yes, I believed there was magic in my app. I believed my mom was picking the matches, pairing up people who really needed each other. But me? I was closed off. Not willing to find that one person. Because I already found him and he left me.

But we weren't talking about him. Not when I had a date with another man.

I took a seat at the end of the bar and waited. My date said he would be wearing jeans and a black tee with a red stripe across it. I liked that he told me what he was wearing instead of asking what I would be wearing. It meant I was the one in charge of us actually meeting.

Hudson scowled at me when I told him I was meeting someone and delivered a club soda with a splash of cranberry juice and a lime twist.

"Is it your ex?" he asked.

"Oh, God, it better not be." I hadn't even considered that Xavier could be the guy I was talking to.

"Isn't he going to be here tonight?"

"Why would he be?"

"The guys usually come. Ian started bringing Trent when he moved here, and Trent's started bringing Xavier. Seems like a nice enough guy, but he hurt you so he has an uphill battle here."

I shook my head and sipped my drink. "It's ancient

history. There's nothing left between us, and I don't want you guys to not be friends with him because of me."

Hudson raised a dark eyebrow and waited for me to say something else.

I just stared right back at him.

He finally gave up and shrugged, walking away to handle other customers.

Yeah, okay, fine. I wanted to tell him not to be friends with Xavier, but that wasn't fair. That would have been childish of me. And I wasn't going to do that. I was going to be civil. For Finley's sake.

A man walked in wearing jeans and a black tee with a red stripe across the chest and down the arms. He stopped just inside the door and looked around. He was cute, and familiar, but not someone I could place. I had definitely seen him around town, though. His blond hair was on the longer side, brushing his chin before he tucked it behind his ears. He looked a few years older than me. Fit without being jacked, and tall without being abnormal. He was fairly average, and that was definitely okay with me. Because he wasn't Xavier.

I waited until his gaze caught mine and waved to him. He smiled back and walked toward me, his gaze not leaving mine as he moved through the light Thursday night crowd.

When he made it to me, he said, "Hi, I'm NerdyByNature, also known as Brantley. Are you Queen?"

I reached out and shook his offered hand. It was nice to meet the man who had a hammer as his profile pic. "I am. It's nice to meet you. I'm also known as Karissa."

"Karissa Thomas, right?"

I nodded. "Small town."

He laughed with me. "I get it. Most of the people I meet have kids who either play for me or are dating kids who play for me. I coach cross-country and baseball at the high school."

"Oh, that's right. Brantley Pierce, right?"

He nodded. "Yep. I hope meeting doesn't ruin things, though. It's been fun talking to you."

"You, too."

He smiled and held my gaze. His green eyes sparkled just a bit, catching on the subtle lighting in the bar. He really was attractive. The kind of guy I wouldn't mind settling down with. He obviously liked kids, and he had a stable job. He was kind and friendly and funny.

And with all of that, I still didn't feel an instant spark like I wanted to. Like I felt when I met Xavier all those years ago.

But I didn't need a spark. I was thirty-eight years old. Thirty-nine was staring at me, which meant forty was right around the corner. I couldn't afford to be picky anymore. Not if I wanted to share the rest of my life with someone.

"Should we get a table?" Brantley asked.

I nodded and let him guide me toward a booth on the other side of the bar. We sat down, and almost immediately, a server came over and asked if we wanted to order anything.

"Do you want something to eat? I haven't had anything yet, but no pressure," Brantley said.

"I could eat. I haven't had anything either."

Brantley nodded and gestured for me to order first.

"Grilled chicken sandwich with cheddar cheese, lettuce, tomato, and ketchup. Fries. And a water, please."

The server nodded and turned to Brantley. "All that sounds great to me. Make it two."

The server nodded again, then walked away.

"So, even though I recognize you, I don't really know

you. Can I ask the boring first date questions?" Brantley asked with a wrinkle of his nose and a charming smile.

"Of course. I feel the same. I think you're a little older than me, right?"

"I think so. I'm forty-four."

"Thirty-eight," I told him. "Thirty-nine soon."

"And dreading forty, aren't you?"

I chuckled. "How did you know?"

"I was the same. My parents were in their forties when I graduated high school and it just hit me that I wasn't anywhere close to that. Made me think about all the things I wanted to have but didn't have."

"And do you have them now?"

A ghost of a smile crossed his lips before he shook his head. "Not all of them."

I wondered what he was thinking about when he said that, but that wasn't a first date kind of question, so I didn't ask.

"I lost my mom a few years ago," I said, "and that really made me think about life differently. She was kind of my rock."

"She's in the mural on the side of Cracked, right? Over-looking the square?"

I nodded. "She is. She worked there forever. A lot of people in town knew her."

"She was always giving me advice. She's definitely missed around here. I'm sorry for your loss."

"Thank you," I said.

We paused our not first date talk while the server delivered our drinks and an appetizer I had no doubt Hudson sent over. When I looked up, I saw him watching us. I smiled and lifted my drink, and he nodded back.

"Are you friends with Hudson?" Brantley asked.

"Yeah. We were three years apart in school, but I live down the street and spend a lot of time here." I paused and tilted my head. "That's probably not something I should admit, is it? That I spend a lot of time in a bar?"

Brantley chuckled. "You won't get any judgement from me. I get it. Especially when you're friends. He seems like a good guy."

"He is. What about you? Other than coaching, what do you do?"

"I teach physics at the high school. I stay pretty busy during the school year. Summers are a good break, but I teach summer school most years and I volunteer with the town sports teams."

"Wow, really?"

"Yeah. I don't like to sit still. My mind gets the better of me when I don't have something to occupy it."

"I understand that. I feel like I'm always thinking of ways to improve my apps or new ones I could develop."

"I didn't know you designed apps. That's pretty awesome," Brantley said.

I almost admitted I designed the one we both used to meet, but for some reason, I kept that to myself. "I enjoy what I do."

"That makes a big difference. I had a job I really didn't like for a while. I didn't come right back here after college and worked closer to Syracuse at a bigger district there. I hated it. The politics of the district were bad. When the job here came up, Valentina sent it to me to apply."

"You know Valentina?" I asked. It didn't surprise me given the town, but for her to have sent him a job said they were much closer than acquaintances.

He sipped his water and nodded, avoiding my gaze. "Yeah, we graduated together and, uh, ended up at the same college. We bonded, being the only two from here. I actually introduced her to Dawson."

"Really? Did you and Valentina ever date?"

He shook his head immediately and wiped his mouth on his napkin. "Nah. We were always just friends."

I nodded, wondering if I was picking up on something that wasn't there or if I was right and Brantley had a thing for Valentina.

"What the hell is going on?"

I looked up at Xavier, towering over our table with clenched fists and furious eyes.

"Can I help you?" Brantley asked, drawing Xavier's attention to him.

"Xavier, what the hell is wrong with you?" I asked him.

"You know him?" Brantley asked.

"Yeah, and I have no idea why he thinks he can interrupt our dinner." I glared at Xavier, waiting for an explanation.

"You were with me earlier today, and now you're with this guy?"

I huffed a laugh and shook my head. Both men waited for me to say something.

"I ran into you at Cove Bakery this morning, and your *daughter* invited me to go on a boat tour with you guys because she wanted to know more about my job. You're acting like we were on a date, which we were not."

"And you're on a date with him?" Xavier spat.

"I am. And you have no right to act like it's any of your business. We are not dating or sleeping together or even friends, Xavier. We were over many, many years ago."

"And I live here now."

"Listen," Brantley said, rising to his feet, "I think you should go. She said she doesn't want you butting in, and you need to listen to her."

"You don't have any right to talk to me about her. You don't know her at all."

Brantley nodded. "You're right. I don't. But I'm here trying to get to know her, and I'm listening to what she has to say. And one of the things she said was she wants you to leave. So please do."

Xavier brushed Brantley off and stormed toward the door, not looking back at all.

Brantley sat back down a minute later and reached across for my hand. "Are you okay?"

I nodded, squeezing his hand. "Thank you. I'm sorry about him."

"You have nothing to be sorry for." He released my hand and smiled. "We can't make people love us or make them move on. But I'm sorry you're having to deal with someone who won't accept that you aren't interested."

I was silent for a minute, thinking about what he said.

"Or maybe you are still interested?"

I shook my head immediately. "No. There's too much history between us for there to be a present or a future."

"I don't really believe that's ever true. I think it can be hard to get over what happened in the past, but if people are really meant to be together, they should be. No matter what."

"I don't think I should be with him. Especially not when he acts like that. I don't even know who that was."

"It was a man who was jealous because he saw the woman he loves on a date with someone else."

I snorted. "He does not love me. Jealous might be it, but that's only because he thought moving here after seventeen years apart would fix all the lies he told me when we were in college."

"Ouch. Yeah, I don't blame you for not forgiving him."

I breathed a laugh. "Let's finish our date and not worry about him anymore."

Brantley smiled and nodded. "Sounds good to me."

"He did not do that," Elise gasped Sunday night at book club.

I'd just finished filling them in on everything that happened with Xavier Thursday. From McJenna inviting me to sit with them at Cove Bakery and go on the tour with them to Xavier pissing me off, then my date with Brantley and Xavier's interruption.

"He did. He really showed his ass," I said.

"Wow," Sofia said. "I have to admit I'm a little jealous that no man has ever gotten emotional like that over me, but I also wouldn't be able to handle the attention of it. What did you say?"

"I told him we weren't together, and he had no right to tell me what I could do. And Brantley told him to leave," I told them.

"Good for you. And for Coach Pierce," Goldie said. "My son runs cross-country for him. I can't think of him as Brantley."

"Is he a good guy?" Finley asked Goldie.

Goldie nodded. "Absolutely. Paul loves him. Says he's very encouraging and helpful. Paul's always loved to run, but Coach Pierce offers tips to make it easier and helps the kids who aren't natural runners."

"I'd be one of those kids," Blake said. "I'm only going to run if it's life and death. And maybe not even then."

The rest of us chuckled and nodded in agreement.

"Brantley said he knows Valentina," I told them. I was

totally fishing because I already knew we were better as friends.

"From Cove Bakery?" Piper asked.

"Yeah. He said they graduated together, and he introduced her to her husband," I said.

"Interesting. I didn't realize he was her age. But I have seen him in there. Gavin and I try to go in at least once a week. Have you guys tried her specials?" Piper asked.

"So good."

"I'm hooked."

"Everything she makes is amazing."

"I think Brantley has a thing for Valentina," I told them.

"She's married," Melody said.

"I know, but it was just a feeling I got from him," I said. "He's a nice guy. I'd hate to think of him pining for her."

"Are you saying that so we won't pressure you to go on a second date with him?" Finley asked.

I shook my head. "No. We're definitely better as friends. He's nice, and he's cute, but our date was just okay."

"You deserve better than just okay," Zoey said. "I settled for okay for a long time, and it wasn't worth it. Not when I could have had what I have now."

"But you have Cameron and Alexis," Piper said.

Zoey nodded. "And I'd never trade my kids, but I wasn't happy."

"I'm kind of tired of being alone," I admitted. "I haven't had a serious relationship since Xavier and I broke up, and that was forever ago. I want what all of you have. A partner to go through life with."

The single ones nodded with me, and the attached ones looked ashamed.

"I don't want any of you to feel bad for being happy. You've inspired me to try. To get out there. And I went into my date with Brantley with an open mind. But Xavier interrupting us just told me I don't want to be with someone who isn't sure. I spent too many years with Xavier before he changed his mind about everything and left me. I'm not willing to risk that again, but I'm also not willing to have someone in my life who doesn't make me feel the way he does."

"The way he *does*?" Finley asked.

"The way he did," I clarified. "All he does now is make me angry."

The lie was easy enough to tell, but none of them bought it. I slipped. And knowing my friends, they weren't going to let me get away with it forever.

But for now I could pretend when Xavier came up to our table my heart didn't race with excitement and my palms didn't sweat in anticipation and my core didn't clench with desire. One day I might have to confess that, but for now, it was my secret.

8

XAVIER

"WHAT EXACTLY ARE YOU TELLING ME?" I HELD BACK AS MUCH of my anger as possible even though the idiot on the other end deserved all of it.

"We can't do what you asked us. It's just not possible."

"Then why in the fuck did you take the deposit for my order?" I barked.

Genevieve jumped up from her seat and walked over to me. She raised her brows and waved her hand at me like she wanted me to hand over my phone.

"What?" I hissed at her.

"Give me the phone. Now."

I sighed and handed it to her. "See if you can get some answers out of those morons."

"Hi, Mr. Alvarez? Yes, this is Genevieve. I'm the one who placed the order with you. Well, see, this is a big project. An expensive project. And it's not acceptable to not have a sign outside the theater. You understand that, don't you?"

I almost snickered at the condescending tone of her voice. Almost. If I wasn't so angry, I might have.

"Yes, well, see, the problem we have is that you've been

sitting on that order for weeks. Holding on to our money, earning interest on our money. We have been under the assumption that deposit would eventually pay for itself when you delivered what you promised when I placed the order with you. Since you said you would. If you're canceling on us now, you owe us our full deposit plus twenty percent for wasting our time."

I heard his shouts before Genevieve pulled the phone away from her head. She rolled her eyes and waited until he quieted down, flashing a glare at me when I tried to take the phone back.

"Quite frankly, Mr. Alvarez, I don't give a fuck what you think. You stole from us. You took our money with no intention of delivering the product we paid for. You can either agree to return every penny we paid you, plus interest, or the next call you will be getting will be from our legal team."

I stared at her, wondering what legal team she was going to sic on him since we didn't have one. She smiled and tilted her head, pouring on the sugar.

"Well, thank you so much, Mr. Alvarez. I appreciate your help. I'll be waiting for that check to arrive, and I'll be sure to let you know exactly when it gets here. Have a great rest of your day."

She hung up and flipped off the phone before handing it back to me.

"He's going to send a check out today."

"Twenty percent?" I asked.

She shrugged. "We're going to need to pay someone to expedite this. It's going to cost more. We wouldn't have been dealing with that if he hadn't agreed to do a job he wasn't capable of doing. I have no patience for people who steal from hardworking business owners. And I figured the big boss probably has a few lawyers on speed dial if we really needed someone to get involved."

"What did he say when you told him that?"

"He shut up real quick. I have a feeling he's not totally above board. I'm sorry I hired him. This can come out of my check."

I shook my head. "This isn't on you. We thought we had someone who was going to do the job we paid him for. There's nothing you need to worry about. We just need to find someone else who can do a sign for us."

"I'll ask around. Maybe David's guys can do something?"

"Maybe, but it has to be what's allowed by the town. And weatherproof and all of that."

"I'll find out. You need to go to Al's and get the supplies, by the way."

"Oh, crap. Thanks. I'm going to grab some lunch while I'm out. You want anything?"

Genevieve shook her head. "Teddy and I packed lunch today so we can eat together. But thanks."

I waved and headed for the door. When Trent and I worked together, we needed our space from each other and never had lunch together. It was clearly a different situation when you worked with someone you were in love with.

The drive through town was quick. Traffic was busy for MacKellar Cove, but that was still nothing compared to Niagara Falls. I was getting used to being able to get anywhere in town in less than ten minutes. Much less in many cases.

I parked in the lot next to Al's Hardware and looked above the door at the sign. It was simple but effective. It was bright enough to be clear without being garish. I wondered who made their sign and if they were still open for business.

It was well-weathered and had definitely been there for a while.

I pocketed my keys and got out of the car. I hadn't gotten into the habit of leaving the keys in the car yet, but I didn't lock it. That was the closest I came to small town lifestyle so far.

I still wasn't sure how I agreed to Genevieve's plan for us to paint the lobby and create a display board for the town, but I was at Al's Hardware buying the paint Genevieve ordered and picking up all the supplies she asked for. There were a few people in line, so I waited my turn so I could ask the guy behind the counter about the order. When he asked what I needed, I told him I was picking up the order for Genevieve.

He laughed. "You're the new guy, huh?" He extended his hand.

I reached automatically and shook. "New guy?"

"You're the one fixing up the theater. That's great. You work for Trent MacKellar?"

"Uh, yeah. I'm Xavier Hogan."

"Nice to meet you. I'm Knox Randall. I own this place. Anything you need, you let me know. I'm happy to help out. I know David's crew has been ordering stuff, but if you need anything else, I can get it, even if I don't have it in stock." Knox came around the counter and pointed to the aisle on the far side of the store.

"Thanks. I appreciate it. I'm still learning my way around and figuring things out."

"I get that. Everyone probably knows more about you than you've ever admitted. And half of it is probably not true."

I laughed, wondering if that was the case.

"Did you really hit on Genevieve during your interview?" Knox asked.

"What? No. Of course not. That's illegal, and she wears a wedding ring. That's not me."

Knox nodded and stopped in front of a cage. He flipped through a large keyring before unlocking the gate. "I figured that one wasn't true. Why would she work for you? How about Trent MacKellar? Did you two have a thing? That's another rumor. Or that you and Trent weren't sure who was the father of Finley's baby until he was born and it was pretty obvious."

"None of that is true," I said firmly. "Wow, this town."

"Yeah. All the guys who come in here are worse than women at the hair salon. They want to tell me everything they think they know. There's also the one about you and Karissa. That you two dated in college and you broke her heart when you decided not to move here."

I froze, unsure how to respond to that one.

Knox lifted a bag of supplies and turned to hand it to me.

I hesitated, still reeling from what he said, and he paused.

"Whoa. That happened? You knew Karissa?"

"I, um... It was a long time ago."

"The way I heard it, you made plans to move here and then bailed on her. Is that true?"

My cheeks heated under the other man's cold glare. What happened between Karissa and me years ago was no one's business. Except when we both lived in her hometown and everyone wanted to protect her.

"Shit. I didn't expect that one. Are you here for her?"

I shook my head. "She's not interested."

"Can't say I blame her."

"Have you ever made a mistake? Done something that you second guessed almost immediately, but you couldn't change it?"

"Sure, of course."

"That's kind of how it happened. I got offered a job out of college. A really good job. The kind of job I thought I'd never get. I had to choose."

"And you chose the job," Knox said.

I nodded. "I did. I had been looking for jobs, but there was nothing around here. At all. I applied for other jobs for experience so when I found something I would be prepared. I didn't think they would offer it to me."

"Was it worth it?"

I sucked in a breath. It was the biggest question life had to offer. Was it worth it? A person could ask that about anything they'd ever experienced. Things they said yes to and no. The hard part was you never knew what would have happened if you made the other choice.

"I don't know."

"You have a daughter, right?" Knox asked.

I nodded.

"You wouldn't have her if you'd chosen differently."

I smiled, thinking of McJenna. The grin on her face when we went on the tour was worth everything. And her excitement at planning another day out for next week was special. She'd been grilling Finley about things to do and was making plans for the last few weeks of summer.

"I think that's your answer," Knox said. "Listen, I get it. It's not easy, but you have to make tough choices in life. A lot of us here don't understand someone wanting to live somewhere else. I grew up here. My dad owned this place. When he retired, it was a given I'd take it over. I never thought about doing something else because I love it. But it's not always easy living in the same place I've lived forever. I'm single because I grew up with all the single women in town. I've never been married or had kids. I love my town and my job, but there are times I've considered leaving so I could have more of a private life. But I don't want to. Some people might say I'm stuck, but I don't know. I just love being here. Where I can walk to the back and have a conversation with someone new to town and I know my customers who came in while we were back here left money or a note on the counter so I know what they took."

"Seriously?"

Knox chuckled. "Yeah. I guarantee it. And that's what I love about being here. Everyone knows everyone, and it's home. You know?"

I nodded slowly, wondering if I'd ever feel like it was home. I liked the idea, but Karissa was the key. If she gave me another chance, I wouldn't screw it up again. She was my home.

"So, is there anything else you need?" Knox asked, locking the cage again and carrying some of the supplies back to the front.

"Actually, we need someone to make a sign for outside the theater. We thought we had it done, but the company pulled out this morning."

"Not good. Um, what kind of sign are you looking at having done?"

"I really like the one you have outside. Something like that would be great. Wood or metal with clear lettering. We'd probably need lights since the theater will be open at night. But nothing too flashy. Simple and elegant is what Genevieve says."

Knox nodded thoughtfully and rubbed his jaw. "I could probably do that."

"You?"

"Yeah, I made that sign. What size are you looking for?"

"Whoa, really?"

"I mean, unless you want to hire a general contractor or a sign company."

"No. I just want something that looks good and meets all the town code and legal requirements. We have specs for the sign we already had on order. Genevieve can send them over to you and you can take a look. We're open to ideas."

Knox nodded. "That sounds good. I close here at five today, but tomorrow I close at three. How about I come by the theater after that and we can work everything out? That work for you?"

"Absolutely. Thank you. Really. And you're very talented."

Knox's cheeks reddened beneath his five o'clock shadow. "Thanks. Let's get you rung up for all of this."

"Genevieve will be so happy to get started."

Knox chuckled at my less than enthusiastic tone. "I bet she will be."

GENEVIEVE WAS FAR MORE creative than I knew and by the end of the day, I could finally see her vision. The display she wanted to set up would be a place to celebrate MacKellar Cove, a perfect addition to the theater set up and run by two men who weren't really a part of the town.

Trent was getting there, but I was an outsider by everyone's standards.

I made it home for dinner and sat and talked with Finley, Trent, and McJenna. Our dynamic had changed since Finley moved in, but she was blending right into our mashed up family well.

"Are you still using the app to talk to women?" Finley asked after McJenna left the table.

I shook my head. "Is nothing secret around here?"

"Nope. Not really," Finley said with zero shame. "Listen, I like you, Xavier, but you hurt my friend by showing up here. I don't want you to do it again. She's the queen of that app, and she deserves to be treated well."

I nodded. "I know. When we were together, I did treat her well. At least, I think I did. Changing things the way I did was shitty, and I know that, but I was young and thought I knew what I was doing."

"What's your excuse for coming back here?" she asked pointedly.

I stared at her for a long minute. Finley hadn't questioned me so directly before. Sure, she asked what the hell I was thinking, but this was different. This was searching.

"I came here for McJenna. To give her a better life. But I knew that was possible because Karissa is here. Because she'd never call this place home unless it was as special as she is."

"So you still love her." It wasn't a question. It was a statement. A truth.

One I couldn't deny.

"I never stopped. Denise was the opposite of Karissa in every way, and I wanted the pain to stop. I knew I'd regret not coming here with her forever, but Denise was a way to soothe that ache. Just a little. I loved her in a way, and McJenna was the best thing that's ever happened to me. I don't regret Denise because she gave me J, but I have wished many times that she was mine and Karissa's."

"What are you going to do to win my friend's heart back?"

"Excuse me?" I blurted.

"I think she still loves you. I don't think she ever stopped, either. And I think you two would be good together. If she'd ever let go of her bruised ego and wounded pride."

"I can't make her do those things."

"No, but you can get her to fall in love with you all over again. She wants to let herself love you. You just have to stop pissing her off so she will."

"And how do I do that?"

Finley shrugged. "If I knew, I wouldn't be asking you what your plan is."

She was right. I needed a plan. A way to get back into Karissa's heart.

"Thanks, Finley," I said, getting up from the table.

I went up to my room and ignored the feeling of dread in my gut. She was the one I wanted. Which meant signing up for a dating app, even if it was the one she created, was a bad idea. I needed to delete it.

I opened the app to close my account, but a message popped up from one of the women I'd been chatting with for the last few weeks.

QUEEN

You never told me. Is Newbie because you're new to the area or new to online dating?

I hesitated. I could ignore the message, but...

Finley said Karissa was the queen. Could it possibly be her messaging me? For weeks?

NEWBIE

Both actually. I haven't lived locally for long, and I never thought about online dating until I moved here. But a friend had great success and I couldn't resist.

QUEEN

Well, that's good to hear.

NEWBIE

Have you met anyone here?

QUEEN

A few people. I like that we're anonymous though. Great profile pic.

NEWBIE

LOL! Thanks. I guess I'm prickly like a porcupine.

QUEEN

Maybe you're just misunderstood.

NEWBIE

I'd like to think so. I'm a pretty simple guy. I like spending time with the people I love and enjoying life.

QUEEN

What about work? Do you enjoy your job?

NEWBIE

I do, but I've learned there's a lot more to life than work. It's cost me in the past, and I'm not willing to lose anyone else I care about because of work.

QUEEN

I'm the opposite. I've put family and friends ahead of everything and it cost me.

NEWBIE

I don't think that's a bad thing. Being around for the people you care about.

QUEEN

Maybe. But I might have missed out on something that could have been great. A life I wished I'd lived. I don't have regrets, but I do wonder what might have been.

NEWBIE

That's normal. I'm the same. Maybe a second chance will come your way.

QUEEN

Maybe you're right.

9

KARISSA

I turned off my phone and smiled. Newbie was funny. It was nice chatting with him. Familiar in a way, but not. He made me laugh, and he made me feel like I could talk to him. Like sharing that a part of me still wished I'd chosen Xavier instead of my hometown all those years ago.

I was a mess when I first came home from college. My mom tried to be there for me, but I was inconsolable. I wanted Xavier, but I wanted the life I planned. The life we both planned. My dad died when I was in high school, and I wanted to live in MacKellar Cove by my mom and raise my family close to her.

I built a life on my own. Not the life I thought I would have with Xavier, but a good life. I became friends with Finley, Blake, Elise, and Laura over the years. All facilitated by my mom. Finley and I moved in together, and my mom reconnected with Eddie, and life moved forward.

But through all those years, I wished Xavier was there to share it with me. I did things I hoped he would have been proud of. I created things I wanted to tell him about. I made the best life I could, but it was a lonely life.

And it was going to get even lonelier.

I went to bed in my far too quiet apartment and tried to decide what I should do with Finley's room. I could move my desk in there, but I didn't always sit at a desk to work. I could turn it into something else, but I didn't have any hobbies.

It could have been a nursery.

The thought was drifting away as quickly as it appeared, but it still stung. I'd always wanted kids. I knew at thirty-eight it was still possible, but after my surgery a year ago and my lack of romantic prospects, I'd given up on that dream.

I laid down and tried not to think about all the things Xavier and I planned that I never got to have. Kids. A house. A partner in my life. Vacations and love and laughter. I had some of it, but it was different. And after all this time, I was different, too.

I woke up the next morning ready for my day. I had a meeting with a potential client who wanted me to design an app for their e-commerce company. It was a smaller company and would be a lower payout than the project I lost the week before, but I needed an income so I couldn't afford to be picky.

After breakfast and my shower, I checked my hair and put on a peach top that complimented my dark skin and always made me feel good. My mom got it for me when we were in Hawaii for her wedding. It was my version of a power suit.

When it was time for my meeting, I sat at my desk so the owner of the company would see the solid wall behind me instead of my unmade bed and dirty laundry.

I smiled as the computer dialed, the beeps and dings

making me tense as time ticked by waiting for the owner to answer.

Three rings. Four. What if they weren't going to hire me because of the rumors going around, too? Maybe they were just going to ghost me instead of answering the call. ·

"Hello. Hello! Sorry! Hang on." The picture was fuzzy. A shirt? No, pants. I could see pockets. And behind the person who was walking quickly down a hallway, I saw a dog trying to chase them.

A door closed, and the computer was moved. Finally, a person came into view.

"Hi, Ms. Thomas. I am so sorry I wasn't ready for your call. It's so nice to meet you. I'm Bex."

"It's nice to meet you. And please, call me Karissa."

"Karissa. Excellent. My youngest is home sick today and my wife couldn't take the day off, so I'm trying to work while also taking care of a sick kid. And a busy dog who thinks it's play time since my son's here. It's been a day."

"We can reschedule if you need to. I completely understand."

"No, no. I have been so excited to meet you. I love the apps you've designed. I've been looking at a few of them and am so impressed with you."

I leaned back, feeling much better about the call. "Thank you. So much. I really appreciate that."

"You're talented. There's no way around that. I'm probably screwing all of this up by gushing, but I couldn't play it cool. That's just not me."

I breathed a laugh, appreciating Bex's honesty. "I'm not like that either. I have been looking into your company. I love what you're doing."

"Thank you. I'm really passionate about creating products that celebrate diverse families. There are so many companies that started out with just one idea and have grown, and I'm seeing why. I never predicted the kind of growth I've seen over the last eight months."

"That's great news. You're giving people a way to express themselves. To share who they are. It doesn't surprise me that it's taking off."

"Thanks. It's been a lot of fun. But customers are asking about an app, for e-commerce to start with."

"What other things are you considering?" I asked. I wanted to make sure I built in the framework for future expansions if it was something I could do.

"Maybe a community, a place for people to share how they used our designs in their lives. A place for people to connect. Maybe something where we can offer suggestions of other companies that have the same mission of showing the world that all families are normal, no matter how they're formed."

"I love it," I told her, scribbling ideas. "It sounds like you have lots of plans."

"I definitely have shiny object syndrome." Bex chuckled, tossing her long twin French braids behind her back.

"Well, I love what you're doing, and I'd love to work on a proposal and get back to you in a few days, if that's okay."

"Oh, yeah. Um, okay, cards on the table?"

I nodded for her to go ahead.

"You're the only person I want to work with. I'm not interviewing other designers. It's you or no one. My wife said I shouldn't tell you that, but I want you to do this. I'm open to whatever creative interpretation you want to do. I can send you my logo and hex codes for colors and whatever else you need, but you're it."

"Wow," I breathed, leaning back in my chair. I set my pen down on the notepad I was using to take notes. I'd had business owners tell me they wanted to work with me before, but they'd all interviewed others with me and most of the time, they chose someone else. This was different.

"I don't know what you can do for my budget, so if that's a concern, maybe we can work out some kind of a step-by-step plan based on your hourly rate. I'm not asking for a discount. I just want to make sure it's perfect, even if that takes a little longer."

"Um, okay. Thank you. I really appreciate that. And if that's the case... You said you were open to ideas?"

"Yes, absolutely. I know it needs to sell things, but that's it."

"Let me think about this and try out a few things and I can have a few options for you to look at in a week? Does that work?"

"Absolutely. Yes. That would be wonderful. How do I pay you for that work?"

"I will work up a proposal for you. Usually my per project cost is lower than a per hour cost, but I'll see what I can do. I have your budget, and I'll make sure I stay within it."

"Oh, my God, thank you. I'm so happy to be working with you. Thank you so much, Karissa."

"You're so welcome, Bex. Thank you for the opportunity."

"You're the best. We'll talk soon."

"Bye."

I hung up the computer and stared at the screen for a long minute. I went into the meeting dreading it, wondering if I was going to get anything out of it. And I got a job and a huge fan. It was going to be a good day.

> Want to join me for lunch today?

I STARED at the text for longer than I should have. One of my best friends wanted to have lunch. Why was I second guessing that? I adored Finley, and I wanted to see her more, not less.

Finally, I replied that I'd love to join her and asked if she wanted me to pick something up.

> I'm going to put in an order. Italian?

> Always up for Italian. Thanks!

> Thanks for joining me. See you soon!

I smiled and admitted to myself that I was happy for Finley. Yes, things had changed, and I wasn't sure what I was going to do with the empty bedroom in my condo, or if I was going to stay there, but I wanted her to be happy. With Trent and George. She deserved it.

I finished up my work for the morning and changed out of my pajama pants and into pants that matched with my peach top. The black linen pants were perfect for the summer day. I felt damn good as I walked the few blocks from my apartment to Finley's shop.

"Karissa?" I heard from behind me as I got closer to the shop.

I turned and found McJenna half a block behind me. "Hey, McJenna. How are you?"

She shook her head. "I've been better. I came to work with Finley today and was trying to meet some people, but no one my age is out. And then I got lost. And I'm starving and hot and—"

"Whoa, calm down. Are you okay?"

She shrugged, looking more like a kid than a sassy teenager.

"Why don't you come with me? I was going to have lunch with Finley."

"No! I don't want her to hate me for coming back so soon."

"Finley will not care."

"It's fine. I'll just go get some food somewhere. It'll be better after that."

I looped my arm through hers and tugged her toward Book Boyfriends Unlimited with me. "It'll be fine. We have plenty of food coming. And it'll give us all a chance to talk."

McJenna hesitated, but she bit down on the inside of her lip and nodded.

Finley was with a customer when we walked in, but she smiled at both of us and waved. I led McJenna to the couches toward the back where we camped out for book club. "I'm going to grab some drinks."

She nodded and picked at her nails.

I grabbed three bottles of water and carried them back to where McJenna was talking to an older lady.

"I don't know you, lady. I'm not telling you where I live," McJenna said.

"Hi, Mrs. Zachary," I said, realizing who it was and moving in quickly. "This is McJenna Hogan. Her dad is Trent MacKellar's best friend. They're living with him and Finley at the Estate."

"Don't tell her where I live," McJenna snapped.

"It's okay," I assured her. "I've known Mrs. Zachary my entire life. In a small town, people want to know who's who."

"She asked if I lived here and where when I said I did."

"She doesn't recognize you," I said.

"I'm sorry I caused trouble," Mrs. Zachary said. "I was just trying to be neighborly."

"I know, Mrs. Zachary. McJenna is still adjusting to living in a town where everyone knows who she is," I said.

"You people are weird," McJenna mumbled.

"Yes, we are," Mrs. Zachary said. "And we like life that way. Next time I see you, McJenna, I will say hello. And you have to introduce me to your father. I hear he's quite a catch."

McJenna's eyes went wide as the woman turned and hobbled away with her cane leading the way.

"Was she just...?"

"Yes," I answered.

"Ew."

I snorted. Another hazard of small town living. Even the older people needed dates. And fresh meat was fresh meat.

"Water?" I asked her.

"Yes, please. I need to get that out of my head. Can I dump it over myself?"

"Only if you want Finley to kick you out forever."

She nodded sharply. "Good point. She's my only ally. I think I need her to like me."

"I'm not your ally?"

McJenna shrugged. "I don't know. You kind of ditched me last week at the castle place."

I closed my eyes and sighed. She was right. It was a shit move. "I'm sorry about that. It had nothing to do with you."

"I know. My dad said he made you mad."

My brows shot up. "He said that?"

"Yeah. He believes in telling me the truth. Even if it's not something I really want to hear."

"Wow. Okay. I give him credit for that. But I'm still sorry. And I want to be your ally."

She shrugged again but didn't reply before Finley joined us.

"I flipped the sign. Let's go to the back and eat. Glad you could join us, J. Are you hungry?"

"I could eat, but it's okay if you don't have enough. I ran into Karissa outside. She invited me."

"And I told her we always have enough food," I said.

"We do," Finley agreed. "Come on. Let's eat."

Finley led the way to the break room where the food was on the counter. She grabbed paper plates from one of the cabinets and plastic silverware. We opened the containers of food, including a dozen breadsticks, a salad that would serve four, and our two entrees. Lasagna and manicotti.

Finley cut the lasagna into three pieces and I divided up the manicotti. We added breadsticks to each plate and a large serving of the salad.

"Whoa, you weren't kidding," McJenna said when we set the plates down on the table. "This is a ton of food."

"It is. And there's more," Finley told her. "We love ordering from Gino's. It's delicious and always too much food."

"It's really good," McJenna said around a mouthful of lasagna.

Finley and I smiled and nodded.

We all dug into our lunch. Again, I missed out on a chance to spend time with Finley, but I couldn't say I was upset about McJenna being there with us. She looked more than a little lost when I saw her on the street. The food and the company seemed to be doing wonders for her.

When we finished eating and cleaned up the break room, Finley asked McJenna how things were going and if she'd met anyone around town.

"Nope. No one is out. They probably all know each

other, anyway. None of them are going to want to hang out with me."

"Not true. Let's go get some dessert. Finley needs to get back to work, but we can go out for cupcakes. Besides, I got a new job today and I want to celebrate because I really like the company I'm going to be working with," I said.

"I'm jealous. Say hi to Valentina for me," Finley said.

I nodded. We waved bye and headed toward Cove Bakery as Finley let in a customer.

It was much quieter than the last time I saw McJenna there with Xavier. We walked straight up to the counter and said hello to Harriett.

"How are you ladies today?" Harriett asked cheerfully.

"We're doing well. How about you?" I asked.

"Oh, I'm hanging in there. What can I get you two?"

"Cookie dough cupcake for me," I said. "You?"

"Do you have any of those eclairs?" McJenna asked.

Harriett and I laughed.

"Those sold out in a hurry. They were good, weren't they?" Harriett asked.

"So good."

"Let me see what Valentina has in the back. She might have something special for you." Harriett got up to go to the back, but she didn't get far before Valentina was pushing her way through the doors with a tray in her hands.

"I told you to call for me if you need something," Valentina chastised her boss. "You need to be resting that knee."

"I'm fine. It gets stiff if I sit too long."

"The doctor said to stay off of it. Now, what were you coming to the back for?" Valentina looked at us and grinned. "Hey, Karissa. How ya doing?"

"Good, Valentina. Do you remember McJenna?" I said.

"It's nice to see you again, McJenna. We didn't get to chat much before. Are you going to MacKellar Cove High School in the fall?"

"I am. I'll be a sophomore."

"My older daughter is a sophomore, too. Her name's Bianca. You should meet up," Valentina said.

"I wasn't sure how old Bianca and Sam were. McJenna hasn't met anyone. She moved here after summer started," I told Valentina.

McJenna stared at the floor, likely wanting to die from embarrassment.

"And obviously, she's really happy I'm telling you this because she feels dumb," I said.

Valentina chuckled, a husky laugh. "I get it. My girls would die if I talked to someone else their age. How about this, McJenna? Bianca comes in here with me on Friday mornings to work. Every Friday she's here until eleven. Why don't you come by Friday a little before eleven? We'll stage a meetup that no one else knows about so you and Bianca can meet. Does that work for you?"

McJenna looked up at me and nodded. Then she looked at Valentina. "Are you sure?"

Valentina smiled. "Absolutely."

"You won't tell her?"

"Not unless you want me to. I might tell her I met you today, but not that you're going to be here on Friday."

"Okay," McJenna said. "Thanks."

Valentina squeezed her hand. "My pleasure, hun. Now, what sweet treat are you hoping I have in the back? I heard Harriett say I might have something special back there."

McJenna looked up at me.

"She was hoping for an eclair," I whispered.

"Ooh, a girl after my own heart," Valentina said. "I think

I've got one or two back there. But you can't tell anyone else where you got them or I'll get in trouble. I'm trying out a few flavors. Strawberry, chocolate, or lemon?"

"I had chocolate, so strawberry," McJenna said, her smile wide and bright.

"Coming right up," Valentina said. She was back a minute later with an eclair on a plate for McJenna. She handed it over and said, "I'll see you Friday. I'll have some new stuff for you to try. If you're willing to be a tester for me."

"Hey, how come I don't get that offer?" I asked.

"Because you like everything," Valentina told me.

I nodded. "True."

McJenna inhaled the sweet scent of the eclair and nodded at Valentina. "I'll be a tester."

I smiled. That was a much better look for her than the one I found her with. And Friday would be even better.

10

———

I buried myself in work for the next two days. I finished the project I'd been working on and turned it into the company a week before the deadline. They were so happy with it that they gave me a bonus for completing everything they asked for ahead of schedule and on budget.

As soon as that was finished, I dove into my proposal for Bex. I had ideas coming at me since we spoke, but I knew I needed to finish my other project before I could really dive into hers.

By the middle of Friday morning, I was dying for a break. And it was right on time for McJenna's pre-arranged meetup with Bianca. I was her excuse for being there, which meant I had to get moving.

I was dressed but hadn't tackled any makeup yet, or decided if I wanted to, when my phone pinged with an alert from Book Boyfriends Wanted.

NEWBIE

If you had a superpower, what would it be?

I laughed out loud at the question. He'd been asking me

all kinds of weird things, trying to get to know me. It was funny, and enlightening.

QUEEN

I'd love to be invisible.

NEWBIE

Really? Why is that?

QUEEN

Then I could hide from people and do what I want without anyone asking me for anything.

NEWBIE

LOL! I was thinking it was so you could spy on people without them knowing you were there. That's why I would want it.

QUEEN

Who would you spy on?

NEWBIE

My kid for one. I always wonder what she's thinking and never feel like I know.

QUEEN

That would be tough. I was super close to my mom growing up and told her everything, but my dad was always in the dark. We had a good relationship, but it was different.

NEWBIE

I'm all she has, but I never feel like it's enough.

He reminded me of Xavier and McJenna. Dad and daughter alone against the world.

NEWBIE

But I'm doing the best I can.

QUEEN

And I'm sure she knows that. What would your superpower be?

NEWBIE

Mind reading. Definitely. Then I wouldn't have to wonder what was going on with her. Or anyone else.

QUEEN

That's not bad. Unless you found out something bad. Like your boss hates you or your girlfriend was cheating on you.

NEWBIE

I'd rather know. Life's too short to be dishonest.

I wholeheartedly agreed with that statement.

QUEEN

Sorry, but I need to go. Meeting a friend. Talk later?

NEWBIE

I'm looking forward to it.

I tucked my phone away and rushed out of my condo. Makeup was no longer an option if I was going to actually make it on time. McJenna texted me that she was at Finley's shop. I hurried down the street, crossing my fingers that we wouldn't be late getting to Cove Bakery.

"Let's go," I said, waving to her when I got close.

She was standing outside the door, looking both ways for me to get there. She opened the door and called inside to Finley, then hurried over to me. "I thought you weren't coming."

I shook my head. "I'd never do that to you. I got tied up

in work and didn't realize what time it was. I'm sorry. But we're still good. Plenty of time."

McJenna didn't look convinced, but Cove Bakery was almost empty when we got there.

We both ordered chocolate croissants and paid for our treats. We claimed a table while Harriett went to the back to get Valentina.

We were halfway through our chocolate croissants when Valentina and Bianca walked over. Bianca looked a lot like her mom with brown skin and wavy hair. She had the same smile and brown eyes, too.

"Hi," Valentina said. "It's good to see you two again. I heard my taste testers were here."

McJenna clammed up immediately, her lips turning up in a strained smile as her gaze flickered between Valentina and Bianca.

"We are ready," I said. "We needed a sweet fix today. McJenna has been hanging around Finley's this morning while I got some work done."

"You know Finley Jameson?" Bianca said.

McJenna nodded. "She's marrying my Uncle Trent."

"That's really cool. I love her store. I'm obsessed with reading, and she has so many cute things in there. Oh, I'm Bianca, by the way."

"McJenna. It's nice to meet you."

"You, too. Are you visiting for the summer?"

McJenna shook her head. "No, I moved here after the school year ended. I'm going to be a sophomore next year."

"Oh, sweet, me, too. We should totally hang out. Can I get your number? If that's okay with your mom."

I shook my head. "Not her mom, but I'm sure her dad would be okay with it. I know your mom. He's been in here, too. It's impossible to resist coming here."

Bianca groaned. "I know, right? All my friends want to work here when they get older, but they don't know how hard it is to be here and not eat everything. I think I've gained ten pounds since summer started."

McJenna laughed. "I've done the same, but that's just from sitting around all the time."

"You have to come out with us. Mom, can McJenna come over this weekend?" Bianca turned a pleading look on her mom.

Valentina just laughed. "I have no problem with that. I think your dad is out of town, but that's okay. Why don't you let McJenna ask her dad?"

"Yeah, do you want to? I'm actually done working here in a little while. Do you want to hang out with me this afternoon? We can grab lunch and walk around. Some of my friends are going to be hanging out in the park later. If you want."

McJenna grinned and nodded. "Yeah, that would be awesome. Thanks."

"Yay, I'm excited."

"First, you need to finish cleaning up," Valentina said, her voice firm but not harsh. "And these two need to finish their treats. These are s'mores bites. Graham cracker crust, marshmallow, and chocolate. In a cookie form. I've gotten good reviews so far, but you two will tell me if it's good enough to sell."

McJenna picked one up and raised it to her lips. She took a bite and groaned. "Oh, man." She pulled it away, the chocolate and gooey marshmallow leaving a string between her mouth and the treat. She brought it back to her lips for another bite. "That's sooo good."

Valentina chuckled. "That's one yes. Karissa?"

I lifted the other one and took a bite. The sweetness of

the marshmallow and the bitterness of the chocolate paired perfectly. The graham cracker had just enough resistance to hold the whole thing together, but not so much that it squished out like a regular s'more. The soft, gooey center was perfect, like a cookie that was slightly underbaked but crunchy on the outside.

"Wow," I said. "That's perfect."

"Yeah?" Valentina asked.

"I told you it was, Mom. Dad doesn't know what he's talking about," Bianca said.

Valentina's smile dimmed just slightly. Her eyes lost their glow of excitement. She recovered, bringing her smile back, but her eyes said Bianca's words hurt. Not because of Bianca but because of her husband.

"Anyone who said this isn't amazing is wrong," McJenna said, shoving the rest into her mouth. "It's so good."

"I agree. These would be huge sellers," I told Valentina.

She smiled brighter, her eyes lighting up once more. "Thank you both. I think they might have to go on the menu with praise like that."

"Definitely."

"We'll let you finish, then you girls can go wander for a while," Valentina said. "Thanks for coming in."

Valentina winked at us, then pushed Bianca back to the kitchen, both of them smiling.

"She's really nice," McJenna said. "Do you think she's going to like me?"

"I think she already does," I told her. "It sounds like she likes to read as much as you do."

McJenna smiled. "That's good. Most of my other friends thought I was a nerd for reading."

"Being a nerd is not the worst thing in the world. But

having someone like you for who you are is the best thing in the world."

McJenna grinned. I had the feeling she didn't have a lot of people who believed in her. I was sure Xavier did, and Trent, but aside from them, I got the feeling she was never told how smart and capable she was. She could do anything she wanted. I had no doubt of that.

We finished our treats, then Bianca came back out without the apron. She asked McJenna if she was ready to go, and they were off.

Valentina walked out a minute later and sat with me. "Thank you for bringing her back here. I think they hit it off."

"I do, too. Thank you. She's so excited."

"Bianca is, too. She loves making new friends."

"Good. McJenna definitely needs someone to be her friend. She's had a boring summer."

Valentina laughed. "Well, no more with Bianca around. That child can't keep still for longer than a few minutes. She'll have McJenna wishing for her quiet back."

I laughed. "I'm not so sure. They might be a great match."

"I hope so. She seems like a good kid. And her dad is pretty good-looking."

"Oh, no. Don't start that."

"Start what?" She tried to play all innocent, but she wasn't fooling me.

"I'm going to say thank you and go before I get myself into trouble with you. Bye, Valentina!"

"Bye, Karissa! See you again soon!"

I laughed and walked out, looking for the girls. They were standing on the sidewalk, talking animatedly, both with big smiles on their faces. That was good to see.

McJenna texted me later that day, thanking me for going with her to meet Bianca. I told her it was all my pleasure. I was happy she was finally feeling a little more at home in MacKellar Cove.

> My dad said thank you, too.

> Tell your dad he's welcome, too.

> Maybe he can take you out to dinner to thank you.

> Is that your dad asking or you, McJenna?

> Does it matter?

> Goodnight McJenna. I'll talk to you later.

I hated to admit the idea of going out with Xavier held some appeal. I didn't want to still be attracted to him, or still in love with him, but I was struggling to hold on to my mad lately.

Finley talked about Xavier every chance she got. I didn't think she was doing it on purpose, but she was always telling me about something amazing he was doing. As a father or a person or a friend or at work. I didn't really want to hear it, but she told me anyway.

To be fair, she also bragged about Trent and how great of a father he was, but there seemed to be a lot more moments where Xavier was the star than Trent. Or maybe I was imagining things.

I thought about reaching out to Finley to see what she was up to over the weekend, but I resisted the urge. I had to get used to being alone, and it needed to start now.

Friday night was quiet for me, a movie and bed early. Saturday I went for a walk early to get outside and enjoy the fresh air. I treated myself to breakfast at Cove Bakery and walked home as I ate my croissant and blueberry muffin.

I did some work on the proposal for Bex, then settled in for the rest of the day. I was content not to leave home again.

I hadn't decided if I was going to stay in my condo or if I was going to move. Rentals in the area were hard to come by since it was a small town, but there were usually homes for sale. I'd looked a few times over the years, but I'd never been serious. As forty got closer and closer, I knew I wanted something I had control over. A place where I knew who was there and who wasn't. My neighbors weren't bad, but they weren't all great either. Like the guy on the ground floor who didn't always think he needed to wear shoes to get his mail. Or shower. Or the woman on the top floor who liked to yell into her phone, on speaker, when she walked up and down the stairs.

I spent about an hour looking at possibilities but not falling in love with any of them. Or even liking them more than where I was. The added expense of taxes, maintaining the outside, and having to take care of everything was daunting. I wanted more, but I wasn't sure I was really ready for it.

I tossed my computer to the side and turned on Netflix. There was a movie I'd been wanting to see, and it was a good night for it.

The movie was halfway done, and not as good as I hoped it would be, when my phone dinged.

NEWBIE

What do you value most in life?

QUEEN

Honesty. Without a doubt.

NEWBIE

That's a good one.

QUEEN

What about you?

NEWBIE

Love. And family. But they go together for me. I love my family.

QUEEN

Are you close to them?

NEWBIE

My parents, no. We haven't been in touch since my daughter was born. But I have a friend who's like a brother to me, and I'd do anything for him.

Okay, seriously, the more Newbie talked, the more I thought he might be Xavier.

The urge to look it up was strong. I could have the answer in a few minutes. I would know everything about him, right down to his IP address.

But I promised my friends I wouldn't do that. For them. But for me...

No, I couldn't. I didn't want to. Not really. If it was Xavier, it would change everything. But if it wasn't, I would be violating the privacy of a perfectly nice guy. A guy I really enjoyed talking to.

NEWBIE

Are you close to your family?

QUEEN

Both my parents have passed. No siblings.

For some reason, I didn't want to tell him about Eddie. Even though Eddie was my step-dad and I adored him, it felt like I would be revealing information that would make it possible for him to figure out who I was.

NEWBIE

I'm sorry. That sucks.

QUEEN

No more than you not being in touch with yours. Mine didn't have a choice. Sounds like yours are just shitty people.

NEWBIE

LOL! You tell it how it is. I can't say I disagree.

QUEEN

Sugar coating is only good if it's actual sugar and it's coating something like chocolate.

NEWBIE

So, I'm guessing you have a sweet tooth?

QUEEN

Nope. I have sweet teeth. All of them!

NEWBIE

I have a kid that's the same. I can barely drag her out of a bakery.

QUEEN

A girl after my own heart.

NEWBIE

What's something you've always wanted to do but never did?

QUEEN

That's tough without getting too personal. Are you sure you want to know?

NEWBIE

> I want to know anything you want to tell me.

I smiled at his answer. It was a very Xavier thing to say. I could be wrong, but a part of me really hoped it was him on the other end of the phone, texting me.

I decided to find new matches because I was determined to forget about him and move on. I thought that was the best for me. But every time I turned around, he was there. I was punishing myself for loving him by not letting myself love him.

Maybe the guy I was chatting with wasn't Xavier. Maybe it was someone else. At the end of the day, it didn't matter because I wanted it to be him. Which told me I needed to start seriously thinking about giving him another chance. About giving us another chance.

QUEEN

> I always wanted a family. A husband, kids, a house with a yard where I could have friends and family over and enjoy life together.

NEWBIE

> And you think it's too late for any of that?

QUEEN

> Partly. I'm not sure I'd want to have a baby at my age. And no, I'm not telling you how old I am. The husband and house are still things I'd love to have, but I'm also pretty set in my ways. I'd have to find someone who's willing to figure out how we fit into each other's lives.

NEWBIE

I struggle with that, too. Finding someone
who isn't going to want to change
everything, especially with my kid. She
comes first for me, always will. It's hard to
think about changing that.

QUEEN

You shouldn't have to. The right person will
know your kid is your priority.

NEWBIE

You'd be surprised how many women would
not agree with that statement.

QUEEN

What's the worst date you've ever been on?

NEWBIE

Oh, boy, are you ready for this story?

I settled in and laughed as he told me about a woman who wanted to send his daughter to boarding school after their first date. Then another who refused to acknowledge the kid at all. And a third who decided they were both too much work before the date even started.

I was starting to get his concerns.

We talked for hours, sharing stories of failed relationships and dates, the dreams we gave up somewhere along the way, and what we hope our futures might look like.

When I fell asleep early in the morning, with my phone still in my hand, I really wanted to know who he was. And if maybe I'd finally found the magic.

11

XAVIER

"ALL I'M SAYING IS NONE OF US WOULD BE HERE WITHOUT Karissa," Trent said, raising his glass.

The rest of us followed suit, even McJenna with her pop. Finley and Trent sat on one side of the square table. Blake and Ian were next to Finley. McJenna and I were across from them, with me next to Trent. Karissa sat next to McJenna with Hudson on the same side as her. Karissa and McJenna had definitely bonded since Karissa introduced J to Bianca the day before and my kid had a friend in town. We were like one big happy family, sort of.

"To Karissa," everyone said at once, making us all laugh.

I brought my glass to my lips and sipped my water. Out of the corner of my eye, I watched Karissa try not to grin. She had every reason to be proud of the work she did to create her app. It was definitely made with some kind of magic since it brought her and I together again.

Well, I was pretty sure. I hadn't actually gotten confirmation, but it was hard to imagine she was not Queen.

"Thank you all for being here tonight," Trent said, commanding the attention of everyone again. "Finley and I want a wedding that really feels like us. We want George involved somehow, and we want all of you to be a part of it. I hope you're all willing to help us out."

"Of course," Blake said for the group. She reached over and squeezed Finley's hand. "We'll do anything to make it the perfect day."

"Thank you," Finley said.

Trent smiled at her, everything about him saying how happy he was. I'd never seen him so relaxed around people other than J and me. He kept his guard up most of the time, wondering what people wanted from him, but with this small group of Finley's family and friends, Trent was the guy I knew him to be. She saw him, really saw him, and he let her.

As I watched them, I decided I wanted to do something special for them. Sure, I was Trent's best man, which meant I'd have a role in the wedding, but I wanted something that would show them how much they both meant to me. The only problem was I had no idea what it could be.

"Our friends are all getting married, it seems," Karissa said.

"And we all have you and Book Boyfriends Wanted to thank for it," Finley said.

"That's the magic of Mom," Karissa said.

"Mom?" McJenna asked.

"My mom was amazing at connecting people. She brought us together." Karissa gestured to Blake and Finley. "I'm older than they are so we didn't know each other growing up, but my mom worked with Blake, and Blake and Finley grew up together. She introduced us all. And she nudged Ian to finally tell Blake he was in love with her."

"Really?" I asked. Looking at the two of them, I couldn't imagine Blake and Ian not being together. The way they talked and responded to each other, it was like they could read each other's minds.

"Yeah," Ian answered. "She was dating someone else for a long time, and I was just dick—uh, messing around. The last time I visited Georgia, she told me I'd better confess how I felt to Blake or I needed to move on."

"That's gutsy," I said.

Karissa shook her head. "That was Mom. She saw things the rest of us couldn't. After college, she told me—"

Karissa ducked her head, the smile on her face fading. It told me everything I needed to know about what her mom said about me. That I wasn't worth it and that she needed to find someone else. And she was right. Karissa deserved better than me. But things had changed. I'd changed. I wasn't that same man. And I was going to prove it to her.

"What did she tell you?" McJenna asked, unaware of the tension around the table.

"Um, J, maybe we can talk about it later," Finley said quietly, trying to diffuse the situation.

"It's okay," I said. "Karissa can say it. It's not a secret that I wasn't who she needed in her life back then."

"And you are now?" Ian asked.

I turned to look at him. We'd only met a few times, but I got the feeling Ian was the kind of guy who appreciated honesty. Even if he was too chicken to give it to Blake when he was pining for her.

"I don't think I'll ever be good enough for Karissa. She's an amazing woman. She's smart and creative and passionate and stunning. I don't have much of anything to offer her or any other woman. But whether or not I'm someone she needs in her life is a decision she has to make. Not me or you or anyone else. My guess is Karissa doesn't need anyone in her life, but wanting something and needing something are not the same thing." I sipped my water and kept my gaze on Ian's.

He raised his brows and nodded in approval of my response.

"My mom told me Xavier might be someone who was only meant to be in my life for a short period of time, or that we might meet again one day. She said only I would know if it was right to walk away more than once, but that I should always be open to love in whatever form it comes," Karissa said, breaking the silence.

Everyone was quiet as we looked at her. Karissa forced a smile, her gaze averted from everyone else.

"Are you open to loving my dad again?" McJenna asked.

Karissa's eyes went wide before I drew the attention back to me.

"I think we've grilled her enough for tonight. Finley, tell us what plans you have set for the wedding," I said.

Finley latched on to the change in subject and dove in. Everyone else followed, asking questions and keeping the focus on the wedding instead of on Karissa.

When we finished eating and cleared the table, Blake and Ian made their excuses to leave. Hudson wasn't far behind them, claiming he needed to check in on the bar. McJenna went up to her room, likely to text Bianca, leaving Finley, Trent, George, Karissa, and me. It wasn't long before George started to fuss.

"Don't leave yet," Finley told Karissa as she carried George inside. Trent was right behind her, tag-teaming the crying baby.

"I'm sorry about what McJenna asked you," I told Karissa when we were alone.

"It's fine."

I shook my head. "It isn't. She shouldn't have put you on

the spot. I shouldn't have either. You had every right to keep quiet about what your mom told you. I just got the feeling you wouldn't have thought twice about sharing it if I weren't here."

She turned to look at me and studied my face for a long minute. "I wouldn't have thought twice. And there's a part of me that has no problem with you knowing what she said. But I'm not the same person I was back then. I'm a lot more jaded and cynical than I used to be. We were barely old enough to drink, and we were making plans for a future that was never meant to be. That foolish girl is gone. She's lost her parents and the love of her life and she's grown up."

"Was I the love of your life?" I asked, my heart racing as my breath slowed to nothing.

She looked out at the water, staring past me. I waited, needing the answer. Finally, she nodded. "I thought you were."

"But you don't anymore?"

"I don't know if I can forgive you. If I can get past what happened. Not that what you did was horrible, but it was really hard to accept that you were planning a future without me when I thought we were planning a future together. There's a part of me that wants to be open to love like my mom always told me to be, but I've lost too many people. I'm not sure I'm going to be able to trust you again."

"Then how about we start with something small?"

"Like what?"

"I want to do something for Trent and Finley. For their wedding. I don't know what yet, but something that will show them how much they mean to me. Would you be willing to help me figure out what to do? Or what to get if I decide on that?"

She took a long moment to consider my question. "Yes, I will help you."

I exhaled a breath I didn't know I was holding. "Thank you. And maybe we can work on building that trust and getting to know each other again. What do you say?"

"I can try."

I grinned, unable to stop myself.

She laughed, smiling with me. "Stop it."

"I can't help it. I'm happy you're willing to try. How about dinner? Tuesday night?"

"We just agreed to be friends."

"Yes, and to get to know each other again. If you're going to help me, I'm guessing we're also going to need to get together somewhere other than where Trent and Finley live to talk. So, dinner?"

She breathed another laugh and nodded. "Fine. Dinner."

"Sounds good. I'll pick you up at seven."

She raised her brows. "I can get myself to dinner."

I shrugged. "I know, but I want to pick you up. See where you live. Get a little peek into who you are now."

"You think I'm going to show you that after one date?"

"Oh, so it's a date now?"

She laughed again and shook her head. "I'm going to stop talking."

I smiled and leaned back in my seat. I had a date. With my Queen.

I COULD BARELY HOLD back from telling everyone I knew about my date with Karissa. I got the feeling she didn't want anyone to hear about it when Finley and Trent came back and she made her excuses to leave right away. Trent asked what I said to her, but I told him we had a nice conversation and left it at that.

Waiting for our date was painful, but it was made easier by our chats online. Especially the one the night before our date.

QUEEN

Do you believe in second chances?

NEWBIE

Absolutely.

QUEEN

Why? If someone hurt you, why would you give them another chance?

NEWBIE

Things change. I wouldn't blindly trust, but I would have a hard time flat out rejecting someone I cared about.

QUEEN

Is there ever a time you would?

I sucked in a breath when I read that line. It felt like she wanted to reject me but was debating.

NEWBIE

Not me, no. If someone came back into my life and wanted to reconcile, I'd go slow, but I wouldn't say no. I'd need a reason to say no.

QUEEN

What if there was someone else in your life who didn't trust the person?

I thought of J and Denise. The only reason to let Denise back into my life would be to give her a chance at a relationship with J, but I'd never force my kid to have a relationship with the mother who abandoned her the first chance she got.

NEWBIE

> It would depend. If I trusted this other person, I would hope they could be honest with me about their reasons. But I wouldn't choose someone who hurt me over someone who hadn't.

QUEEN

Love makes us do crazy things.

NEWBIE

Always.

I couldn't help but wonder if Karissa was asking about us. If she was thinking of giving me another chance, a real chance.

Every time I saw her, she was acting more and more like the woman I used to know. I loved seeing it come out in her. Seeing her be true to herself instead of hiding who she was.

Honesty was always important to Karissa, which was why my choice to take the job and leave her was so bad. It was the right choice at the time, but I should have been honest with her from the start about looking for jobs outside the area. The fact that she was talking to me about it now and willing to try to start over made me feel like things were changing. God, I hoped they were.

Maybe I needed to ask her mom for a little magical help in that area.

When it was finally time for me to pick up Karissa for our date, she was standing on the sidewalk outside her condo. She walked over to my car and got in before I could get out and open the door for her.

"I was going to get that."

"Yeah, but then everyone in town will see us together and know we're going out."

"And you don't want anyone to know." I wasn't mad, or hurt, not really. She had her reasons, and I was invading her safe space. I didn't mind treading carefully.

"It's not that. Not entirely. I've spent years wishing things had been different between us. You being here has been hard in ways I never imagined because we're different. If you'd moved here after a year, or even two, I probably would have forgiven and forgotten and built a life with you. But you didn't. And it's been a long time. And there's still that part of me that wants to forgive and forget, but there's a louder part of me that wants to make you suffer."

A laugh burst from me.

Karissa sighed. "I know. It's crazy, but—"

I put my hand over hers. "No. It's not crazy. You were my world. I was willing to do anything for you. I planned to move here, and I was going to give up my dream of being a TV producer, but that job... I told myself I could take the job and have you. That you would choose me the same way I was willing to choose you. When you got angry, I wasn't willing to talk about it. I decided what we had was one-sided because you weren't willing to give up our plans for me the way I always said I'd give up my plans for you."

"I thought our plans were your plans," she said softly.

"I know. I loved you too much to tell you otherwise. We were young, and I wasn't willing to rock the boat. I thought I could make it all work, figure something out, but I couldn't find anything until I looked farther away. And I couldn't see past what I wanted after pushing it aside for so long. I ruined us, and I'm really sorry about that, Karissa."

She shook her head. "It sounds like we both did."

My hand was still over hers, and she put her other hand on mine, linking our fingers together. I smiled and held onto her while I drove south to a restaurant outside of town so no one would see us together.

We talked about the wedding and Finley and Trent on the twenty-minute drive. When we made it into the restaurant and sat down, she looked up at me and chewed on her lower lip.

"I have something I need to tell you," she said.

I tried not to panic, but those were words no man ever wanted to hear. "Okay."

"I'm Queen."

"Excuse me?" I wasn't sure if she meant what I thought she meant or if she meant something else.

"I think we're paired together on my app. On Book Boyfriends Wanted. My screen name is Queen. You're Newbie, right?"

"How in the hell did you figure that out?"

She chuckled. "I wasn't entirely sure, but you mentioned a teenage daughter and her struggling to find friends. That was my first clue. I was sure after we talked about second chances the other night."

"I was trying not to tip my hat," I admitted.

"You knew who I was?"

"I thought it was you. Finley said something one day about you being the queen of the app. I thought she was saying it because you designed it, but then we were chatting and I wondered if she was telling me in case we were paired up."

Karissa breathed a laugh. "Probably knowing her."

"Is that why you started talking to me more? Because of the app?"

Karissa hesitated, then nodded. "The app is good. And if

we were paired after all this time, maybe there's something still there. I figured it's better to find out. But I need you to be honest with me."

"I will. I promise."

"About McJenna's mom."

"Denise? What about her?"

"If she comes back, I don't want to be in the middle of a love triangle."

"Why would you ever worry about that?"

"Your message the other night. You said you'd always give someone a second chance. If she came back—"

"No. That's...no. If she came back, I would never stand in the way of her having a relationship with J, but Denise and me? We were over a long time ago. She was... I was with her because she was nothing like you. I was trying to forget you. To move on. When she got pregnant, I told myself it was the Universe trying to get me to commit and not go back to you like I'd been thinking about. I thought I could build a life with Denise. I told myself I loved her, and I know a part of me did, but it wasn't the same as it was with you. When she left, I didn't really care. I was too tired to care. But I knew I couldn't show up here and ask for your forgiveness with another woman's baby. I had to put McJenna first."

"And you did. She's an amazing kid. Smart and strong and so kind."

"Thank you. I'd do anything for her. And anything meant giving up the life I wanted. The life I gave up being with you for."

"What do you mean?"

"I passed up promotions and job opportunities that would have forced me into a different schedule or city over the years. J doesn't know. I wanted her to have stability. To know she was the most important thing to me. To do for her what I couldn't do for you."

Karissa put her hand on mine, and I turned mine over to hold on to her. She smiled. "She was the one you needed to be there for. I had my mom. And now I have Eddie, too."

"Who's Eddie?"

She grinned. "My step-dad. He's amazing. And he's going to put you through the ringer."

"I can take it. Anything to prove I'm not the man I once was. For you."

Karissa chuckled. God, that was a beautiful sound. I was happy to hear it again.

12

KARISSA

KNOWING XAVIER FIGURED OUT WHO I WAS ON THE APP WAS A relief. I worried he would be mad that I didn't tell him when I first figured it out. And knowing he wasn't interested in a second chance with McJenna's mom made letting him in an easier choice.

Not that I was ready to marry him and build a future together, but I was open to figuring out if we were still as compatible as we once were.

Xavier and I talked through the rest of dinner, catching up on each other's lives over the years. It was strange to hear about him after the stories I told myself about who he was. I imagined a whole life for him, a future that was happy and full of everything he ever hoped it would be. That wasn't the reality of it, and instead of feeling vindicated, I was sad he was in the same place I was wishing things had been different.

"I'd never change having J," he said, "but I definitely wish I'd had kids with someone who was a partner. Trent is awesome, but there was only so much I could count on him for."

"What do you mean?" I asked.

Xavier shrugged. "Sex."

A laugh popped out of me.

"It's true. Having a kid and raising her was never easy. Trent made all the big parts easier since he was there to co-parent and help with discipline and homework and things like that, but it was lonely for me."

"You didn't date?"

He shook his head. "I was too busy. I made the choice to put J first in every way, and that meant no relationships for me."

"None. At all. Since her mom."

Xavier nodded. "I had a few one-night stands, and some flirtations, but nothing that became more than that."

"Except the one who wanted to send her to boarding school after your first date," I said.

He laughed. "Yeah, she was the one who convinced me I couldn't even take a chance on dating. I wasn't willing to risk someone else thinking she should come ahead of my kid."

"That's admirable," I told him. It really was. Not a lot of men would sacrifice a personal life for their kid. Not a lot of anyone would.

"I don't know about that, but it was the right call for me. I have a tendency to jump in with both feet. If I did that and J got hurt in the process, I never would have forgiven myself. It was better that I didn't jump at all."

"That makes sense."

I set my silverware on my plate and pushed it away. Dinner was amazing. And the company was even better.

"What about you? Any relationships in the last seventeen years or so?" Xavier asked.

I shook my head.

"None?" His voice and raised brows said he thought I was lying.

"Nothing serious. I've dated some, but whenever we were on the edge of something serious, it never felt right to take the plunge."

"You always did like to think things through. And to do things your way."

I chuckled. He was right. I hadn't changed.

"I think that's why I fell for you so hard. You made me see things in different ways. I jumped in and figured things out from the inside, but you would hang back and understand before you started."

"You sped me up."

"And you slowed me down."

We smiled at each other. My mind went back to the first night we spent together. We'd been dating for a few months. All my friends were having sex and not thinking twice about it, but I wasn't sure it was right for me. It was the one and only time Xavier wasn't in a hurry. He never said anything about it. He let me make the decision, and when I told him I wanted to, he still took it slow. It was a night I never forgot.

"What are you thinking about?" he asked. His voice dipped low, the rumble vibrating through my entire body. Even from across the table, I felt him.

"Our first time," I confessed.

"That was a special night."

I nodded.

"I knew I loved you that night."

"After we had sex?"

He smiled and shook his head. "No. Before. You were so scared. You were fidgeting all night, and I knew something was going on. I thought you were going to break up with me, and all I could think about all night was how I would convince you to give me another chance. To keep dating me. I had never felt that way before, or since, and I knew that was love for me. Not wanting to live without you in my life."

"But you did," I said. The words came out without a thought, breaking the spell of the conversation. "I'm sorry. I shouldn't have said that."

"It's the truth. We aren't going to hide from it. We never did, and if we try to now, it's going to end whatever this could be before we even start."

I drew in a breath and held it. He was right. I didn't want to keep throwing it in his face, though. That wouldn't make it easier, either.

"It's not fair to you. We both made choices back then that separated us. We both hid things and said things. We're different people now. And I really want us to start over, as much as we can."

He nodded slowly. "I'd like that a lot."

We left the restaurant and decided to take a walk around town. It was a beautiful night, and I didn't want the night to end just yet. It felt like he was thinking the same thing.

Xavier grabbed my hand, then asked if it was okay.

"Yes," I said, smiling up at him.

We walked in silence for a few minutes. Then he said, "Tell me about your mom. I'm sorry I wasn't here for you when she passed."

"Thank you. It was hard to watch her suffer, but it wasn't long. By the time she realized she had breast cancer, she was beyond treatment. She only lasted a few months. And she enjoyed those few months."

"What did she do?"

I laughed. "Everything. She worked until she couldn't stand the long hours. She tried to go part time, but she didn't want to leave when her shift was over. Eddie and I talked her into quitting so she could have downtime, but she just decided to take up hobbies."

"What kind of hobbies?"

"Matchmaking was always a hobby of hers, but she started painting and she tried to write a romance novel, and she went to a studio and made pottery."

"Wow. That's impressive."

"She was horrible," I said, barely holding back my laughter.

"At which one?"

"All of them!"

Xavier laughed loudly with me. "No. She had to be good at something."

"Nope. It was so bad. She tried one of those painting classes where they walk you through how to do it. The instructor asked if she followed any of their directions."

"They did not."

"Oh, they did. She had no eye for it. It looked like a toddler did it."

"Wow."

"Yep. The pottery wasn't any better. If she'd walked away with a lump of clay, she could have said it was a rock, but she wanted to make something. She made me a cup for my desk. To put pens or whatever in. The thing wobbles. I'm not even sure what it was supposed to be, but it has a face. And it's the weirdest colors you've ever seen. She must have blended her own, but they all look like shades of brown."

"Seriously?"

"Oh, yeah. It's like a hollowed out turd on my desk. She said it was a statement piece, but I'm really not sure what statement it's supposed to make."

Xavier shook his head and laughed again. "She always sounded like she would have been a lot of fun."

"Yeah, she was," I said quietly. "I miss her. It's been four years since her wedding. She and Eddie got married in Hawaii. When they found each other again, they thought they had time to be together. Neither of them were in a rush, but when they found out about her cancer, they wanted to get married. Mom always wanted to see Hawaii, so we took her there for her wedding. Laura's friend's friend lives there and works at a wedding planning company. He and his wife gave up their wedding so Mom and Eddie could get married. Sawyer and Kiana will forever have my heart and gratitude for that."

"That's a really special memory."

"It is. Laura, Finley, Blake, Elise, and Ian went with me. All of Laura's friends were there, too. And the friends in Hawaii. It ended up being a big thing, and perfect for Mom. She was in her element, and she loved Hawaii. When she died, she told me that was where she was going to spend eternity. In Hawaii."

"Have you been back since the wedding?"

I shook my head. "I'd love to, but I haven't taken the time."

"We should go." Xavier cleared his throat. "I mean, I'd love to go if you ever want to go back."

I breathed a laugh and smiled. "That sounds nice."

We were silent as we continued walking. Hawaii drifted through my mind. Mom was right. It was perfect there. And if she and Eddie could find each other and have a second chance, maybe Xavier and I could, too.

We wandered a little longer, then decided to head back home. Xavier insisted on walking me up to my condo, holding my hand as we climbed the stairs. When we got to the door, I asked if he wanted to come in.

"As much as I'd love to see the poop pen holder, I'm

trying not to rush things. I want you to know I'm here, and I'm in this, and I'm willing to wait for you to catch up to me. So, yes, I'd love to come in, but I'm not going to. Not tonight."

I was a little disappointed, but it made me want him that much more. Again, he was thinking of me.

"I am hoping I can get a kiss from you, though."

I nodded and tilted my head back to look up at him as he stepped closer.

It all happened in slow motion, like time paused so the moment would last longer. He cupped my jaw, his fingertips grazing the sensitive skin behind my ear. I breathed him in, the familiar scent of the man I once knew bringing back long-forgotten memories. He leaned down, pausing when our lips were just barely separated, letting me close the distance between us.

The first brush of his lips was as familiar as his scent, soft and firm and perfect. He licked the seam of my mouth, asking for more. I opened for him, taking a taste of him.

My arms circled his waist, bringing him closer to me. He leaned against me, pressing my back to the door as he covered my body. He hardened between us, but he kept his hips away from mine. I ached to pull him inside with me and never stop kissing him.

Just as I had the thought, he eased back and put some distance between us.

"I'm going to lose all my sense of honor if I don't stop now."

I laughed. "I feel the same way."

"Then it's definitely best if I say good night and thank you for going out with me."

"We never talked about something for Finley and Trent."

He smiled and shook his head like he forgot all about

the reason we went to dinner. "I guess we're going to have to do this again, then."

My lips turned up, and my cheeks hurt from smiling so big. "I guess we will."

He squeezed my hand, then released me and took another step back. "Good night, Karissa."

"Good night, Xavier."

"We'll talk soon, Queen."

I laughed as he waved and walked away.

Xavier Hogan was back in my life. Maybe for good this time.

THREE DAYS LATER, I was still smiling when I walked into O'Kelley's for my weekly lunch with Trinity. She was sitting at the bar, talking to Hudson when I got there.

"What's with the face?" Hudson asked.

"It's called a smile," Trinity said. "She had a date. And I take it the date went well."

"How did you know that?"

Trinity snorted. "Please. Nothing is secret in this town, especially when you're kissing outside your condo and my husband, the cop, walks by."

"Dammit. But you love saying husband, don't you?"

Trinity grinned, a silly, dopey grin that matched mine. "Yeah, I do."

"Oh, shit. I'm out of here. I can't handle all of that," Hudson said.

"You know you love it," Trinity teased him. "One day you'll have this look on your face, too. You're a catch, Hudson, and any woman would be lucky to have all of your attention."

The front door opened and drew Hudson's gaze. He scowled, making me turn and snicker when I saw Anna Charlotte walking in. She and Hudson had a tentative truce since she worked for Finley and her son worked for Hudson, and they saw each other regularly.

"I'm here to pick up our order. Finley said she called it in twenty minutes ago and it should be ready," Anna said with very little emotion.

"I thought she was going to come get it," Hudson said. He had plenty of emotion, none of it good.

"And she asked me to. Are you going to let me have our food?" Anna asked. She smiled sweetly at him, a smile some people would see as kind but I knew was all for show.

I liked Anna, and she seemed to be the only person in town who got under Hudson's skin on a regular basis. He was usually an even-tempered kind of guy, but with Anna, his default was tense and frustrated.

Hudson grabbed the bag of food and thrust it at Anna. "Here."

"Thanks so much. I'm so happy I got to witness your smile today."

Hudson rolled his eyes. Anna did the same and turned on her heel and left, the door slamming behind her.

"That woman makes me nuts," Hudson muttered.

"Okay, then," Trinity said. "Can we order some lunch? Or should we sit at a table and wait for someone?"

"No, I'll take your order. What do you two want?"

Trinity ordered a burger and cheese curds, and I got a chicken sandwich and fries. We both asked for water and went to a booth so we could sit and talk while our food was being made.

"What do you think is going on between them?" Trinity asked.

"Between Hudson and Anna? Nothing. I think they drive each other crazy."

"James and I were the same. I could barely stand to be in the same room as him before we started sleeping together. And after."

I snorted. "You and James are interesting."

"And you and Xavier are what?"

I stopped with my water halfway to my lips. I set the glass down. "I don't know exactly. It was one date, but it felt good."

"Really?" She dragged out the word in a teasing tone.

"Not that kind of good. We just kissed. I meant the date. Spending time with him. I haven't let my guard down with anyone since him."

"And you're ready to let him back in?"

I shook my head. "I don't know. A part of me thinks it's nostalgia that's making me a little crazy, and a part of me thinks it's just the connection we have. I've always felt like we were meant to be together."

"Maybe you are."

"Yeah, but maybe we're not. Why were we both alone for so long if we were supposed to be together?"

"I can't answer that, but do you need an answer? Is that important enough to stop you from finding out where things can do now?"

I shrugged. "No, I guess not. I feel like we missed out. Like life would have been different, better, if we had been together all this time."

"Maybe, but maybe not. You never know what could have happened. You might not have been here for your mom, and we might not know each other. You and Xavier might not have stayed together. And McJenna wouldn't exist. I know it's hard to let go of what might've been, but I don't think it'll do you any good to wish for it."

"I know. You're right. He was my one big regret. Not going with him. I told myself his life was better for it, but I always regretted not being brave enough to choose him."

"You chose yourself, Rissa. That's even braver. Most of us take the easy path and put someone else first, someone we love. It's harder to stick to what we really want deep down inside. That's why I almost left here when I first moved. I wanted something different when I met Ms. Georgia, but moving here was because of her. When I found out she was gone, the easy choice was to move home to where my mom and grandma were. It was still different, but it was a safer version of different. Staying here was a hard decision, but there was a part of me that knew deep down this was where I was supposed to be."

"I never thought of it that way," I admitted.

"Life is not a straight line. You and Xavier weren't ready for each other when you were in your twenties. You might not be ready now, but unless you try, you won't know. I think you should give him a chance. And yourself."

I smiled. "Thanks, Trinity. I think you might be right."

"Of course I'm right! Just like I'm right about Hudson and Anna. You just wait and see."

"Are you taking over for Mom and matchmaking people now?"

"Well, we do share the same birthday."

"True. Very true."

13

———

After my lunch with Trinity, I sat at the bar and talked to Hudson for a few minutes. He scowled at everyone who walked by, and he looked like he needed a break.

"What's going on with you?"

"What do you mean?"

"I mean, you look like you're going to rip someone's head off. What the hell?"

"I'm fine," he snapped.

"Yeah, and you sound like it, too."

"Finley knows Anna makes me crazy. Why would she send that woman over here to get their lunch?"

My brows shot up. "Seriously? This attitude is still because of Anna? What is your deal with her?"

"She just gets under my skin. I don't deal well with her. And Finley knows that."

"Don't get mad at Fin. When's the last time you had a day off?"

"I don't get days off. I own the place."

"Hudson, you need time off."

"Rissa, I love you, but please don't tell me how to run my life."

I saw the exhaustion and the frustration in his gaze, but more than anything was the determination. He was going to do things his way, no matter what anyone else said. Period.

I nodded. "Got it. Sorry. Have a good day."

He nodded sharply and went back to wiping down the counter.

Maybe Trinity was on to something about Hudson and Anna. But I was not getting in the middle of it. I had enough going on in my life.

I spent the rest of my day working on the app I was developing for Bex's company. I was incredibly happy with the progress I was making and loved the freedom Bex gave me to run with the idea she chose. My creative block was definitely coming to an end.

I was finishing up my day when my phone buzzed with an alert. From Book Boyfriends Wanted.

NEWBIE

What are you doing right now?

I smiled. It was a very Xavier thing to ask. Not tonight, not next week. Right now.

QUEEN

I just finished work.

NEWBIE

Does that mean you're not busy?

QUEEN

Yes, it means I'm not busy. Why?

NEWBIE

Can I show you something?

> QUEEN
>
> Sure.

NEWBIE

Meet me out front of your building in five. Is that enough time?

> QUEEN
>
> I'll make it work.

Thankfully, I hadn't changed after going out to lunch and was still wearing clothes suitable for being in public. I grabbed my purse, locked up my condo, and headed downstairs. Xavier was pulling up as I walked out the front door, and I jumped in.

"Hi," he said, smiling as he waited for me to buckle my seatbelt.

"Hi. Where are we going?"

"Well, first, I'm hoping I can get a kiss from you. Then we're going to the theater."

"You're going to show me the theater?" I gasped. I'd been wondering what he was doing to it, but I didn't want to ask.

"Kiss later," he said, chuckling as he put the car in drive.

"I'm sorry." He was already pulling away from the curb. "I'm really excited. I haven't heard anything about what you're doing."

"That's good. We want it to be a surprise, so you can't tell anyone what I show you. But I wanted to get your opinion."

I bounced in my seat like an impatient child. Xavier shook his head and smiled, letting me be excited and weird.

When we stopped in front of the theater, I was wowed. It had already changed a lot. The old dingy windows were gone, replaced with new glass and framed out so they no longer looked into the lobby of the theater.

"Are you going to do something with those?" I pointed to the windows before we went inside.

"Yes," Xavier said. "They're going to have the movie posters and whatever else we decide to draw people into the theater."

"Like storefronts?"

"Exactly. We're still working on ideas, but we're going to focus everything around movie posters and go from there."

"That's cool. Good idea."

Xavier laughed and opened the door for me. "I take zero credit for that. It was all Genevieve. She's been most of the creative genius on this project."

"Well, that's good to know. Wow." I gasped and looked around. The place was very different. All the flooring was new, the walls had a fresh coat of paint, and the whole space was opened up and welcoming. The old snack bar was on the other side of the room and completely out of place in the upgraded room.

"It's very different. Obviously, I don't know what it looked like when it was operational, but I wanted to change all of it. We moved the snack bar for better traffic flow. A new one arrives in a few weeks, but that's the location for it. Right now, it's our office space. When people come in, we want them to move through the area, so having the snack bar over there will encourage them to keep going instead of hanging out by the door."

"Smart," I told him. The lobby opened up a lot with it moved. The whole space seemed twice the size it was before. "Is this tile?"

"Vinyl plank flooring. Very durable and easy to clean. We ran the same flooring through the theaters, too."

"Okay, I can see that. Are there still two theaters?"

"Yes." He didn't elaborate at all, just a single word.

"Why does that feel like a loaded answer?"

"It is. But first, let's finish out here. What do you think? What would you change out here?"

I stepped back toward the door and looked around. I wanted to really give him my opinion, so I wasn't going to hold back.

Overall, it seemed okay. It was boring, but I figured that would change once they had movies to show and could decorate based on the shows. But it felt a little empty.

"Are you putting anything else out here?"

"Like what?"

I shrugged. "Seating? Video games? Anything else? Are you going to offer parties here and maybe have a party room?"

"We talked about seating, but decided against it because we only have two theaters. The showtimes will be set so there isn't overlap between when people will show up for a movie and when the earlier one gets out. Probably six and nine or five and eight. Something like that."

"That's a good idea. But the money in a movie theater is usually made in concessions. Are you sure you should do that?"

"We'll talk about that in a minute."

"What about parties?"

"We're going to offer parties for off-hours, like weekend afternoons. If someone wants a party that's during a regular movie, we can make that work."

"How?"

"Let's go into the first theater," he said cryptically.

I followed him into the theater and stopped as soon as we walked inside. "What the hell?"

He chuckled. "What do you think?"

"Um, this isn't like any theater I've ever been in." The

floors were the same gray vinyl as the lobby, but the rest of the room was full of color. Stripes criss-crossed the walls, making them bright and vibrant. The wall sconces were all different, each one a color that matched the stripe it was over and each unique. There were no seats, and it was clear from the funky table and chairs tucked into the corner there weren't going to be.

"That's the point," Xavier said. "We want this to be a special kind of place. This theater is for families. We're going to exclusively show movies that are G or PG. Nothing that would be inappropriate for all ages of viewers. The table we have over here is going to be one type of seating, but we're going to have flexible seating options so people can feel like they're watching a movie at home and be comfortable."

"Don't you think that's going to make people talk? When I'm at the theater, I'm quiet, but when I'm home, I talk."

"We thought about that. For some, it might, but we're going to make it dark in here, dark enough that people will feel like they're in the theater. We have lighting in the floors that will guide people to the door if they need to leave during the show. We're going to have tables and more relaxed seating like bean bag chairs and recliners. Each family will get their own section so the kids will be encouraged to stay close to their parents or guardians."

"This is interesting," I said. I wandered through the space, taking it all in. It was big without the furniture there. I wasn't completely sold on it, but I was not an expert in what families with young kids needed. Having a space where they could explore a little might not be a bad thing.

"If someone wants a party, we're going to have a group seating option. They will have to reserve it in advance so we can set everything up, but we're thinking it'll be to the one side."

I walked over to the one table on the side and sat in the chair. It was red plastic molded to look like a hand. A blue one was across the yellow table. "Are you going to be able to fit as many people in here as a normal theater?"

Xavier shook his head. "No. But the old theater went out of business because they needed to sell eighty percent of their seats and only sold about forty. The way this is set up, we also need to sell eighty percent, but the total number is much lower. We're going to offer family packs of tickets that include concessions, and we're going to make it more of an experience to come here instead of just show up and watch a movie."

"That's why you don't want anything in the lobby."

"Exactly. The lobby isn't the attraction. The theater is. We want people to come in, buy their snacks, find their seat, and watch the movie. We're considering having a way for customers to order food from their seats and getting it delivered to them so they don't have to leave during the movie to get a refill."

"Now, that's a great idea."

Xavier smiled and brushed his dark hair from his forehead.

"This is not what I expected. You're making it a lot more fun than a regular theater. I think it's going to do well."

"Thank you. I hope so. Want to see the adult theater?"

I raised an eyebrow. "Adult theater?"

"Not like that. The other theater is where we're going to show PG-13 and R-rated movies. Not so family friendly."

I nodded for him to lead the way and might have stared at his ass as I followed him to the other theater.

"Whoa," I breathed. This one screamed adult. From the rich colors on the walls to the low-backed sofa in the corner.

"We want a different feel in here. The other room was fun and quirky, but this is sophisticated and elegant. At least, that's what Genevieve tells me."

"It really is." I walked over and ran my hand along the short-pile carpet that lined the walls. It was mounted in horizontal stripes that carried my gaze around the space. The house lights were bright enough to see just how huge this theater was compared to the other. The matching sconces were all black with amber shades, giving a seductive glow to each area.

"We're going to serve alcohol here, only allowed in this theater. People will have to go to the counter to order it, no delivery of that, but it'll be an option. The seating in here is going to be casual but raised. No floor seating options. Some bar top tables, some couches, whatever we find."

"You don't have it all picked out?" I asked.

Xavier shook his head. "We're looking at options. We don't want everything to be the same, but all the couches are going to stay in this wine, gray, black theme."

"Do you know those are the MacKellar Cove High School colors?"

Xavier nodded. "I did. That's why we went with them."

"Good plan."

"I thought so." He walked closer to me. "So, what do you think?"

I moved to the couch and sat down. I ran my hand over the firm cushion, the fabric soft under my palm. I looked at the wall where the screen would be, imagining a movie playing just for us.

Xavier sat on the couch next to me. He didn't say anything as I considered my words.

"It's growing on me. I think it's going to be a huge success."

"Really?"

I nodded. "I do. It's different, but in a good way. It's special. There's nothing like this anywhere around here. I think it's smart to have the theaters designed differently and to make one more suited for kids. That's going to be a huge hit with parents. And this one is going to be really relaxing for adults."

"That's what we were going for." He reached across the couch and grabbed my hand. "Thank you for coming here tonight. I really wanted another opinion, but I didn't want to talk to Trent about it. It's his money, but he keeps telling me he trusts me to make the right decisions."

"You definitely made the right decisions. It's going to be nice to have a place to go in the evenings without having to leave town."

"Good. And maybe I can take you on a date here sometime."

"Maybe," I said.

He leaned closer and tilted my head back. His lips grazed mine, a ghost of a kiss that was so much more. He shifted his body closer and slid his hand over my hip. He moved in for another kiss, his tongue darting out to taste mine as I opened my mouth for him.

My hands went around his neck, drawing him closer. He didn't hesitate to close the distance between us. His hand squeezed my hip.

I was so lost in our kiss, I wasn't paying attention to what else he was doing until his fingertips brushed the outside edge of my chest. I pulled back, stunned to find his entire hand cupping my breast.

He froze. He stared at me, his brows knitting together in confusion.

I jumped up off the couch and paced to the other side of the theater.

Shit. Shit, shit, shit.

I didn't plan for things to go that far. For him to touch me. To touch them.

It had been almost a year since my double mastectomy, and aside from my doctor, I was the only one who'd touched them. The doctor said it might be uncomfortable or different, that I might have heightened sensitivity or none, but until that moment, I didn't think about it.

Until Xavier cupped my breast and I didn't feel it, I told myself the feeling would come back. But it hadn't.

"Are you okay?" he asked tentatively. He was still on the couch, watching me as I had my mini-panic attack.

"My boobs are fake," I blurted.

"I'm sorry?"

I drew a breath and let it out slowly. "My mom died of breast cancer. The doctor said if I had the gene, I was highly likely to do the same. I got tested. I have the gene, so I made the decision last year to have a preventative double mastectomy. There was no evidence of cancer, but I didn't want to wait around until there was. But in order to still feel like me, I chose to have implants put in."

"Okay." Xavier stood from the couch and started to walk toward me.

"I didn't feel it when you touched me. At all."

"Oh."

"I understand if you don't want to keep this going or if you just want to pull back. It's weird and I don't really feel like myself anymore because I'm not...entirely, and—"

"Karissa," he said firmly. His hands gripped my biceps, holding me until I looked up at him.

"Yeah?"

"You made a decision that probably saved your life. A choice that made it so you could have a life. There's no reason to be ashamed of that or upset by that. And what the hell kind of man would be upset with you for doing that?"

I shrugged. "I just haven't...um, you know, since, and I wasn't sure, and then I didn't feel anything and I just, I don't know."

"We can take things slow. We don't have to do anything. And if you don't feel comfortable about anything, we stop."

"It's just that I used to..."

"I know," he said.

"And now..."

"It's okay. There are a lot of fun ways to tease you and get you ready for an orgasm besides playing with your breasts. And I'm happy to explore all of them. When you're ready."

He pulled me into his arms, and I laughed against his chest. I took a deep breath, feeling like a huge weight had been lifted off of me.

I didn't know how either of us would react when we got to that point, but it was less of a thing than I thought it would be. He wasn't running the other way, and even though it was a disappointment that I couldn't feel anything, I would have a lot of fun figuring out new places where I could feel everything. With Xavier.

14

XAVIER

"WHAT ARE YOU DOING?" GENEVIEVE ASKED FROM RIGHT behind me.

I slammed the laptop shut, but obviously not before she saw what was on my screen.

"Are you buying a house? I thought you lived with Mr. MacKellar. What's going on?"

I turned to face her, laughing until I saw the look of terror in her eyes. "Whoa, calm down."

"Calm down? Don't you know you never tell a person who's freaking out to calm down? It doesn't help anything. What the hell is going on? Am I losing my job?"

"Genevieve, everything is fine. I promise. Why are you losing it?"

"Because I'm pregnant," she blurted, then burst into tears.

It took me a beat longer than it should have for her words to sink in and make their way to my brain, and for my brain to actually respond. When it finally did, I pulled my crying assistant into my arms and hugged her until she stopped sobbing all over both of us.

She pulled back and sniffed, then straightened her shoulders and looked up at me. "I'm sorry. I didn't mean to blurt it out like that."

"It's fine. I promise. How are you feeling?"

"Like a train wreck."

I chuckled, and she managed a small smile. "How far along are you?"

"Almost thirteen weeks. We aren't supposed to tell anyone yet. It sort of fell out."

"It's okay. I won't say a word."

"Yeah, but you're my boss. And we're getting to the end of this project, and if things don't work out, and you can't afford to pay me, and—"

"Genevieve, sit down," I told her, gesturing to the chair I'd just vacated. "You're not going to lose your job. Trent has signed off on you staying on at your current salary with quarterly evaluations to talk about raises. You have nothing to worry about."

"Then why are you looking at houses for sale? Is he firing you? I don't think I can do this alone. Especially not when I'm pregnant. And I like working for you."

"I'm not going anywhere," I said calmly, being careful to also avoid her question.

"Are you sure? Did you have a fight? Is he kicking you out? We can get people to boycott the theater. No, wait, that would mean we were out of jobs. Shit. What do you need me to do?"

"Your job, Genevieve. That's it. There's nothing wrong with Trent and me. He's not firing me or closing the theater or anything else. You have nothing to worry about."

"Then why are you looking at houses? Are you moving?"

"No."

She stopped the nervous blabber and glared at me,

finally realizing I'd been dodging her question the whole time. She crossed her arms over her chest and looked up at me with the look every kid feared from his mother.

And I caved.

"I need to be able to stand on my own two feet. I haven't had my own place in forever. In college, I had roommates. After college, I lived alone for a little while, but it was really only about a year. I moved in with McJenna's mom shortly after we started dating because she got pregnant. And after she left, I moved in with Trent. He's been paying for everything for a long time, and even though he assures me he doesn't mind, I do."

Genevieve was silent for a long minute. "I give you a lot of credit. Most people would be content to let someone else handle things."

I shrugged. "I have tried for years to move out, but whenever I brought it up, he would get upset. The three of us have been a family J's entire life. But now…"

"Mr. MacKellar has his own family, and you feel like yours needs to give him space."

I opened my mouth to contradict her, but there was nothing to say. She was exactly right. I nodded.

"Let me see the house."

I shook my head as she reached for the computer and opened it.

"Put in your password and let me see it. I used to be a real estate agent. I can tell you the tricks so you know which houses are actually worth your time to go see."

I typed my password as she spoke, and she spun the computer back to her. She looked at the house I'd been checking out with the high ceilings and big backyard.

"This is a decent one. It's older, but a lot of things around here are. It looks like it's in good shape. But it's kind of far outside town. It wouldn't really be walkable for McJenna. I'm guessing you want something closer so she can walk into town and hang out with her friends, right?"

I nodded. "Ideally, yes. But I'm not sure I can afford one of those."

"I'll find you something." She tapped on the keys and did another search. She scrolled through pictures of houses until she found one she liked and opened the listing. "How about this one? Two bedrooms, two bathrooms. Decent kitchen. Big living room. The backyard is nice and already has a deck and a fence. These floors are amazing. It's super cute. What do you think?"

She pushed the computer toward me, but I already knew it wasn't going to work. It was only two bedrooms, which meant there wasn't space for Karissa's office.

Even worse than having Genevieve find out I was looking at houses to buy was having her find out I was planning to move Karissa in with us without Karissa knowing first.

"Um, yeah, it's great. Looks nice."

"But you don't like it. Okay, I'll keep looking."

I tried to tell her she didn't have to, but she ignored me and kept going, showing me listing after listing of houses that simply weren't big enough.

"What's wrong? You don't like any of them. Are you sure you want to move out?"

"I was just thinking we might want more space. A third bedroom wouldn't be a bad idea."

"It's going to be more expensive, and unless there's a real need for it, I think that's something that'll push you past your budget. McJenna is graduating in three years. Why do you need a third bedroom?"

Dammit. I knew it was going to be tough to explain, but I

didn't expect her to come out and ask me directly. "Um, I just thought it would be nice to have a home office or a workout space or something. A little extra space."

"But do you need it? This last one has a really big living room and you can totally fit a desk in the corner. Or a piece of gym equipment. You can also join a gym here. It's pretty affordable. Teddy's a member if you want to go with him sometime."

"Thanks."

"So, this house?"

I looked at the pictures again and nodded. "I'll think about it," I lied.

She was good. She narrowed her eyes and stared at me until I shuffled my feet and started to feel incredibly uncomfortable. "There's something else. Are you leaving for real? Starting a new business? Having a kid? Getting married?" She paused. Her eyes widened, and she looked up at me. "That's it, isn't it? You're planning for someone else to live with you. Who is it?"

"It's no one."

"No? It's not Karissa Thomas?"

My cheeks heated under her careful gaze, and a smile lifted her lips until she could have doubled for the Cheshire Cat.

"Really? I didn't know it was that serious between the two of you. It's only been three dates."

"How do you know that?"

Genevieve shrugged like it was common knowledge. "Small town, boss. Your first date was down to A-Bay. Smart. Second was when you brought her here over the weekend. And third was last night when you met for dinner at O'Kelley's."

"Are you serious?"

Genevieve shrugged again. "Everyone knows. Karissa is adored around here. Her mom was a fixture. Ms. Georgia was friendly to everyone and loved by everyone. She had a way of getting you to talk and knowing exactly what you needed. She's the one who got me and Teddy together. I never would have thought twice about him. I'm not a work with her hands kind of girl, but Ms. Georgia said he was a good man and to start with a conversation. I realized he was funny and kind and smart, all things that I wanted in another person. After that first conversation, it was like we'd been together forever and I couldn't imagine my life without him."

"She sounds like she was someone special." I hated that I never knew Ms. Georgia. If I'd come back to MacKellar Cove with Karissa after college, I would, but I didn't make that choice.

"She was very special. And so is Karissa. If you mess things up with her and break her heart again, you're going to be run out of town. I hope you know that."

I chuckled, but the look on Genevieve's face said she wasn't kidding.

"People here are protective of their own. She's one of us, you're not yet. I adore you, but not everyone knows you as well as I do."

"I don't want people to pick me over Karissa. But I also don't want to mess things up with her."

"Good," Genevieve said. "Then maybe you should talk to her about a house before you buy one for the three of you."

I smiled. "Probably a good idea."

Two days later, I was still working up the nerve to talk to Karissa about a house. We weren't there yet. Not even close. And I knew it. Which was why I was not even considering talking to her, even though I was considering buying a house.

I was looking through more listings when the front door to the theater opened. I closed the laptop before anyone else caught me and looked up.

Knox Randall was standing just inside the door and looking around the wide open space with a smile. "Damn. This place looks amazing."

"Thanks," I told him, walking over to shake his hand. "Want a tour?"

"Hell, yeah. You open in three weeks, right?"

I nodded. "We were supposed to open next week, before Labor Day, but it was just too much."

Everything was coming together. David's crew worked hard to finish all the projects we handed them. They'd moved on to another job, which was great news because it meant the majority of stuff was finished.

"The lobby looks good," Knox said. He walked over to the local bulletin board. "What's this for?"

"Any local events. We're going to post flyers about other things going on and anything that should be celebrated. The high school winning something, someone getting a big scholarship, whatever. This was the project Genevieve roped me into a few weeks back."

Knox nodded. "I like it. Bring the community in. You going to use that for a concession stand?"

"Definitely not. We have a new setup on order. It's supposed to be delivered in two weeks." The old concession stand Genevieve and I had been using as a desk was wobbly and dirty. The glass on one part had been broken long ago.

We considered ripping it out on day one, but we needed space to use for planning and didn't want to bring in a table we would just trash eventually.

"Nice. What food are you selling?"

"We're working on a liquor license. It should be in on time. Genevieve has been talking to some of the local restaurants about supplying orders for food. We talked about selling food here, but we decided it would be better to support other businesses, so we're trying to get them to agree to take orders through our site and deliver everything at once since the movie times are set. We are also going to offer snacks, candy and popcorn and stuff like that, but we wanted to have a dinner and a show kind of experience for guests."

"That's different. It'll be a good place for a date."

"That's what we're hoping." I walked toward the adult theater. "This is one of our theaters. We're still waiting for some of the seating to come in, but this is where we're going to show PG-13 movies and above."

"No kids?"

"We have another theater that's going to be family friendly."

"This is a weird place. They do things differently in the city."

I chuckled. "This was all Genevieve's idea, actually. I think it's brilliant."

"Tables and chairs?" Knox asked when we walked into the theater.

The house lights were up, making the theater brighter than it would be during a show or before and after. All the house lights would only be on at the end of the night for cleanup. But it gave Knox a good view of the theater.

"Huh. Not what I expected. So, I order dinner online,

from someplace local, and it'll get delivered here, and I can sit and eat my ribs or steak and watch a movie with my date. At a table or on a couch or whatever?"

"Exactly."

"I think I like it. It's unique."

"We would have had to do major renovations to make the theater like the big ones. We don't have the vertical space for stadium seating, but this gave us the option to offer a different kind of experience. We have higher top tables in the back so people are a little more elevated and can still see the screen. The middle is standard tables. Up front is the lower seating. It gives the illusion of stadium seating without actually changing the elevation."

"Smart. One question."

"Yeah?"

"Where's your screen?"

I laughed. "I knew we forgot something."

Knox raised an eyebrow at me.

"They're on order. It was a long lead-time for them, but they should be here the week we open. Genevieve has been in touch with the company every week, and they keep saying everything is on schedule, so we're crossing our fingers."

"I know how that goes."

I nodded. "Want to see the other one?"

"Yeah, why not? Might be the only time I'm in there."

"No kids for you?" I asked as we went next door.

"Eh, we'll see. For now, it's not looking like it'll happen."

"You never know," I told him. I certainly didn't plan to have a kid when I did, but I understood the disappointment when you wanted something and it didn't happen. Trent lived with that for years before he met Finley. I did, too, after I walked away from Karissa.

Knox laughed when we walked into the family theater. Bar top tables were at the back with high chairs and carseat frames for adults who needed a place for their kids to sit. Just like the other theater, next came standard height tables and couches, still with high chairs and carseat frames. Beanbag chairs, low couches, and futons were at the front. All the seating was easy to clean and brightly colored so it was fun for families.

"This is cool. I like it. Can I come in here?"

"Of course. We wanted families to be comfortable, but that doesn't mean adults can't be here, too."

"This is funky. I definitely get the vision a little more. And if you have food delivered, it's easy for the parents to enjoy a night out. This is kind of genius."

"I agree."

Knox wandered around the theater a few more minutes, then went back to the lobby. "Did you want signs for the theaters? Something so people know which one to go to?"

"I never thought about that, but it's not a bad idea." I closed the doors so he could see the outside. "We tried to make the doors hard to mix up, but when they're open, it's not so easy to tell which theater is which."

"I could make up something real quick, if you want. No charge."

"No, we'll pay you. I like it. Did you bring the sign for outside?"

"Yeah, it's in the truck. I wanted to show it to you, but I'll be back tomorrow to get it up in the air, if that's cool."

"That'll be great. Yeah. Let's take a look."

I followed Knox outside and was blown away by the sign he created. MacKellar Theater was spelled out in big block letters cut out of a thick slab of wood. The letters were outlined in white with a tight mesh screen behind the openings.

"This looks great," I told Knox.

"Thanks. The mesh hides the lightbulbs when it's lit up. There's a board between the two sides so you don't see both at the same time. That way, whichever direction people are driving from, they'll see the words."

"That's genius. I never would have thought of that."

Knox nodded, not accepting the praise he deserved.

"This is amazing. Can I take a picture for Trent?"

"Yeah, man, of course. Whatever you want. If he wants something different, I can do that."

I shook my head as I tapped out a quick text to Trent. "No, this is perfect. He's going to love it." I stuck my phone back in my pocket and walked closer to get a better look. The sign was angled in the back of Knox's truck and stuck up above the cab. My guess was it was at least six feet long, maybe more, and four feet high. The letters were big and would be easy to read from a distance. It was exactly what I was hoping we'd get.

My phone buzzed in my pocket. I read the text from Trent and grinned.

"Trent said it's amazing. He really appreciates it and wants to buy you a beer if you're free tonight. We're going to O'Kelley's with a few other local guys if you can join us."

"I don't really want to leave this outside," Knox said, pointing to the sign. "Don't want to risk it getting damaged."

"I can follow you back to the store, or wherever you leave your truck, and you can ride over with me if you want. I can bring you back after."

Knox shrugged and nodded. "That'll work. Thanks, man."

"No problem. Let me lock up here and we can head out."

Knox waited while I turned off all the lights inside and locked the place up. I followed him to the hardware store. He parked in a garage in the back, then jumped in with me. We chatted about the town and the theater until we made it to O'Kelley's. It was clear he knew the other guys as soon as we walked in when they welcomed him into the group more than they'd ever welcomed me. I didn't mind. Knox was one of them. A local. I had to earn that place.

"So, is this where I can ask you how things are going with Karissa?" Knox asked once we had beers in front of us. "Or are the rumors about you two being back together all fiction?"

I froze with my beer halfway to my mouth and looked at the men sitting around me. None of them looked happy. Which meant I had some explaining to do.

15

"You're dating Karissa?" Trent asked. "Why didn't you tell me?"

"We were trying to keep it quiet. We didn't want pressure on us," I told my best friend. He was clearly the last to know since the others had the same angry expressions, but I was guessing for a very different reason.

"It's been weeks since they started dating," Hudson said.

"No, they had their first date last week," James said.

"Are you sure? I thought it was longer?" Ian added.

"Why don't we let the man who's going on the dates talk?" Sebastian said above them all.

They all turned and looked at me.

"Okay, well, we had our first date last week. We went to dinner. Then over the weekend, I showed her the theater. And earlier this week, we had dinner here." I tried to act like it was no big deal, but it was a big deal to me. I didn't want to explain myself to them, but I also didn't want them to put an end to my relationship before it had a chance to get started.

And I had a bad feeling they could if they wanted to.

"Are you two back together?" Trent asked.

I eyed the others and debated how much to share. If it was just Trent and me, I would have told him everything, but it wasn't. It was Karissa's friends, too.

"We're getting to know each other again. Trying to find out if we can build a future together," I said.

"You better not hurt her," Rowan threatened. Coming from a cop, the threat was very real.

"I don't intend to. I made a lot of mistakes in the past, but moving here was one of the few things I've done that wasn't a mistake. I want her back in my life. For good," I admitted.

"Do you think she wants that, too? She's been talking to some guy on that app she has. She seems to really like him," Hudson said.

I nodded. "I know. She's talking to me. We were paired on the app."

Most of the guys chuckled and leaned back in their seats. The others rolled their eyes.

"What does that mean?" Knox asked.

"It means it's all over," Ian answered for the group. "All of us were been paired on the app with our women. Karissa's app has a way of connecting people who are meant to be. If the app paired them, we're not going to argue."

"Seriously? You were all paired on the app with your wives and girlfriends?" Knox asked.

Ian nodded. "Yep. Not all at first, and not always the only one, but eventually, yeah. We don't argue with those matches. Especially when there was already a connection."

"No freaking way," Knox said.

The attached ones all nodded.

"Damn. Maybe I need to sign up for that app." Knox dug out his phone.

"Book Boyfriends Wanted," Ian told him. "You won't regret it."

Trent nudged me. "You weren't going to tell me about Karissa?"

I shrugged. "I didn't want to jinx it. Everyone seems to know everything, and I don't want her to get hurt. I also didn't want anyone else telling her how she should feel or what she should think about being with me again. I know our past is just as public as our present."

"Karissa isn't going to let anyone tell her what to do. She's too smart for that. You should know that about her." Hudson glared at me.

"I know she is, but I also know it's not always easy when everyone else has an opinion about what you should do or how you should feel. She's a private person, and everyone else getting involved in her life isn't what she wants. So, we're trying to keep it between us."

"Does Finley know?" Trent asked.

I shrugged. "I haven't talked to anyone. I don't know if Karissa has or not. That's up to her."

"But you're in this, aren't you?" Trent asked.

I nodded. "I am. She's the only one I want to spend the rest of my life with. If it's not her, it's no one as far as I'm concerned."

"Then I hope it's her."

"Me, too."

THE FOLLOWING week was the last full week of summer. It had gone fast. I was still a little disappointed the theater wasn't opening that week, but I knew it was for the best. There were a lot of other events in town for the holiday weekend coming up, and the tourists were still flocking to the area. It was quieter than it'd been most of the summer, but it was still busy.

I took Monday off so I could spend time with McJenna before school. She was finally looking forward to starting school since she met Bianca and Bianca introduced her to others she would be in school with. They'd all gotten their schedules and were comparing classes. J had lunch with Bianca, which meant I no longer had to worry about my kid sitting in the cafeteria alone all year.

"What are we doing today?" McJenna asked when she came downstairs. She'd finally accepted that I was actually going to be home when I said I was taking the day off. It was a nice change.

"I thought we could get breakfast at Cove Bakery to start the day, then maybe do some shopping for school stuff. Clothes and supplies and whatever else you need. This afternoon, we need to meet Uncle Trent to get fitted for the wedding."

To my surprise, she nodded. Being seen in public with her dad wasn't as much of a travesty as it had once been. Living in a small town where everyone knew everyone else's family meant there was no reason to be ashamed of your parents, apparently.

We got ready to go and headed into town, joining the long line of people waiting to see what Valentina's special treat of the day was. We chatted with the people around us, all of them asking me about the theater and when it would be open.

"Two weeks from Thursday," I told them. "Give the kids a little while to get back into school, and for summer to wind down. We figured no one wants to be inside when the weather is this beautiful."

"I heard it's got tables," one man said.

"I did, too," a woman agreed.

"It does," I told them. "We wanted a different experience. Genevieve is very creative and smart, and she came up with the concept. I hope you'll all come and see what she did with the place."

"Why are you there if she's the one doing all the work?" another woman asked.

"We're working together. I was just saying she's the one who came up with the idea," I explained.

A few people grumbled, but I knew once they saw the place, they would love it as much as I did. The theater was amazing. Knox put the sign up on Friday, and it was perfect. The lighting was solar powered, so the lights came on automatically when it started to get dark.

Genevieve was working on the display windows while I was gone. She said she wanted to do them without anyone around so she could focus. Since she was going to be alone in the theater, I made her promise to check in with either me or Teddy throughout the day, preferably both. She agreed and said Teddy demanded the same thing.

McJenna and I finally made our way to the front of the line and said hello to Ms. Harriett.

"What are you two having today? Besides the special, of course," Harriett asked.

"A chocolate croissant for me, please," McJenna said.

"I'll take one of those, too," I told her. "And two bottles of water."

Harriett rang us up and handed over our plates and waters. We thanked her and searched for a table.

"What is this?" McJenna asked when we sat down.

I shrugged, picking up the gooey treat. It smelled like cinnamon. "Maybe a cinnamon roll?"

"I've never seen a cinnamon roll like this," J said.

We both bit into it and groaned. It tasted like a cinnamon roll, but it had a crunchy outside, like a waffle. The creamy icing added a sweetness to it that offset the spiciness of the cinnamon. Overall, it was just delicious.

"That's really good," J said. "It might be my favorite so far."

We'd gone to Cove Bakery every chance we got, and J was there more often without me. She raved about everything, so for her to say it was her favorite was high praise.

"You'll have to tell Ms. Valentina. I'm sure she'll appreciate the feedback," I told her.

McJenna nodded and finished her cinnamon waffle thing. It was really good. Then we went for our chocolate croissants. We finished breakfast and headed out quickly since there were people waiting for tables.

We wandered around town for a while, stopping into all the stores and checking out what they had. By the time we finished shopping, my credit card was in tears and my arms were sore from carrying all of J's new stuff.

"We got a lot of stuff today," she said as we loaded it all into the back of the vehicle. "Are you sure we can afford all of this? If you're going to buy a new house, maybe we shouldn't have bought everything."

"We're fine, J. I promise. You needed school supplies, and you needed clothes. I wouldn't get things unless we could afford to pay for them. And buying a house is something we'll figure out when the time is right."

"Are you not looking?"

"I am. I'm just undecided about what makes sense right now. And with work, I haven't had a lot of time to find something."

She didn't say anything as we got in the car and headed

out of town. The place Trent wanted to go for a suit was in another town south of MacKellar Cove. We drove for a few minutes before McJenna said anything else.

"I don't think we should move until after the wedding."

"It'll be at least that long. Even if we found something today, we wouldn't be able to move in for a month or two."

"Okay, that's good."

"Why?"

She shrugged. "I just think we should make sure we're around for Uncle Trent and Aunt Finley."

"Aunt Finley?" I asked.

She shrugged. "She said I could call her that."

"Good, then you should. We're always going to be around for them. What's going on?"

McJenna shrugged. "I don't know. I just feel like we're ditching them. I mean, we should move out, but I think we need to talk to them about it first, and I don't want to drop it on them right before the wedding, you know?"

I nodded along with her. "I agree. That's a good idea. We'll talk to them after the wedding and start looking for a house to move sometime in the next year. Does that work for you?"

"Yep, sounds good." She paused and twisted her hands together. "Um, do you think Uncle Trent would mind if I had friends over sometime?"

"He said he doesn't. I wouldn't go throwing any parties, but I'm sure he'll be okay with a few friends."

"Okay, good. Bianca and I were talking about doing something over the weekend, and I mentioned that Uncle Trent was planning his party. I was kind of hoping I could invite her to that."

"I'm sure he'll be fine with it. Let's ask him when we go inside."

She nodded and unbuckled her seatbelt. The formal-wear store was bigger than I expected. We walked in, looking around at the options as we worked our way to the back, where Trent was talking to another man.

"Thanks, Enrique. I think this is perfect," Trent said.

"Hi, Uncle Trent," McJenna said.

"Hey! How was your morning?"

"Good. We bought a ton of stuff. That suit looks good."

Trent grinned. "Thanks. It's mine, but I wanted some new accessories. Something to make it a little different from every day for the wedding."

"Aren't you wearing a tux?"

"Nope. I wear a tux for work stuff. Fancy events. Finley and I wanted a wedding that feels like us. More casual. We're still going to dress up and be fancy, but I'm wearing this suit because Finley really likes it. But don't tell her because she doesn't know I'm wearing this one."

"Um, okay," McJenna said.

Trent and I chuckled.

"So, are you ready to get outfitted?" Trent asked us.

"Both of us?" McJenna asked.

Trent nodded. "You're one of my grooms-people. Your dad is my best man, but you and Ian are my grooms-people. Unless you don't want to be."

"No, I do. I want to be in a wedding. How cool!"

We laughed at her excitement.

"Well, let's see what we have for you two. Dress or suit?" Enrique asked J.

J looked at Trent and me. I shrugged and pointed to Trent. "It's his wedding."

"We want you to be comfortable. You can wear whatever you want. If you want to be in a suit like Ian and your dad, that's cool. If you'd rather be in a dress, that's okay, too."

"I think a suit would be fun," J said.

"Suit it is," Trent said.

Enrique showed us options for suits, all matching the color of Trent's blue suit. McJenna tried on the different ones until she found one she said was perfect. It had a tapered waist and a bright white shirt underneath. The bowtie she added was the perfect touch.

"It looks good on you," Trent said. "Perfect."

McJenna beamed under the praise. I was caught staring at my kid and wondering how long it was going to be before I had to plan her wedding. It was all going too fast, and our conversation in the car proved she was growing up even faster than I realized.

While McJenna was changing back into her regular clothes, Ian showed up. Trent and I showed him the suit McJenna chose before Ian and I had to decide what we were going to wear.

"Do you want us to match?" Ian asked.

"You know how your sister is. She wants everyone comfortable," Trent said.

Ian nodded. "She does. Which is working out well for my wife because Blake was worried she was going to ruin your wedding pictures by being pregnant."

"Not even a little," Trent said. "Has anyone heard from Hudson?"

"Hudson? Why?"

"He's one of Finley's brides-people. But he vetoed wearing a dress or going with her, so I thought he was coming here."

"I haven't talked to him," Ian said.

Before either of them could get out their phones, Hudson burst through the front door and stomped his way to the back.

"God damn woman. Makes me fucking nuts. Sorry I'm late," Hudson spat. He looked up and stopped when he saw McJenna. "And sorry for swearing."

"Nothing she hasn't heard before. Or said, probably," I said.

"Yep," J agreed.

Hudson grunted and rolled his head around to stretch the tension from his neck.

"Rough day?" Ian asked.

"Yeah." Hudson didn't elaborate, and no one asked.

I got the feeling Hudson was someone who didn't get ruffled easily, but when he was, it was bad. Giving him space felt like the right move.

Enrique helped Ian, Hudson, and me find suits to wear for the wedding. We each picked different styles, but all the same color so we matched. With Trent's suit, it was going to look good.

"Mr. MacKellar?" Enrique said, nodding toward the front of the store.

"Oh, hell, no. You're not paying for all of this," I argued.

"It's already done," Trent said. "This is my wedding. Finley and I wanted to pay for as much as her parents will let us. I have more money than George and J can spend in a lifetime. We can spend it."

"Me? Why would I spend your money?" J asked.

I stopped cold, wondering the same thing.

Trent looked around, realizing he admitted something he didn't mean to. "Shit. I didn't mean it to sound like that."

"Like what?" I asked.

Trent took a step closer to me and reached for J. She went to him without a second thought, letting him pull her to his side. "You're her dad, and I don't want to ever replace you. I know you're capable of taking care of her and everything, but she's mine, too. You're my brother, and she's like my kid. So, J's in my will. And I set up a trust fund for her years ago that she'll get when she's twenty-five. You're the executor. And there's a college fund. George has all the same, and we're going to do the same for Blake and Ian's kid, if they'll let us. Finley really wants to."

Ian looked just as shell-shocked as I was. McJenna looked like she was going to cry. Hudson finally let go of his shitty mood. He was the only one of us who seemed to be able to form a coherent thought.

"Well, I think that's pretty damn admirable of you. Having that kind of money is amazing, but sharing it with the people you call family is special. That's awesome."

"Thank you, Uncle Trent," McJenna said. "That's really nice of you."

"You're mine, kid. I've been with you from the start, and I'm not walking away now." Trent hugged her tight.

McJenna wiped tears from her eyes and hugged him back. "Thank you."

"Trent, you didn't have to do that," I said.

"I know, but I've always said she felt like my kid. You were the first family I had. Ever. If I could have set up a trust fund for you, I would have. What's mine is yours, man. Always."

I nodded and moved across the room to hug my brother and my kid. The three of us embraced. I didn't know what I did to be so lucky to have him in my life, but I was glad for it.

"I knew you had money, but I never knew you were that kind of rich," Ian said. "But I'll happily let my kid reap those benefits. That's amazing of you."

Trent smiled and shook Ian's hand. "You're my brother now, too. And you, Hudson. If there's ever anything you need, let me know. I'm not going to hoard my money like I won't make more. It's better to be able to share it."

"Well, you can pay for my suit," Hudson said. "I'm not going to fight you."

Everyone laughed, including Enrique. McJenna hugged me when Trent walked away to take care of the bill.

She whispered, "We definitely need to talk to him after the wedding and before we find a house. I don't want him to think we're abandoning him."

"I don't either, kid. We'll make sure he understands. I promise."

16

KARISSA

"I can't believe you're getting married in three weeks," Blake said. She wiped at her eyes and scrunched up her face, taking in Finley in her wedding dress.

"I know," Finley agreed. "It's crazy to think a year ago we'd never met."

"You just met your fiancé?" Heather, the attendant, asked.

Finley needed alterations on her wedding dress. She found a dress she absolutely loved in stock, and the store agreed to alter it for her in time for the wedding.

"We grew up in the same town, but he's older than me so we didn't know each other. We met on the app my beautiful friend here designed. It wasn't an easy year, but eventually, we figured it out. Our son is three months old," Finley said.

"Whoa," Heather replied with a chuckle. "Yeah, that sounds like a rough year. But congratulations. Obviously, you two were right for each other."

"They're perfect," I told Heather. "And their son is perfect. It's like a fairy tale."

"Now it is," Finley said with a laugh. "It was definitely

touch and go for a while and I really thought I'd be a single mom."

"Wow. Well, I'm happy it worked out for you. I want a love story like that." Heather fluffed the edges of the gown and pinned the hem so Finley wouldn't trip on the dress that was a few inches too long.

"You should sign up for Book Boyfriends Wanted," Blake told her. "I met my husband on there, too."

"Really?"

"Yep. A lot of our friends have met people on the app. It's amazing."

"I'll have to do that tonight. Working here and being single isn't always easy," Heather said.

"I bet," I said. "I'm single, too. And I created the damn thing."

"You're not entirely single," Finley said. "You're dating Xavier."

I shrugged. Dating was one thing, being not single was another. I wasn't sure things had progressed enough to consider myself not single.

"Are things not going well?" Blake asked.

"No, they are. But it's early. We've only been dating for a few weeks. Tomorrow is, like, our fifth date," I said.

"Yeah, but it's not like you're just getting to know each other," Finley said.

"It feels like it. We're different people than when we were in college. I know I'm different."

"You'll figure it out. He seems like he's all in." Finley spun on the riser so Heather could pin the back of the dress. She smiled at herself in the mirror, a wistful look in her eyes.

"That dress is perfect," I told her, hoping we could get

back to talking about Finley and Trent and leave me out of it.

"It really is," Blake agreed. "It's amazing. And so lucky you found something off the rack."

"I was worried I was going to need to wear something I hated. I don't know how I got this lucky." Finley smoothed her hand down the bodice of the dress. The high neck blended into cap sleeves and made the dress look modest from the front. The simple satin bodice was elegant and stunning, hugging her chest before flaring around at her waist. The back of the dress dipped low, ribbons criss-crossing over her exposed spine. It was a perfect blend of sexy and subtle that personified Finley in so many ways.

"It's perfect for you. If you couldn't find something, Trent would have figured something out, though. He wants this to be the best day of your life," Blake said.

"I know. I'm worried he's going a little overboard." Finley wrinkled her nose.

"In what way?" I asked.

"He doesn't think twice about spending money. It's not bad, but there are times I think we could do with something more affordable. It's just not my mindset to spend," Finley admitted.

"I don't think there's anything wrong with that. Have you signed your prenup yet?" Blake asked.

"You're signing a prenup?" I asked.

Finley nodded. "I insisted on it. His lawyer recommended it, since we both own businesses. Even though mine is nothing compared to his, it's still a smart idea. Trent didn't want to, said we don't need it, but I said then it isn't an issue."

"I think I'd be mad if someone wanted me to sign a prenup," I admitted.

"I love him, and I know he loves me. And signing it means he never has to worry that I might have married him for his money. You know how things have always been for him. I don't ever want him to worry. It's the least I can do," Finley said.

"How does that feel?" Heather asked, interrupting our conversation.

Finley twisted and turned, watching the dress in the mirror. "Perfect."

"Good." Heather smiled. "How's the bodice and the waist?"

"I think it feels good. It's not tight, but I don't feel like I might fall out either. The length was really the only thing I worried about."

"Well, perfect. Then I think we can get you out of it and back into your normal clothes. We should have this done by next weekend if you want to schedule your final fitting."

"That sounds good," Finley said, following Heather toward the dressing room. Their voices faded as they walked away.

"You wouldn't sign a prenup?" Blake asked me.

I shook my head. "It's not something I've ever considered. I also don't know anyone with money like Trent's besides him."

"Ian and I talked about it, but we didn't really see the point. But I get why Finley did it. You knew Trent a little in high school. It wasn't easy for him."

"No, it wasn't. A part of me sees it as planning for their marriage to fail." I didn't like that idea. I wanted Finley happy.

"I think she sees it as planning for it to succeed, but knowing things happen. They've only known each other for a year." Blake shrugged like that made all the sense in the world.

"I guess that's true. And if Finley is happy, I'm not going to tell her she's wrong. If they never get divorced, it won't ever matter."

Blake nodded. Before she could say anything else, the dressing room door opened and Finley joined us.

"Do you two have time for lunch?" Finley asked. "Anna's watching the store for me, and I was hoping we could grab a bite."

"I'm good with that," I said.

"Me, too," agreed Blake.

We found a small deli not far from the store. We ordered sandwiches at the counter, then sat at a table in the back corner to wait for our food.

"How's Eddie doing?" Blake asked. "I haven't seen him in a while."

"I'm having lunch with him tomorrow. He's good. Staying busy."

"Good. Tell him he should come into Cracked sometime and see everyone. It's been too long." Blake sipped her drink.

"I will. We should all get together sometime."

"He's coming to the wedding, right?" Finley asked.

"He said he is. How many people did you guys invite?" I asked.

"Fifty. I think everyone is coming. It's going to be a lot at the estate, but it'll be fun." Finley sighed happily.

"It'll be amazing. We just have to cross our fingers that the weather is nice so we can use the property," Blake said.

Finley groaned. "I know! I keep saying that, too. Trent insists he's going to get a huge tent, just in case."

"That might not be a bad idea," I said.

"Yeah, but if it doesn't rain, then I'm going to feel like we wasted the money," Finley said.

"Fin, I think you're going to need to accept that you have stupid money at your disposal now. You're in a different world than you used to be. I'm not saying throw it away, but you can do things with it that make life easier. How much can a tent possibly cost? A few thousand dollars?" Blake looked between us.

I nodded, and Finley shrugged.

"That's nothing for Trent. Don't let it get to you," Blake said.

"A year ago, I was worried about keeping my store open. I thought I might have to close it down. And now, I'm spending thousands on a tent I might not even need. It's an adjustment," Finley said.

"It is," I told her. "But it's not a bad one. Start small. Spend money on something little that you would normally hold back. Maybe buy coffee before work every day instead of making it at home. Or go out to eat more than once a week. Buy yourself a new phone. Something."

Finley looked more and more uncomfortable with every idea, but she nodded. "I'll try."

"Good," I said.

Our food arrived, and we dug in, enjoying the sandwiches as much as the conversation. After lunch, we headed back to MacKellar Cove and back to work.

THE NEXT DAY, I got to Eddie's a little early so I could help him make lunch. I knocked on the door and let myself into the house. He told me ever since he and Mom moved in together that I should always think of their home as mine.

And that meant not having to wait outside for someone to let me in.

"Hey, hun," Eddie called out from the kitchen. "Back here."

I toed off my shoes and left them at the door with my purse. I followed the sounds and scents of something delicious being made.

Eddie was at the stove stirring something when I walked in. He looked over his shoulder and grinned. "How are you?"

"Good," I said, crossing the kitchen to give him a hug. "How are you?"

"I'm still upright," he said with a chuckle.

I leaned against the counter next to him and shook my head. "I was going to help you cook. What are you making?"

"Your mom's spaghetti. I wanted to get started early so it had time to come together."

I groaned. Mom's spaghetti was amazing. Simple, but she made her own meatballs and sauce and added sausage, pepperoni, and ground beef to the sauce. It was spicy and full of flavors, and delicious. It also took hours to cook, which was why she never made it often.

"You definitely should have waited for me. Or told me so I could be here earlier."

Eddie shook his head. "You're busy, kid. I'm not going to interrupt your life."

"You are not an interruption."

He smiled at me.

"Blake and Finley asked about you."

"How are they doing? I haven't seen them in a while. I'm not getting out as much as I used to."

"They're good. Finley's getting ready for the wedding. Blake's getting ready for the baby."

"Good, good. I'm looking forward to seeing them. Three weeks, right?"

"Yep. Finley was getting her dress altered. We had lunch yesterday."

"Good. That's nice. How are they doing?"

I looked at Eddie. "You just asked me that. Are you okay?"

"Of course. Why wouldn't I be?"

He didn't turn to look at me, which wasn't a big deal, but something didn't seem right.

"Eddie?" I asked, putting down the piece of pepperoni I stole from the counter. "Are you okay?"

"Yeah, sure. How are you?"

"Eddie? What's wrong?" My heart pounded hard. Something was not okay. He wasn't acting like himself.

He looked up at me. His eyes were glazed. He tilted his head to the side, like he couldn't see me. "When did you get here?"

I took his arm and guided him to the table. He didn't resist me at all. He still held the spoon he was using to stir the sauce.

"Sit here for a minute."

"But I need to finish cooking lunch. We were going to eat lunch. I didn't want to bother you since you're so busy."

"I'm never too busy for you," I told him. Guilt tore through me. He was the only parent I had left, and he thought I was too busy to be there for him.

I turned off the stove, making sure the burners were out. I did the same with the oven, even as Eddie protested. I grabbed the spoon from him and stirred the sauce, then I went to the front of the house and grabbed my phone.

I was already calling nine-one-one when I got back to the kitchen.

Eddie was back at the stove, stirring the sauce.

"Nine-one-one. What's your emergency?"

"My step-dad needs help."

"Okay, what is going on?"

"I'm not sure, really. His eyes are unfocused, and he seems like he's in a trance. He's repeating himself. I don't know what's happening."

"Is he coherent? Can he form complete sentences?"

"Yes, we were talking. He just doesn't remember what we talked about."

"Does there appear to be any weakness or loss of function anywhere in his body?"

"No, I don't think so. He's walking and trying to make lunch. He got mad at me when I turned the stove off, but now he doesn't seem to remember."

"You turned the stove off?" Eddie blurted.

"Yeah, because we need to go to the hospital," I told him.

"I don't need a hospital," Eddie argued.

"Ma'am, I'm sending someone out to do a wellness check on him. If the EMTs think he's okay, he can stay home, but we will let them assess him. They'll likely transport him to St. Lawrence Medical. Is that okay?"

"Yes, that's fine. Thank you."

"Would you like me to stay on the line with you until they arrive? They should be there in less than five minutes."

"No, I'm okay. Thank you. I appreciate your help."

"You're welcome, ma'am. I hope he's okay."

"Thanks."

I hung up the phone and stared at Eddie's back. He was stirring the sauce like nothing weird was going on.

I checked that the stove was off, then went to the front to open the door and wait for the paramedics. I was just checking outside when the ambulance pulled up, followed immediately by a police car driven by Rowan.

"Hey, Karissa," Rowan said when he got out. "Is everything okay?"

"My step-father is acting strange. I don't know what's going on, but he seems like he's not all there."

Rowan nodded. I stepped back to let him and the paramedics into the house. "Has he had any falls lately?"

"Not that I know of. I don't live here. He lives alone."

The paramedics moved past me toward the kitchen, where I pointed. Rowan hung back. I didn't know him well, but Willow was a completely new person after meeting him and I knew he was a good man and a good cop.

"Why are you here?" I asked him.

"It's required that a cop shows up when a call goes out to nine-one-one. I was closest. But I'm glad I'm here for you. Want me to call Willow or someone else?"

I shook my head. "Not yet. I want to know what's going on with him. I haven't been here as much as I should have been."

"Don't do that to yourself. Let's worry about getting him better and we'll go from there."

Rowan gestured for me to go ahead of him to the kitchen. The paramedics had Eddie sitting in a chair with oxygen on. He looked up at me when I walked in.

"Karissa, when did you get here?" he asked, his face breaking into a smile.

"Just now," I told him, forcing a smile. The paramedics looked at me and I shook my head. "Twenty minutes ago."

The female paramedic crouched in front of Eddie and waved a penlight in front of him. "Hi, Eddie. I'm Danielle, and this is Rick. Can you follow this light for me?"

Eddie stared at the light.

"Response is sluggish. Still impaired." She looked up at me. "Do you know if he's been drinking?"

I shook my head. "No, but I doubt it. He's never been a big drinker."

"Do you know if he ate today?"

"I don't know. I don't live here. I was just coming over for lunch."

"There's bruising on his right arm. Looks like an IV. Do you know what that's from?" Rick asked.

"What?" I blurted. "No. I have no idea."

"I think we should take him in and get him checked out. Just make sure everything is okay." Rick looked at Danielle for confirmation, and she nodded. "Do you know who his primary care physician is?" he asked me.

"Yeah, I have all the information on my phone," I told him.

"Okay, great. Do you want to ride with us, or would you rather meet us there?" Danielle asked me as Rick left the room.

"I'll meet you there so I have my car," I told them. My hands shook as I reached for my purse.

Rowan stepped away and pulled out his phone.

I stared at Eddie as Danielle continued to examine him. He looked around the room like he didn't know where he was. I couldn't lose another parent. I just couldn't.

Rick came back in and nodded to Danielle.

"Okay, Eddie," Danielle said. "We're going to go for a ride. Do you think you can get to the door with us?"

I stepped to the side with Rowan while Rick and Danielle helped Eddie walk to the front door. Rick had a hold of Eddie the entire time, with Danielle walking in front of him, holding his hands.

Rowan and I watched as they helped him onto the

stretcher just outside the door and loaded him into the ambulance. They waved and took off.

"Want me to help you clean up before you go?" Rowan offered.

I shook my head, everything feeling like I was in a dream. "I don't know. Shouldn't I go now?"

"It'll take a little while for them to get him checked in. You can take a minute. Even if it's just to sit down and take a breath. I can go with you if you want. James and I can bring your car to the hospital later."

I took a deep breath and let it out slowly. "I'll be okay. Cleaning up is a good idea."

Rowan followed me back inside to the kitchen. We worked silently together to put up the food Eddie had out. I offered some to Rowan for him and Willow to share, but he declined.

"You guys are going to need something to eat when he gets home."

"Do you think he's going to be okay?" I asked, hating how shaky my voice was.

Rowan nodded. "They weren't in a hurry. They let him walk out. If it was something bad, they would have rushed him out of here much faster and raced off with lights and sirens."

For the first time since I called the ambulance, I felt like it was going to be okay. "Thank you, Rowan. I never thought of that. Thank you."

"You're welcome. Let's finish this up so you can go find out what happened."

I nodded, grateful he was there to help. It was good to not be alone.

17

BY THE TIME I MADE IT TO THE ER, EDDIE WAS IN A ROOM and hooked up to more machines than seemed sane. They beeped, but nothing alarmed, so I took it as a good sign. Eddie looked like he was sleeping, so I sat in a chair and stared at him.

A nurse came in shortly after I arrived and introduced herself as Bonnie.

"How's he doing?" I asked her.

"So far, so good."

I noticed the Fall Risk band on his wrist. "Why is he a fall risk?"

"He was unsteady when he came in. The paramedics said his walk to the door at home was uneven. It could be from his age, but just in case, we put that on there. It only means he's not allowed to be up and walking without being supervised."

"Do you know what's going on yet?"

She shook her head. "Not yet. The doctor has tests ordered. There's no sign of a stroke, which is a good sign.

The bruising on his arm is from the heart cath he had done on Monday."

"What?"

Bonnie looked at me and smiled sweetly. "He didn't tell you?"

I shook my head.

"I'm sorry, hun. Dads aren't always good at admitting they're vulnerable. They're supposed to be our heroes, and saying they're not the same guy from when you were a kid is tough."

"He's my step-dad. He and my mom got married four years ago. My mom died of breast cancer a few months later."

"And I wouldn't change a bit of it," Eddie said softly from the bed.

"You're awake," I gasped, turning to him.

"Hey, kid. What's going on?"

"You're in the hospital. You weren't feeling well. Why didn't you tell me something was going on with your heart?"

"I didn't want to worry you."

"Eddie, I'm always going to worry about you."

"You're too young to have to think twice about me. I'm fine. The doc said it was all good. Gave me some new medicine."

"What new medicine?" Bonnie asked.

"I don't remember. Everything should be in a chart somewhere."

Bonnie looked at me for help.

I pulled out my phone and opened the notes app where I kept all of his information. I turned the phone so Bonnie could read the information. "That's his primary care and all the medication I'm aware of. I have power of attorney for him and am his health care proxy."

"Thank you," Bonnie said. She recorded all the information, then left with a promise to be back soon.

"Why am I here?" Eddie asked a minute later.

"You weren't feeling well," I told him. I pulled the chair next to the bed and held his hand. "I was worried about you."

"I don't want you to worry. You should be out living your life."

"You're a part of that life, Eddie. I need you here with me."

He smiled and squeezed my hand. We sat back and watched the silent TV in the corner and waited for an update from the doctor.

AN HOUR BECAME TWO, and that became three before the doctors had any real answers. Eddie was taken for tests, each time wheeled back in to wait. When the doctor finally arrived, we were more than a little tense.

"Well, it looks like the new medicine was the culprit," the doctor said. "The beta blocker you're on lowered your blood pressure a bit too much. I've spoken with the prescribing doctor and we agreed that you still need the medication."

"Is that a good idea?" I asked.

"He was having some instances of arrhythmia. The heart cath and EKG he had earlier in the week were to make sure there wasn't anything else going on. We might be looking at a pacemaker at some point, but for now, Dr. Carlyle thinks the meds are the right move."

"Not if he's going to pass out when he's home alone," I

argued. Eddie was too important for them to ignore what was going on and not do their jobs.

"I agree," the doctor said. "But Eddie is dehydrated. He said he didn't eat breakfast, and the dehydration looks like he may not have had any water today and probably not enough yesterday."

I spun on Eddie. "What? Why would you do that?"

He shrugged, looking small in the hospital bed. "I don't love water. And I wanted to get lunch going. I didn't think about anything else."

"The IV he has is giving him fluids, and we want him to eat before we release him. If he takes the medication as prescribed, and we have no reason to think he hasn't been, and he eats and drinks as he normally would, the medication shouldn't cause anymore issues for him."

My cheeks burned with embarrassment. I was ready to blast the doctor for being dismissive, and the treatment was eating and drinking instead of starving himself. I felt like such a fool. "Thank you, doctor. We appreciate it."

"Of course. I'll have a nurse come in with a menu and you can order whatever you'd like. We want to keep him here for a few more hours to make sure, but as long as nothing changes, we should be able to discharge him tonight."

"Thank you."

"You're welcome."

The doctor left the room, and I turned on Eddie. "What were you thinking? You know you need to take care of yourself."

Eddie looked ashamed. "I'm sorry. I really just forgot. I was going to eat something once I got the sauce started, and then I was busy getting things done. By the time I thought about eating again, I knew you'd be there soon and we would have spaghetti. Man, I hate that I ruined lunch and that sauce."

"The sauce will be fine," I told him.

"Not sitting out all day."

"I put it away before I left. I knew you'd be mad if you made it home."

He chuckled. "A little low blood pressure isn't going to take me out, sweetheart. You're stuck with me for a while longer."

"I hope so. I'm not ready to lose you just yet."

"That's good. I'm not ready to go just yet."

I hugged him, relieved he was going to be okay.

The rest of his stay was uneventful. After he ate, he looked more like himself and the doctor discharged him late-afternoon. All he talked about on the drive home was the sauce and finally getting to have the spaghetti.

I got Eddie settled in the living room, even though he argued with me about wanting to help, and pulled the sauce out of the fridge. With it warming on the stove, I started the water for spaghetti. When everything was finished, I carried two bowls into the living room and sat with him in front of the TV.

Eddie groaned after his first bite. "Man, this is good."

I chuckled. "Yes, it is. It reminds me of Mom."

Eddie smiled at me. "Me, too. It's hard to believe it's been almost four years since we lost her."

"Yeah. I miss her."

"Me, too. All the time. But she's still here with us. We're never without her. She's in everything we do. She would be proud of you and all you've accomplished."

"I hope so."

Eddie and I were quiet for a few minutes while we ate. I

kept peeking at him to make sure he was doing okay, but he looked like his normal self.

"I'm surprised you're free tonight. I figured you'd have plans on a Saturday night."

"Oh, shit," I breathed.

"Uh oh," Eddie said.

I jumped up from the couch and snatched my purse from the front hall. I dug out my phone and carried it back to my seat, flipping through texts and messages from Xavier. They ranged from *are you ready for our date* to *is everything okay, I'm worried.*

"Shit, shit, shit," I mumbled.

"Did you forget about a hot date?" Eddie teased.

I ignored him, unsure how to answer his question. Where my mom was in the middle of all the town gossip, Eddie was oblivious. He had no idea I was dating someone, let alone that Xavier had moved here.

"You had a date? With who? Invite him here. We have plenty of spaghetti."

I looked up at Eddie, wondering if he'd lost his mind again. "Invite him here? We've only been dating for a few weeks."

"So? You need to grab life by the horns and enjoy every minute of it. I missed out on time with your mom because we thought we had all the time in the world. You never know when your time is up. Don't wait to love someone."

"I don't know."

"You can go if you need to see him. I will be okay."

I shook my head. "No. I don't want to leave you right now."

"Then invite him over. I promise to be on my best behavior."

I chewed my lip and debated my options. If I wanted to

see Xavier, which I did, I had to invite him over. To my step-father's. A few hours after he got out of the hospital.

I tapped Xavier's name on the screen and lifted the phone to my ear. It rang, and rang. I got nervous and jumped up from my seat. Eddie watched me as I paced to the other end of the room.

"Are you okay?" Xavier asked as a greeting.

"I'm fine. I'm sorry."

"You're sorry. Shit. Okay. Can I talk you out of it?"

"Out of what?"

"Ending things. We said we were going to try to move forward, and I still want to. I want you in my life, Karissa. I have always wanted you in my life. And now that we live in the same town, I'm not willing to walk away from you. I know it's seventeen years too late, but I love you. I want to build a future with you. Please give me another chance."

My lips turned up in a goofy grin with every word he said. When he was done, I was so shocked I couldn't speak.

"Where are you? Can I come see you? We can talk in person."

"I'm at Eddie's," I finally said.

"Your step-dad's. Okay. Did he say something that changed your mind about us?"

"No."

"Then what did? What happened? I want to fix this. I'm not going to lose you again. Not without doing everything possible to make this right."

"Do you want to come over for dinner?"

"What?" he blurted.

"Dinner. We were just having dinner. I came here for lunch, and Eddie was acting weird. He started a new medication this week, and his blood pressure dropped really low and he had to go to the hospital. I went with him and forgot about everything else, including our date tonight. We were just having dinner, and Eddie said he was surprised I was free, and I remembered we were supposed to go out tonight."

"And that's what you were apologizing for."

"Yep."

"And I made a complete fool of myself. Awesome."

I breathed a laugh. "Thank you."

"I meant it, Karissa. I love you."

"Good."

He waited a beat, then laughed. "Okay, so dinner? Is there anything I can bring?"

"Nope. We already started eating. Do you like spaghetti?"

"I love it."

"Good. I'll text you the address. See you soon."

"Yep."

We hung up, and I still couldn't stop my grin.

"Sounds like that went well," Eddie said, watching me from across the room.

"He said he loves me."

Eddie's brows jumped up. "And you didn't say it back?"

"I want to say it to his face."

"Well, good for you, sweetheart."

I smiled. "I wish Mom could have met him."

"I'll tell her all about him."

"Thanks, Eddie."

I turned on the outside lights and got another bowl of spaghetti ready. When Xavier rang the bell, I was unreasonably nervous.

Eddie stayed in his chair while I went to answer the door. Xavier was wearing jeans and a pool blue shirt that stretched across his upper body. His scent hit me as soon as

I opened the door. But it was the look in his eyes that did me in. Part concern, part nerves, and all love.

"Hi," he said.

"Hey."

"How is Eddie?"

"He's better."

"Good. How are you?"

I smiled. "I was terrified."

He stepped forward and wrapped his arms around me, pulling me against his chest without hesitation. He pressed his nose to my neck and held me for a long moment.

I finally breathed deeply, letting go of the anxiety I felt all day. Eddie was home and okay. And Xavier was there, and he loved me.

"I love you," I whispered.

He pulled back, meeting my gaze and smiling. "Did I hear you right?"

I nodded.

"Hell yes."

I laughed with him. He pressed his lips to mine, careful not to push too far since we weren't alone. "I love you."

"Good."

He chuckled. "Introduce me to Eddie."

I nodded and took his hand, leading him to the living room. Eddie looked up at us with a wide grin.

"Eddie, this is Xavier. Xavier, this is my step-father, Eddie."

Xavier let go of my hand to cross the room to Eddie. He shook Eddie's hand and said, "It's so nice to meet you. I'm glad you're feeling better."

"You and me both, son. Karissa has told me absolutely nothing about you, so grab some food and join us. You can spill."

I laughed and rolled my eyes. Xavier just nodded and agreed.

The three of us settled in front of the TV, Xavier between Eddie and me. I listened while the two of them talked about everything from childhood to college to sports. When the conversation turned to McJenna, Eddie asked about moving her here in the middle of high school.

"She wasn't happy," Xavier admitted.

"I can imagine. It's a pretty good place to grow up, though. She'll meet friends next week when school starts."

"Thanks to Karissa, she met one a few weeks ago. She's a whole new kid."

Eddie looked at me.

"Valentina's oldest is the same age. She and I helped arrange a casual meeting without Bianca knowing they were being set up."

"That's a good idea. It's not easy being the new kid. Especially when everyone else knows each other."

"The beginning of summer was tough," Xavier admitted. "I was working a lot of hours, and she was bored out of her mind. I started working a more normal schedule and taking a day off every other week, and Karissa introduced her to Bianca, and it's like I have a different kid at home."

"I'm happy to hear that. You'll have to bring her by sometime so I can meet her," Eddie said.

"I'd like that," Xavier replied.

Both men turned to smile at me. I looked between them and just laughed. "Are you two already conspiring?"

"Of course not," they said together. We all laughed.

Xavier and I stayed with Eddie until he declared he was tired and going to bed. I made sure the kitchen was cleaned up and everything was put away, then we said good night to Eddie and headed out.

"Do I have to kiss you on your step-father's driveway, or am I going to be able to continue this night with you?" Xavier asked when we reached our cars.

"I was thinking maybe you could come back to my place. It's still early. Unless you have to get home."

He shook his head slowly. "McJenna is having a sleep-over at Bianca's tonight."

"Really?"

He nodded.

"Which means you're in no rush to get home."

"Not in the slightest."

"Hmm. What are you going to do with yourself?"

He stepped forward, pressing my back to the side of my car. "I have a few ideas."

He leaned down and kissed my neck. The cool evening air was no match for the heat he built inside me. I moaned and tipped my head back.

"I could do this for a little while." He nipped at my collarbone. "And that." His tongue slid up my neck, and he suckled on the soft spot behind my ear. "And that."

"I like all those options," I whispered.

"I have a few other ideas, too, but I should probably wait until we're behind closed doors for those."

"I like the way you think."

He chuckled against my skin, sending goosebumps over my body.

"I do love you, you know."

He nodded and pulled back. "I know. And I love you. I never thought I'd be able to say that to you again, but I can now. I'm going to make you a little crazy with how much I say it."

I grinned. "I don't think so."

"Good. Because I love you." He kissed my lips. "I love

you." He kissed my neck. "I love you." He kissed my ear. "I can't wait to make love to you."

I nodded.

"I'll follow you. I love you."

I smiled as he backed up and moved toward his car. "I love you."

18

XAVIER

THE FIVE-MINUTE DRIVE TO KARISSA'S APARTMENT FELT LIKE it was three hours long. I just wanted her in my arms, but there were stop signs and people crossing the street and no parking spaces. I was about to crawl out of my skin.

We finally managed to get there and park, and we met in front of her building. I took her hand, and we hurried up the stairs. It was good to know she was as impatient as I was.

Karissa fumbled with her key in the lock. I barely resisted the urge to bring her into my arms while we were standing outside her door, then she finally got the key in and let us inside.

As soon as the door closed, she pushed me against it. Her hands slid under my shirt, lifting it up and away, her nails scratching my skin. I groaned and yanked my shirt off when she abandoned it around my chest so she could touch me.

I was not about to complain.

Her fingertips grazed my nipples, then slid down over my abs. I sucked it in, knowing I didn't look the same as when we were in our early twenties. She leaned down and licked my sternum, the tip of her tongue the only thing in contact with my skin. She kept moving up, over my throat and chin until her lips closed over mine.

Damn, the woman knew how to drive me crazy.

I cupped her jaw and held her in place while I fucked her mouth with my tongue. My cock throbbed in my jeans, begging to be out and inside of her, but she was the one running the show. I was just a very willing participant.

She took a step back, drawing me with her since our mouths were still attached. She didn't bother with lights as she moved us through her condo. She made a turn and a minute later, she stopped at the edge of a bed.

I wanted to see her, to watch her, to take in everything. "Lights."

She broke away from me and turned on a lamp next to the bed.

I looked around the room, taking in all the pieces of her I saw. The colorful curtains, the oversized dresser with a few scattered pieces of jewelry on top, the simple desk in the corner with the poop pen holder from her mom. If Karissa was a room, this would be it, right down to the queen bed that was neatly made with a comforter that looked like sunlight itself had stained it.

"I'm nervous now," she admitted. "I wasn't a minute ago, but now I am."

"We're just two people who love each other," I said. "Nothing has to happen if you're not ready."

"Trust me, I'm ready. But it's been a while."

"Seventeen years."

She chuckled. "Yes, but I just meant in general."

"How long?" I tucked a lock of hair behind her ear and waited for her answer. I didn't want to think about her with another man, but I knew she hadn't been completely alone either.

"More than a year. And then my surgery." She hid her gaze from me, chewing on the inside of her cheek.

I lifted her chin with a fingertip and waited until she was looking at me. "I wouldn't care if you had nothing there. Knowing you're safe and healthy and have the best chance for survival as possible is the most important thing."

She nodded. "I agree, but I'm not all me. When you touch me there, you'll be touching skin covered sacks of fluid."

"But it's your skin, Karissa. That's what I'm touching. That's what I want. Just you."

She nodded again. When she reached for the edge of her shirt, I put my hand on hers.

"Let me."

She took a breath and released the fabric.

I dropped to my knees in front of her and lifted the hem. A thin strip of brown skin was visible, just enough for me to see and taste. I ran my tongue over that bare skin, loving how she moaned softly in response.

I lifted more, exposing her skin inch by inch until I reached the bottom of her bra. A stretchy band wrapped around her, no wires. I found a clasp in the back and lifted her shirt the rest of the way off.

She sucked in a breath, just like I did when my shirt came off, but all I saw was the most beautiful woman in the world. I kissed her, holding her body tight against mine while I drove us both crazy with need.

Her hands slid up and down my back, nails scraping my skin with her impatience. I eased the clasp on her bra apart and stepped back to let it fall to the floor, then brought her body into contact with mine again.

"Karissa," I moaned.

"Please," she whimpered.

She didn't have to ask me again. I knew her enough to know she was wet and ready and needed to move things along.

I dropped to my knees again and slid her shorts and panties down her thighs. She stepped out of them, spreading her thighs in the process. I took advantage of the movement and slid a hand up her the inside of her leg.

She froze, her hands on my shoulders. She stepped wider, just enough to tell me she wanted me to keep going.

I looked up at her, watching her face as my hand reached the apex of her thighs. She bit her lip and closed her eyes. I traced her lips, spreading her wetness around her silky skin.

"Xavier."

I gently pushed a finger inside her, groaning when her body sucked it in deeper. I pumped in and out, slowly, getting a feel for how tight she was. I couldn't wait to fill her up.

She spread her thighs wider. I withdrew my finger and dragged it up to her clit, circling the sensitive nub before plunging into her core again.

"Oh, God."

"Lie down," I told her, nudging her toward the bed as I fucked her slowly with my finger.

She took a step back and reached behind her, lowering herself onto the bed with her knees hanging over the edge. I pressed her thighs wide and hooked her feet over my shoulders so she was spread out for me.

Fucking hell, she was beautiful. Her skin glistened with her wetness, her clit plump and ready for me. Her core dripped every time I withdrew my finger.

I added a second finger to her, and she moaned long and loud. Her thighs tightened around my neck, but I pressed on them until she dropped them again. Then I leaned forward and got my first taste of her in far too long.

The flavor of her exploded on my tongue, bringing me back to when she belonged to me. I couldn't hold myself back once I had my tongue on her and lashed at her clit with quick, pointed strokes intent on sending her up and over the edge as quickly as possible.

She moaned and thrashed on the bed, urging me on with her incoherent sounds. Her hips moved with my fingers, fucking me back as hard as I fucked her. My cock throbbed, dying to be in on the action, but I wasn't done with her taste yet. Not even close.

"Oh, God, Xavier. Oh, God."

She whimpered and thrust against me. Her hands grabbed the back of my head, then immediately pulled back. I took her hand with my one free one and put it back on my head. I wanted her to show me exactly what she needed.

She grabbed my head and pulled hard, shoving my face into my pussy. I licked and sucked and fucked her until her entire body went still and she let out a moan that turned quickly into a scream.

Her arms went lax, and I took a breath, drunk on her scent and taste and touch. I needed more of her, and my woman could give it to me. She always did.

I flicked the tip of her clit with my tongue until she jerked and moaned again. I thrust my fingers deep into her again, bringing her back to me so I could send her flying again.

"Yes," she breathed.

Yes, indeed. I rasped my tongue over her clit until she

panted and reached for my head again. Then I sucked her clit hard into my mouth and she went flying. Moans and cries and nails down my scalp told me she wasn't done yet. She was still going, and she needed more.

I added a third finger to her core, and she relaxed her entire body.

"Fuck me," she breathed.

"Yes, ma'am," I said against her flesh. Everything was wet. Come poured from her, filling my hand as I fucked her hard and fast. She pumped her hips against my hand, taking what she needed. I sucked her clit, doing my best to keep up with her movements. Every time I got her in my mouth, she gasped and moved her hips faster.

"Please," she begged, her voice strained.

I pressed my hand to her thigh and my face tight to her body and sucked hard on her clit. I moved with her, not letting her get away from me as she retreated to fuck my face and hand. I cupped her hip with my free hand and rode through her orgasm as she finally let go.

"Yes, oh, God, yes. Fuck! Xavier! Yes!"

Her body shook and thrashed and bucked until I had no choice but to move or risk hurting her. I wiped my face on the back of my hand and stroked inside her gently until she looked down at me and smiled.

"Damn, that was amazing."

I smiled. "Hell, yes."

"Why are you still down there?"

"It's an amazing view."

She grinned. "A better one would be you inside me."

I slid my fingers from her body, watching as she let me go. Her body trembled.

I stood and stripped the rest of my clothes. I moved close

to her and positioned myself between her thighs, then stopped. "I almost forgot a condom."

When we were in college, we never used them. She was on the pill, and we got tested after a few months. After that, we were only together.

"Xavier," she said softly.

I stopped and looked back at her. She nibbled her lower lip and shrugged.

"You have to say it, Karissa."

"You don't have to wear a condom. I'm still on the pill. I'm clean."

I closed my eyes and grabbed my cock, stroking it once, then a second time. "I want nothing more than to sink into you without anything between us, but I know it's been a long time."

"I want you. I just want you."

"I'm clean. I promise you. I haven't been with anyone in almost four years. At all. I've been tested. And I always wore condoms, except with Denise after she was pregnant."

"I trust you," she said.

Those three words were more than anything else. I closed my eyes and let those words sink into me. I moved back over to her, pressing her thighs wide and fitting myself between them.

"I trust you," she said again. "I love you."

"I love you," I told her. "Just you, Karissa. Always you. Love you. Trust you. Need you."

She repeated the words to me, hooking her legs around my hips.

I lined up at her entrance and held my cock still. I looked up at her, my gaze locked on hers while I plunged deep into the love of my life.

"Oh, God," she breathed.

"Yes." I looked down, watching as my cock reappeared between her legs. In again, vanishing into her perfect pussy. She stretched and let me in, her body wrapping tight around mine.

"Fuck," she whispered.

"Let go for me," I told her.

She nodded and slid her hand down her body. Her fingers spread over her clit, then dipped lower to feel where I entered her.

"Fuck," I grunted when her fingertips touched me.

I spread her thighs wider and watched us fuck. It was raw and beautiful and everything I'd been missing in my life. It was Karissa. It was us. I was never going to lose her again.

Her fingers slid back up her body to her clit, and she pinched it between two of them. She groaned and pressed one finger to the swollen nub. Her channel tightened around me, and I nearly blew right then.

"Xavier," she whispered.

I looked up at her, loving the look of pure bliss on her face as she made herself come. Her lips twisted and her mouth parted in an O before she released, her core clamping down on me as her fingers flew over her clit and she came with a scream that spurred me to the edge.

I held her ankles and let go, fucking my woman until my throat tightened and my entire body locked up. I stared at her entrance, slamming hard into her and groaning when her fingertips touched my cock again and I came hard, grunting and moaning and wondering how in the hell I ever walked away from her.

Never again. She was mine, and I was hers, and nothing would ever change that again.

My thighs ached from standing while I came that hard,

but I wasn't ready to leave her body just yet. I stood there for a long moment, watching her as she came down from her high. Her eyes blinked open and peered up at me with a sleepy, sex-drunk smile that made her look seventeen years younger.

"God, I've missed that."

I chuckled. "Is that the only reason you agreed to a date? You're using me for sex?"

"Um, no?" Karissa said with a grin.

"Not fair," I protested. "I have so much more to offer than just good sex."

"It's not good sex," she teased. "It's fucking amazing sex."

My cock twitched inside her, and she moaned.

"Oh, yeah. See? That's what I'm saying."

I laughed with her. I'd never laughed during, or after, sex with anyone else. Karissa was the only one who ever made me feel like I could be myself in every moment we were together.

"I need to pee. You have to let me up," she said, pushing at my chest.

"I don't want to let you go."

She looked up at me. "Never."

I leaned down and kissed her hard, spearing my tongue into her mouth. I needed her to know what it meant to be with her again.

She smiled against my lips when I gentled the kiss. She stood and waddled to the bathroom, leaving the door open. It was like seventeen years hadn't passed and we were soon-to-be college graduates planning a life together all over again.

When she flushed and turned on the water to wash her hands, I went into the bathroom to clean myself up. She leaned against the counter and watched me, a smile on her face.

"What?"

She shook her head. "I just never thought we'd be together again."

I nodded and pulled her into my arms. "Neither did I. I never thought you'd forgive me. I still don't forgive myself."

She pushed away from me. "No. You can't say that. The choices you made back then were the right ones for you at the time. It hurt, a lot, but we can't start this with regrets. You have to forgive yourself."

"We missed a lot of time."

"And we're going to miss more if you let old decisions ruin what we could have. I love you. I've always loved you. I've never let another man into my body without protection. That's a big one for me. You're it for me, Xavier. Forever. You always were, and I know that's why I never settled down with anyone else. I was waiting for you and hoping we'd find a way to be together. But you can't look back. We have to look ahead to our future."

I drew a deep breath and let it out slowly. She was right. She was always right.

"Okay."

"Good," she said. "Now, I think we need something to eat. I'm running out of fuel, and we have a full night ahead of us. I plan to use you for more sex before the sun comes up."

"I love the way you think," I told her.

I washed my hands and chased her out of the bathroom into the kitchen. I loved that she didn't bother to put on any clothes, just wandered around completely naked. Open and ready for me. Heart, body, and soul. I was a lucky man.

19

KARISSA

"Why do you look like you're floating?" Blake asked when I walked into book club.

"Probably because Xavier didn't come home last night," Finley provided for the group.

"What?" they all gasped.

"It's no big deal," I said, even as my cheeks warmed and my entire body flooded with joy. God, it was so dumb, but I couldn't stop smiling.

"You two are officially back together?" Melody asked.

I nodded. "We are."

"Is this like a permanent thing, or is it casual?" Sofia asked.

"Not casual. I can't say it's permanent, but I hope it is," I told them.

"Wow. Good for you." Piper smiled widely.

"Thank you."

"How was the sex?" Elise asked.

"Only you," I said, laughing and shaking my head at her.

"I was wondering, too," Willow said.

Elise and Willow fist-bumped.

"Maybe she doesn't want to tell us," Finley said.

"Oh, no, I definitely do," I said, making everyone laugh. "I haven't had a good story to share in forever. And even then, it was always a fumbling, random story. That's not how it is with Xavier."

"I love when it's like that," Goldie said. "When it feels like you know each other inside and out and can anticipate what the other person is going to say or do."

"Why did your marriage fail?" Trinity asked.

"Trinity!" I gasped.

"What?" She had the decency to look ashamed. "Sorry. That was bad to ask. You just sounded like you had a really good sex life. Why did everything go wrong?"

Goldie shrugged. "We weren't right for each other in the end. I thought we were. We had good sex and good conversations and we have an amazing son, but..." She paused and looked around the room.

None of us knew Goldie well. Her sister worked with Laura, and they hit it off when they met. Goldie helped Finley with some events a year ago that secured finances for the store for a while. She was talented and smart and funny. I wondered why her marriage failed, too, but I didn't have the guts to ask her.

"My ex is gay. well, bi, I guess. He wasn't out when we got married, and I had no idea. He was kind and giving, and we connected. But as the world has become more accepting, he finally felt safe to be his true self."

"Holy shit," Elise said. "That's not what I expected you to say."

Goldie nodded. "I don't talk about it because it's painful. Not that he's bi, but that he lied to me about who he was for so long. I loved him. I still do, but in a friendship way. I want him to be happy, and he is now, but it's hard because I'm alone now. I thought he was it for me."

"I'm so sorry," Trinity asked. "I shouldn't have asked."

Goldie shook her head. "It's okay. He doesn't live around here, so not many people know. Paul took the divorce hard. He adored his dad, and to find out Charles was lying to him his whole life was really tough for Paul to take. He didn't care that his dad was gay, but he's still a kid who wants his parents to be together forever."

"It's not easy," Sofia said. "When my parents split up, I was so mad at my dad. Their lives just didn't align, but I thought he should change so he could be with my mom. She told me once that she didn't want a man who was different, but she couldn't live with the man he was. I didn't get it at the time. I was young and believed if you loved someone, you did everything for them. Love works both ways, though, and I only saw where he wasn't willing to change, not how she wasn't willing to change since I'm a lot like she was."

"I can understand that," Goldie said. "I wasn't willing to stay in a marriage I knew was one-sided, even if he asked me to. He didn't, but if he had, I would have said no. I want to know the person I come home to at the end of the day is just as excited to see me as I am to see him." She paused and took a bite of her cake. "I should probably get a dog and be done with men."

We all laughed, but I completely understood her thought.

"I'm more of a cat person," I admitted. "Less maintenance."

"True, but you have a man now," Goldie said with a warm smile. "I'm happy for you."

"Thank you."

"Now, tell us all about your night. Because I need something good." Goldie bobbed her head from side-to-side and grinned widely.

"It was like we'd been together all these years," I admitted. "It was weird, but it felt normal. Like we had just spent time together."

"Does that mean the sex was good?" Blake asked. "Pregnant sex is better than I thought it would be, but new relationship sex, when we were committed and fresh and shiny, was damn good."

"It was amazing. I told him I'm only using him for the amazing sex," I confessed.

"No, you didn't!" Finley said.

I nodded. "I did. He laughed. He knew I was joking. It was like it used to be. It was fun."

"Wow," Laura said. "I'm so happy for you. You deserve happiness. After your mom, I was so worried you wouldn't open yourself up to anyone else. How's Eddie?"

I hesitated, knowing exactly what she meant. When my mom died, I was done. I wasn't sure I would survive. I cried for days. It was the worst month of my life. Eddie was there for me, but it wasn't the same for him. He loved my mom, but he'd lost a wife before and knew life would go on. For me, it was a blow I didn't know if I'd recover from.

I'd lost my dad, but losing my mom was different. Losing my dad hurt, but I was always closer to my mom. She was there for me when Dad died, and through everything else in my life. She was my constant. My best friend in a way no one else had ever been. She was the first person I wanted to share something with. Always had been.

When she died, I felt like I'd lost myself. I knew it was coming, but I still wasn't prepared. I wasn't sure it was possible to ever be prepared. But it was worse than I imagined.

Opening myself up to that pain again... Laura was right. Xavier was quickly becoming my number one person. The thought of losing him stole my breath and made everything hurt.

"Rissa? Are you okay? Did something happen to Eddie?" Laura asked.

I snapped out of it and looked around the room at my friends. The looks on their faces went from worry to fear.

"What happened?" Elise asked. "Is Eddie okay?"

I finally nodded. "Yeah, he is. Sorry. I figured everyone knew. He went to the hospital yesterday."

"What happened?"

"Is he okay?"

"Are you okay?"

"We're fine. He's fine. He was having some heart palpitations and minor discomfort and had a heart catheterization on Monday and started some blood pressure meds. It dropped his blood pressure, and he didn't eat and was on his feet and ended up in dangerous territory."

"Oh, my God," Finley said. "Why didn't you call me?"

"He was okay. I figured I'd tell everyone when we were here. He was in the hospital for a few hours, but once he had food and was hydrated again, he was okay. I took him home, and we had dinner."

"I thought Xavier had dinner with you last night? When he left, he said he was meeting you," Finley said.

"He was. He did. We had plans, but with Eddie, I forgot. When I finally remembered, I invited Xavier to have dinner with us."

"So, he met Eddie?" Finley asked.

I chuckled. "Yes, he met Eddie."

"How did that go?" Blake asked.

"Good. Eddie really liked him."

"And how's Eddie today?" Elise asked.

"He's good. He promised me he's going to eat regularly. He set a timer on his phone to make sure he eats and drinks so he doesn't end up in the hospital again."

"What a scare. People don't realize how much what we eat and drink can influence our bodies. Of course, cake doesn't count." Laura shoved a big bite into her mouth and chewed slowly.

The rest of us laughed and nodded with her.

"Less than three weeks to the wedding, Finley. Are you ready?" Melody asked.

Finley smiled. "I am. I'm really looking forward to it. You guys are all coming, right?"

Everyone nodded.

"And your significant others, kids, whoever?"

"Are you sure?" Goldie asked. "I don't have to bring Paul."

"If he doesn't want to come, we will not be offended, but there will be other kids there. Valentina is coming with her family. I think Paul knows her younger daughter?"

Goldie laughed. "That might get him to come. I think he has a crush on Sam."

"Romance is alive at weddings," I teased.

"I'm so not ready for my fourteen-year-old to be dating," Goldie said with a groan. "I think there should be a rule that parents and children shouldn't date at the same time."

"Who are you dating?" Elise asked.

"Oh, no one. Just that I'm single. I want to be open to the possibility." Goldie's cheeks turned pink.

"Ah, I don't believe you. At all. What's going on?" Elise pressed.

Goldie shook her head. "Nothing at all. My new assistant is just really flirtatious."

"Your new twenty-six-year-old male assistant?" Laura asked.

Goldie dropped her head into her hands. "That's the one."

"Oh my God, you've been holding out on us!" Elise said. "Tell us everything about the flirty new young thing. And how you're going to flirt back with him."

Goldie groaned. "I cannot flirt with my assistant. He's gorgeous, but he's just too young for me. And he works for me. I worked too hard to get to where I am to risk it all with a sexual harassment lawsuit."

"If it's mutual, it's not harassment," Piper said. "There's no reason you can't be involved with him just because you work together."

"He works for me. He's my assistant. Anything can be seen as wrong. And besides that, I'm not interested in him." Goldie was lying through her teeth.

"That's bullshit," Elise said. "You so like him. We can all see it."

Goldie groaned again. "I'm not allowed, so I'm just choosing mind over matter and I'm going to pretend I don't. Give me that, please."

Elise opened her mouth to argue, but I interrupted her. "Of course. You don't come here to be pressured into something you're not comfortable with. Right, Elise."

Elise grumbled but agreed.

Finley changed the subject back to the wedding, leaving Goldie alone. I offered her a smile and hoped she'd find her own happiness. I finally understood why all my friends were so ready for everyone else to be happy. Finding mine again made me want to see all my friends blissfully in love like I was.

Two days later, I had a status meeting with Bex about the app I was designing for her. I had a mockup already done and ready for her to test out, if she wanted to. Some customers just wanted it done and didn't want to get involved, but I had a feeling Bex would want to see the product live.

I sat in front of my computer and waited for her call to come in. She was three minutes late, but that wasn't unheard of for her, so I didn't worry.

Until I got a text.

> Sorry. Got caught on a call. We need to talk.
> Are you available in thirty?

My heart pounded. She could have just canceled, but she said we need to talk. That was always ominous.

> I'm available. I'll see you then.

> Thx.

I clicked off my phone and took a deep breath. Maybe I was being ridiculous, but something about her tone felt off.

I took the time to get some water and a quick snack, making sure I didn't stay away from the computer too long in case she called early.

When thirty minutes was up, I sat down again and forced myself to take deep breaths. Bex didn't call then. I kept waiting, dread sinking deeper with every passing minute.

The computer finally rang seven minutes late. I exhaled deeply, then forced my lips up into a smile and answered the call.

"Hi! How are you?"

Bex did not look happy. Our first call, she was stressed, but this call she just looked frustrated.

"Not great, to be honest."

"Is everything okay?"

She took a breath and looked up at me through the screen. Our eyes locked, and I knew what was coming.

"Honestly, no. I got a call earlier from a colleague. He heard I was working with you to develop the app, and he wanted to warn me that working with you would destroy my business. I probably shouldn't be telling you this, but I have a lot of respect for you. I'm just confused, Karissa."

"Bex, I don't know what to say. We've been working together for a month. Do you believe what this colleague said over me?"

"That's what I'm struggling with. Normally, he's not someone I'd listen to, but he showed me proof. The reviews on his app are horrible. It doesn't work like it's designed, it crashes constantly. It's a disaster. I can't have that happen to mine. I don't have the funds to pay someone else to redesign it if it doesn't work."

I wasn't positive who she was talking about, but I had a guess. I needed to know if I was right. "Bex, can I ask you who is telling you this? I know that violates his trust, but if I know who this is, I might be able to defend myself."

"I'm not sure that's a good idea."

"I think this person is trying to ruin my business. I had been working up a proposal for another company before you and I spoke. The other company all but gave me a contract, telling me the project was mine. I started designing their app, only to have them call me after weeks of work and tell me they hired someone else because of the supposed word of a former client of mine."

"That's horrible," Bex said.

"It was frustrating, but it happens. However, if someone is trying to ruin my business, I'd like to know who. My guess is Gary Carmack."

Bex didn't say anything, but she sucked in a quick breath. That was all the admission I needed to tell her the story.

"I started working for him three years ago. I'd just finished developing an app that I sold myself. It was very successful. He wanted me to sell that app to him, but I refused. It was a labor of love in a way, and something I wanted to maintain control of. He asked me to develop something else for him. I did exactly what he wanted. The app was perfect. I turned over all the developer files and the background information because he said they had an in-house team that would upload the app. He lied."

"What?"

"His in-house team was really his brother, who was learning how to develop apps. They uploaded the app, but they refused to contract me for regular maintenance. They uploaded it, and I had no access to the files to maintain it. With a team, it wouldn't have been a big deal to do little things, and they could have hired me for major updates, but they didn't. They also didn't have an in-house team or anyone who knew what they were doing. The first update crashed all devices running the app."

"No."

I nodded. "They still had the original files, so they re-uploaded those, but they needed some updates. They tried to hire me to do an emergency update, but I didn't have room in my calendar to take on a project like that immediately. When I wouldn't drop everything and walk away from the clients I was working with at the time, Mr. Carmack said I would regret it."

"Wow," Bex breathed.

"I don't know if that's who you heard from, but I wanted you to know that story, just in case. My understanding is they had to pay double my rate for someone to fix what the brother did to the app, and to do it in a timely fashion because they were trying to launch a new product line. I believe it got done, but the damage was done to the business, and I don't think they recovered. He blames me, even though I had nothing to do with everything being messed up. I'm not sure why he's reaching out to people now to try to ruin my reputation, but I'm guessing it's because there are rumors they are going to have to close. I think he is hoping if he can shift the blame to me, maybe he can sue me or at least save his reputation and name."

"I'm so sorry, Karissa," Bex said. She shook her head. "I should have known he was lying. He told me you were the reason everything crashed, and that he had to hire someone to fix it all. He never mentioned his brother or his lack of a team."

"I figured. I'm not surprised. I wouldn't normally speak so openly about another client, but I figured their fail was public enough that I wasn't telling you anything you didn't know, except for my part in it."

"I didn't know. But I'm glad I do now. Can you forgive me for even thinking he could have been telling the truth? I will understand if you're not interested in working with me now."

I thought about it for a minute. I didn't like that Bex trusted Gary Carmack, but I understood it. He was someone she had other connections with, and I was someone she hired. Trusting me with her business was putting a lot of faith into me, especially when someone else was assuring her it was the wrong call.

"If you are willing to trust me, I'll continue working with you. I've already created a demo I wanted to show you today. The work is almost finished."

"Oh, thank you so much, Karissa. I really am so sorry. I will make sure everyone I know knows how amazing you are so his toxic story doesn't continue to spread."

"Thank you," I told her. It was nice to hear, but it was a bitter pill. Forgive and forget was one thing, but having my values questioned and found lacking was another. I liked Bex, and I trusted that Gary laid it on thick for her, but if I was going to keep my career, I needed to stop relying on others to hire me and do work I loved for people I loved.

Like that app Trent and Xavier talked about for the theater.

20

———

BEX LOVED THE DEMO I CREATED AND APOLOGIZED PROFUSELY. She also made a very public announcement that she was proud to be working with me for the design of her app. She apologized in the announcement for trusting a less than honest colleague and almost ending our partnership and being grateful to me for my honesty and hard work.

I appreciated it, but it didn't change my mind about wanting to design more for myself. I wanted to update Book Boyfriends Wanted and make the app better. I wanted to create other apps I'd considered over the years but never had the guts to do. I wanted to do things for my friends and loved ones.

I was done chasing work from people who could destroy everything I did with a few careful keystrokes and some perfectly placed bad words.

The best vindication I got was when Maxwell Robertson reached out to ask for a meeting. I told him I was too busy right now, but could fit him in a month from now. He said he'd wait and apologized for trusting the wrong person and not giving me the contract he promised me.

I had little intention of working with him, but I was going to take the meeting and see what he said.

While Bex was testing the demo I created for her, I decided to start working on an app for the theater. I figured they would need two, one for tickets and food orders and one for guests inside the theater to order drinks and snacks during a show. Both needed to be simple enough that employees could update them with current information, like movie titles and menu options. Which meant I needed to talk to Xavier about it.

I invited him over for dinner Tuesday night after my meeting with Bex so we could talk through the details. It wasn't complicated to build, and I was sure I could have it done before the theater opened. In nine days. Maybe I was crazy.

"Are you sure you can do this?" Xavier asked.

"I'm going to do my best," I told him.

"We were going to use the website. Trent had his hotel people design it. It works."

"I know, but you wanted an app. And I can create an app. Then you can launch exactly how you want. I just need to know what restaurants you've partnered with and what of their menu they are doing. And what concessions you're going to offer for that side of the app."

"If you're sure about this, let's do it."

"I'm sure."

Xavier pulled me in for a rough kiss. His hand speared through my hair and tilted my head to the side. He leaned his forehead against mine and inhaled. "I love you."

"I love you."

He let me go and sat at the table. We ran through all the options and I made notes on everything. I was really excited about doing the app.

When we finished with the details I needed, he asked if I wanted to order dinner. "Chinese?"

"Sounds good. Where's J tonight?"

"Last night of freedom before school starts tomorrow," Xavier said.

"Ooh, I forgot school starts tomorrow."

"Yep. She and Bianca went out to dinner, but I'm picking her up at nine."

"So, we have time for dinner and dessert?" I teased.

"Oh, yeah."

We ordered Chinese food and Xavier picked it up while I started working on my plans. By the time he got back, I'd repurposed another app and had a first mockup to show him.

"Holy shit. You did this while I was getting dinner?"

I nodded. "It's quick, and it's not close to perfect, but I wanted to give you an idea of what it could look like. If you want me to do something different, I can."

"That's amazing. I mean, I don't know what others there are, but that's unbelievable."

"I can do a lot of things, but I picked this because it reminds me of the theater. Different but still clear what it's for."

"It's perfect."

We sat on the couch and ignored the TV while we talked. "Are you going to be ready to open next week?"

He laughed. "I don't know. There are days it feels like we won't be open for another year, but I know we're really close. All the seating is in. The concession stand is getting delivered tomorrow and will be installed by a crew we have coming in the afternoon. The screens are supposed to arrive next week. We have some minor things to do, but I really think it's almost ready."

"That's great. I know people are excited about it. Is Goldie doing something for the grand opening?"

"Who's Goldie?"

I looked at him, but he wasn't joking. "She's the director of tourism for the area."

"I doubt she'd be interested. This is more for locals than tourists. And she probably isn't here this time of year. Tourists are mostly gone."

I shook my head. "Goldie lives here. She has a fourteen-year-old son. She's a friend of mine. I'm surprised Finley hasn't talked to her about something for the theater."

Xavier shrugged. "It's not a big deal. I think we've gotten the word out well enough. The theaters aren't that big, and we don't want people mad because they can't get in."

"Well, that's true. I didn't think about that."

"Your app will help that. If people buy tickets ahead of time, they will know they have seats."

"I love making things better."

Xavier chuckled.

We finished our dinner and cleaned up the boxes we ate out of. We were standing in the kitchen when Xavier put his arms around me.

"I still have an hour before I need to get J."

I tapped a nail on my chin. "What should we do with that free time?"

He grinned. "I can think of something."

"Oh, yeah?"

He nodded. "You can show me more of that app you're working on."

I huffed a laugh and shoved him away.

He laughed and pulled me back into his arms. "Or we could go to your room and I can show you how much I missed you."

"I think I like that idea better," I admitted.

"Me, too."

He led me to my room with his hand in mine. He stopped just inside the door and turned to face me, bringing his hands up to cup my jaw. He tilted my head to the side and kissed me gently, tasting me softly like it was our first kiss instead of one of hundreds, maybe thousands.

We moved toward the bed slowly, like we had all the time in the world instead of less than an hour. Xavier tugged his shirt off with one hand behind his neck, dropping it and bringing his lips to mine again.

I splayed my hands wide on his chest, enjoying the feel of his soft chest hair against my fingers. His skin was warm. So was his hand on my back, bringing me closer to his body. He lifted my shirt, my belly touching his without a barrier between us.

I wanted more. And I knew if I didn't move things along, I would run out of time for more. I stepped back and pulled off my shirt, then unhooked my bra and tossed that aside. He yanked me back against him, his warm skin pressed to mine.

We kissed like the frenzied teenagers we were when we met. He groaned when I stroked him through his jeans, and I moaned when he thrust a thick thigh between my legs.

"Enough teasing. I need you," he said against my lips.

I nodded. We parted, each of us shoving at our clothes while we struggled to keep our hands on each other. He tripped over his jeans, and I got my panties caught on my foot, but we managed to fall onto the bed together, laughing and kissing and touching.

His fingers dipped between my thighs, spreading me wide as his tongue grazed the tip of mine. I looked at him, eyes open, as he watched me.

"I love seeing you come," he whispered.

I grinned. "I love seeing you come."

"You do?"

I nodded. "Of course. It's sexy and makes me feel powerful that I can make you feel that good."

"Always, Karissa."

He pressed his finger inside me, drawing my wetness back to my clit where he focused his attention. It wasn't long before I was clawing at his back and moaning with pleasure and wishing we had a lot longer than an hour.

"I want to taste you," I said, getting to my knees.

"I want to come inside you."

"I know. I won't take long. Just taste you. I've missed you," I admitted.

His face softened, and he rolled to his back. His cock stood up, curving toward his stomach. Dark hair nestled around it. He put his hands behind his head and watched as I positioned myself between his knees.

I leaned forward, licking the underside of him. He groaned, his eyes slipping closed. I parted my lips and took him into my mouth. I could feel his thighs tighten as he restrained himself. That wasn't what I wanted. I wanted Xavier. My Xavier.

I dragged my nails down his thighs, and he trembled under my touch. When I brought them back up, I held onto his hips and looked up at him.

He was watching me, his eyes full of love and admiration and care. "I love you."

I smiled around his cock, knowing he saw the words in my gaze.

I licked his tip and took him deep again. He groaned, and after a few more strokes, he abandoned his restraint and lifted my hair from my face and held it up so he could control my movements.

"Fuck, Karissa. Oh, God. You feel so damn good."

I mumbled my agreement and let him guide me until he pulled me off him with a pop and dragged me up his body. He replaced his cock with his tongue, fucking my mouth and groaning as my body covered his.

"I've missed you."

I smiled up at him. "Me, too."

I pushed myself up and spread my thighs wide to accommodate him. He held himself upright while I sank down onto him, both of us groaning at the feel of his cock deep inside me.

"Damn. I'm almost there, beautiful. Can I touch you? Help you go with me?"

"Please," I moaned, already feeling the pleasure building inside me. Sucking his cock got me started, but having him fill me up made me damn near orgasmic without any effort.

His palm held my thigh as his thumb pressed against my clit. I pumped my hips, taking him slowly at first, but speeding up with every passing second. It wasn't long before he was grunting and gritting his teeth. His thumb pressed harder, sending me up, up, up until I tumbled over, losing all my strength as my orgasm took over and my body went limp.

"Fuck, Karissa," Xavier groaned. He didn't let up on my clit as he slammed into me from beneath and held me up while he fucked me and finished.

"Yes," I moaned as I felt him come inside me, the warm rush of fluid that almost triggered another orgasm for me.

"Oh, God," he grunted, bringing my body down onto his. He breathed heavily in my ear. My heart raced with his, both of us worn out and well satisfied.

We laid there for a few minutes, holding each other and enjoying the feel of being together. When I felt him slipping from me, I rolled over and went to the bathroom.

He came in right behind me. "Is this weird?"

I shook my head. "Maybe it's weird that it's not weird."

He grinned and leaned down to kiss me.

We cleaned up and got dressed. I was walking to the door with him when his alarm went off.

"Perfect timing," I said.

"Not really. I have to leave you." He cupped my jaw and held me close while he kissed me. I leaned into him, not wanting him to go but knowing he had to.

"I love you."

He hugged me tight. "I love you, Karissa. One day, I won't have to run out on you."

"We'll get there."

He kissed me again, then let himself out. I locked the door behind him and leaned against it. One day felt a lot closer than it had ever felt before.

I SPENT the entire next day working on the app for the theater. I was so excited about it. It did all the things Xavier wanted it to do, and it was even easier than I thought it would be. It wasn't ready for use yet, but it was close. A few more days and I could get it to where they could use it.

I still had to build a data entry piece so Xavier or Genevieve could update the information about the movies, but overall, I was really excited about the app. So excited that I decided to go out and celebrate at the end of my day with a sweet treat from Cove Bakery.

The bakery was busy when I walked in. Full of teenagers

with backpacks. I completely forgot it was the first day of school.

Harriett was behind the counter with a huge smile on her face. "Hello, Karissa. How are you?"

"I'm good. You look like you're in a good mood."

"Oh, I am. I love when the kids come in here. They really liven up the place."

"I bet it's good for business, too."

"It definitely is. I won't say that part doesn't help."

I laughed with her. "It looks like you guys still have a full case."

"Valentina knew it was going to get busy today so she made extras of everything. Even her special for the day."

"Really? What's today's special?"

"It's a caramel cake with a brownie baked inside."

"Seriously?" I asked. My mouth was already watering.

"It's unbelievable. I never baked the way she does. My mind is nowhere near as creative. She impresses me constantly."

"I'm sure she appreciates the opportunity to be creative," I told Harriett.

"I definitely do," Valentina said, coming up next to Harriett. I didn't notice her walking over. "I have the best job ever, and the hips to prove I'm good at it."

"You're stunning," Harriett said. "And any man who isn't willing to see that is a fool."

Valentina's smile faded just slightly. "Yes, well, my baking skills are good. Are you trying the special today, Karissa?"

I nodded. "It sounds too good to pass up."

"And your chocolate croissant?" Harriett asked as Valentina smiled at a customer and excused herself.

"Sure, why not," I said. When Harriett brought my stuff

back to the counter, I lowered my voice. "Is everything okay with Valentina and Dawson?"

Harriett scowled and shook her head. "He's always working and traveling for work. It's just getting to her. She thinks she's not enough of a reason for him to be home anymore. I think he'd be a fool to be stepping out on her, but men are fools sometimes."

I chuckled. "They sure are."

"I hear your man is getting himself together. Sounds like things are going well."

My cheeks warmed, and I nodded. "We're enjoying getting to know each other again."

"Well, good for you. You need some happiness in your life. That McJenna reminds me so much of you." Harriett nodded behind me.

I turned and found McJenna at a table with Bianca and two other girls. They were talking animatedly and laughing, looking like old friends.

"She's a good kid."

"She is. She's been in here a lot with Bianca, and she's always respectful and kind. She's..."

Harriett trailed off and stared behind me. It took me a minute to realize she was watching McJenna.

"What? I'll... I'll be right there. Okay." McJenna's raised voice silenced the rest of the bakery. McJenna hung up her phone and looked at her friends with panic and fear. "My dad. He's in the hospital."

She burst into tears right there in the middle of the bakery.

Her words echoed inside me. Hospital. Xavier was in the hospital.

"McJenna, what happened?" Harriett asked, coming around the edge of the counter.

I watched like it was a movie, unable to move or interact or do anything.

"He was at work and was moving something or installing something. I don't know. They just said something fell on him. He's hurt. He had to go to the hospital. They don't know how he is. What if he's dead? What if he dies? What am I going to do?"

"Come on, sweetheart. We'll take you. Bianca, get your things." Valentina's voice cut through everything else. "Karissa, do you want to ride with us?"

I shook my head slowly. I couldn't. If something happened. If he wasn't okay. I couldn't.

Valentina stared at me for a long minute, then nodded and ushered the girls out the front door. I stood there, watching them, as they disappeared around the corner.

Harriett came up to me and put her arm around my waist. She guided me to a table and helped me sit. I stayed there for hours. Staring at the wall. I couldn't do anything else.

21

XAVIER

HOSPITALS WERE MY LEAST FAVORITE PLACE IN THE WORLD. I hated them. I didn't know many people who loved them, especially as a patient, but sitting there and wishing I wasn't alone was the worst feeling in the entire fucking world.

I shifted and winced at the pain that shot through my body. I was lucky, and I knew it, but it didn't make the whole thing suck any less.

A knock on my door brought my head up off the pillow and hope into me. It only took half a second for that hope to be shattered, like my leg nearly was.

"Hey," Trent said with a lopsided smile. He glanced at the bed next to me and softened his voice when he noticed McJenna sleeping. "How are you feeling?"

"Like the biggest idiot on the planet."

"We all do dumb things like that. You thought you could move it. How were you supposed to know it would fall over on you?"

I looked up at him with barely restrained frustration. I was pretty sure he knew that wasn't what I was talking about.

It took him a second, but then he said, "Oh, you mean Karissa. Why are you writing her off?"

"She's writing me off."

"Did you call her? Are you sure that's what's happening?"

"Ah, man, I knew I forgot to do something. I should just call her and then everything will be fine." I glared at my best friend and tried not to hate him and his shiny happiness.

"Finley said she was at Cove Bakery when McJenna got the call. She freaked out. Maybe she just got scared or something."

"And because she's scared, she's ignored all my calls, texts, and messages?"

Trent shrugged helplessly.

"She's done. For whatever reason, she's done. It doesn't really matter what it is. If she doesn't want to be with me, then it's over. I thought we were building something. I was trying to take it slow—"

"Didn't you tell her you still love her?"

"Yeah, but that was just me being honest. Not me rushing her."

"Are you sure she sees it the same way?"

I growled at him.

Trent held up his hands and moved to the chair next to the bed I wasn't allowed to get out of. Hell, I couldn't even take a fucking piss without assistance.

"I don't know Karissa well. I'm not going to say I can understand what she's thinking. But I know what it's like to be scared. I pushed Finley away every chance I had because things were moving too fast for me. It wasn't even her trying to move them along, it was our reality. Maybe Karissa's scared things are going too fast."

"She said she loves me, too. We were in this. She was working on an app for the theater. She sent me a text saying she wanted to show it to me. I never replied because I was pinned underneath the concession stand, but fuck, dude? I'm not pushing her too far, too fast. Something fucking changed."

Trent shifted, the plastic chair creaking under his weight. He leaned forward. "Want me to talk to Finley?"

"Fuck no. Just go home to your family. I'll be fine for the night. You don't need to be here all night."

"Want me to take J?"

I sighed. My kid freaked the fuck out. I wasn't sure why she got a call like she did, but when the paramedics arrived to get the concession stand off of me, they called Trent, and when he asked if McJenna knew, the paramedic called her. They could have let Trent go to her and tell her, but they took it on themselves to let a teenager know her father was hurt and going to the hospital.

I was too out of it at that point to make decisions about anything. Trent met me at the hospital and was surprised when Valentina showed up shortly after with McJenna, Bianca, and her younger daughter, Sam.

McJenna went crazy, crying hysterically and worrying that I was going to die. Trent had to talk her down and tell her I was going to be fine before she calmed down and listened to the doctors.

Trent told me she also said she would be homeless if I died, which was something we never talked about. She didn't know Trent would become her legal guardian if anything ever happened to me.

There were a lot of things I needed to talk to my kid about when I got out of the hospital, but for the night, all she needed to know was that I would be okay and that she still had to go to school for the second day of her sophomore year.

"Yeah, she needs to get some sleep. Take her out for ice cream. Make sure she knows you're there. I know it's a lot when you have George, but—"

"Don't fucking say that," Trent snarled. "J's mine, too. She's never a lot, and she's never less important than George. I think we could both use some ice cream tonight. Even though it's late."

I smiled. He was always the parent who wanted to keep her in line. I was the one who wanted to spoil J because I felt guilty she didn't have a mom. We balanced each other out most of the time.

"Thank you."

Trent stood and leaned over me, hugging me awkwardly in the hospital bed. "You scared the shit out of me today. Don't do that again. I don't want to lose you."

My throat thickened with emotion. I nodded. "I'm glad someone feels that way."

"Karissa will come around. She just needs time. You'll figure it out."

"We'll see."

"I'll wake J so she can say goodnight. Then we'll head out."

"Thanks."

Trent went to the bed next to me and gently shook my daughter. She stirred and stretched, then blinked her eyes open a minute later and sat bolt upright. She turned to look at me and relaxed.

"You're going to come home with me," Trent told her. "I wanted you to say goodnight to Dad."

"I don't want to go," McJenna said, her voice wobbling as much as her lip.

"I am good," I told her. "I feel good. They just want to keep me here because it's late and they want to make sure I'm stable on crutches before sending me home."

"You can't get up the stairs. How are you going to do that? And the shower? What about the bathroom?" McJenna's voice rose in pitch and volume with each question.

"Hey, come here," I told her, reaching out my hand. "Listen, I'm okay. I promise you. I'm sore, but that's normal. And yes, it will take some getting used to, but I'll figure it out. And I know you will help me. So will Trent and Finley."

"What about Karissa?" McJenna asked. "Why isn't she here? I thought you were dating?"

I ignored the pain slicing through my chest and forced a smile. "I don't know why she isn't here. But it doesn't matter. I'll be okay. You and I will be okay."

"I don't want to move again if you and Karissa break up. Please don't make me move again."

I shook my head. "I won't. I promise. We're staying here."

"Are you sure?"

"Yes. Now, go with Uncle Trent. He said he's going to get you some ice cream."

"Really?" McJenna asked with a smile.

I nodded. "That's what he said."

"Do I get to choose how big of an ice cream?" McJenna asked.

Trent groaned and threw his arm around her shoulders. "I think I'm in trouble."

McJenna laughed. "You might be." She came over and hugged me cautiously, then went back to Trent and let him lead her out of the room.

I listened to their voices as they walked down the hallway. When they were too far away for me to hear, I strained to hear something through the silence.

But nothing came. No one was there. I was truly completely alone.

Fucking hell. It sucked.

BEFORE THEY WOULD DISCHARGE ME, I had to prove I could use my crutches to get around. The doctor didn't want to approve me for work, but I assured him I had an assistant that would kick my ass if I didn't follow the orders he gave me to a T.

I still had to make it around the floor on crutches without help and without stopping, and I had to prove I could use the bathroom without help.

When I passed both tests, the doctor reluctantly signed off on my discharge. He made Trent promise to bring me back if I did anything that re-injured my leg.

Hospital policy meant I had to leave in a wheelchair. With my leg propped up, broken bones and all. I didn't need surgery to fix my leg, but I still broke both tibia and fibula, which meant a longer time to heal before I'd be back on my feet.

"Are you hungry?" Trent asked after he got me loaded into his vehicle. The backseat so I could stretch my leg on the seat. Like I was a child.

"I guess I could eat," I grumbled like the brat I was.

"Any opinion about where we go?"

"Someplace without stairs," I said. Considering I couldn't think of a place with stairs, I figured that went unsaid, but just in case, I wasn't looking to tackle stairs on day one.

Trent chuckled. "Got it. Hey, how are you going to get around at home?"

I shrugged. I'd been thinking about that all night and still didn't have an answer. I knew I could do stairs, but that many wouldn't be easy. Especially since the staircase was wide and I couldn't reach both sides to use the handrails going up and down. I could do it with one crutch and a handrail, but if the crutch slipped...

"I don't know."

"Maybe we can make a bedroom on the ground floor. Wall off part of the living room or something."

"I'll figure it out," I grumbled.

Trent looked at me in the rearview mirror but didn't comment.

I was being an ass, and I knew it, but I couldn't stop the frustrated feeling I had. After Trent and McJenna left last night, I sent Karissa a text and messaged her on the app. She didn't reply to either one. I was almost positive she saw them, but she ignored my messages.

I hated to admit it, but I sent her one before Trent arrived that morning, too. A text asking what I did wrong and why she was mad at me. I felt like a whiney shit asking her, but fucking hell, I wanted to talk to her. I was injured, and the one person I wanted to see was a ghost.

Trent parked in the lot next to Will Work For Burgers. He came around to open the door for me since I couldn't reach it with my leg propped up in the way. Trent grabbed my crutches and held them while I scooted across the bench seat and eased myself out of the car. I was going to be a miserable bastard by the time my leg healed and I could take care of myself again.

I followed Trent inside and sighed when I saw it was blissfully quiet. There were a few customers, but not many, and getting to a table was easy.

We sat and ordered, handing our menus to the server.

He was back a minute later with our drinks and a promise the food would be out soon.

"How are you feeling?" Trent asked. It seemed to be the only thing he knew how to ask anymore.

"Like shit. How was J's morning?"

Trent shrugged. "She's worried about you. She's also worried about Karissa and why she hasn't been around."

"It doesn't matter. Did J pack a lunch? Sometimes she pretends she did but doesn't."

"I know, dude. I've lived with her for her entire life."

"I know. I'm sorry. I wanted to be there for her to start her new school, and instead I was stuck in the hospital after her first day, and I missed her second day. I'm just feeling like a shitty father."

"Why?"

I sighed and looked up at him. "I wanted to get out of there early yesterday. I was hoping I'd have time to see Karissa before I needed to get J. I was moving that old piece of shit out of the way so the install of the new concession stand would be faster. I thought I could do it, but it got caught on the floor and just tipped. But it was stupid of me to try to do it, and it happened because I was trying to put my girlfriend above my kid."

Trent sighed heavily and shook his head. "It was an accident. It wasn't because you screwed up or some cosmic force showed you that you were being a crappy dad. You're allowed to want a life."

"I don't know if I am. J is finally happy. For years, I've been trying to do whatever I could to make sure she was happy, and she's finally there. She has friends here and people she likes spending time with, and all I've done since we got here is think about people other than her. Karissa and myself and work and I've done what I always said I wouldn't do and put my kid last."

"That's not what you're doing. You're teaching her that you can be a parent and be a person. You're showing her that she can be whatever she wants. Being a woman is harder. I see it with Finley all the damn time. She's working full time, and she's a mom. She's amazing at both, but it consumes her. She told me she has to be better at everything if she's going to succeed because there are always people waiting to tell her she's failing. Whether it's other parents who judge how she's raising our son or other business owners who think she's doing something she shouldn't be doing, it's tough. And it sucks because she's amazing. When J grows up, she's going to have the same pressure. Even if she doesn't have her own business, it'll be the same if she wants a family. Teach her now that she doesn't have to choose like you always did. Show her that you made your choice because you knew the right person was out there and you didn't have her in your life until now."

"She's not in my life. Karissa has made it clear she's not interested in continuing what we had going on."

"I still just don't believe that."

"All the unanswered texts I've sent her are pretty definitive proof."

"Nothing is proof until you talk to her."

"I don't know if that's a good idea. I might break down and beg her to give me another chance."

"Then we should go to her place next because I would love to see that."

I snorted and shook my head. "Not gonna happen. After lunch, I need to get to the theater and make sure things are getting done."

"Genevieve can handle the theater."

"Please, Trent. I need to stay busy. I can't sit around the house and hope everything is ready for next week. We open a week from today. I have to be here."

Trent ground his teeth together, but finally nodded. "Fine. But I'm staying with you so I can help with anything that needs to be done."

"Fine."

WE FINISHED OUR LUNCH, and Trent drove to the theater. On the outside, everything looked good. It was clean and quiet and looked ready to go. Inside was a slightly different story.

"What the hell happened?" I asked Genevieve when we walked in.

"Hey, boss. I didn't think you'd be here today."

"So you thought destroying the place would be no big deal?" I barked.

Genevieve stilled at my harsh words. She clasped her hands together and tilted her head. She smiled at me, one of those shit-eating smiles where the person wanted to feed you the shit. "I apologize for the mess. Unfortunately, it couldn't be avoided since the firefighters who moved the concession stand off of your broken leg weren't super careful with how they handled the floors. I have David's crew here replacing the damaged section and completing the installation they didn't get to yesterday due to the accident and not being allowed in on time."

Well, fuck. She was right. And she was right to be pissed at me for jumping on her. "I'm sorry. I should not have gotten upset with you. You're right. I was the asshole who fucked everything up. Are we going to be able to open on time?"

Genevieve still looked pissed. "Yes. We will. I'm doing everything in my power to make sure of it. The floor will be repaired and the concession stand installed today. We didn't have anything else on the agenda. I need to work on the community board, but I will take care of that next week instead of today. The screens are still on track to be delivered and installed on Tuesday. I'm doing my best."

"You're doing amazing, Genevieve," Trent said for me. "What Xavier meant to say was thank you for handling so much in his absence, and you will be receiving a bonus for all the extra work you've taken on. And another one for putting up with his stubborn, sullen ass while he's healing."

Genevieve flashed a genuine smile at Trent. "You're very kind, Mr. MacKellar, but that won't be necessary."

"Please, call me Trent, and yes, it will. Unless you're saying that because he's pissed you off so badly you're giving your notice."

"Fuck," I breathed. "Please don't quit, Genevieve. I'm in a shitty mood, and I'm taking it out on you, and I'm sorry. But please don't quit."

"I'm not quitting. I enjoy working here. And you're allowed to be in a shitty mood. I just...shit." She drew in a shaky breath and closed her eyes. She swallowed roughly, then wiped at the tears slipping from her eyes. "I'm sorry. You really scared me yesterday, and the hormones are making me more emotional than usual, and I feel a little crazy right now. Can I hug you?"

I was taken aback by her request but incredibly touched. I opened my arms and smiled when she hurried over to me, then stopped so she didn't knock me off my feet.

"Are you okay?" she asked.

I nodded. "I'll be okay. I'll be on crutches for at least three months, but I'll recover to do something stupid again."

"Don't scare me like that. Teddy almost had to tie me down to keep me from going to the hospital to see how you were."

"I'm sorry. I really didn't mean to upset you so much. I'm here. And I'm good. And I'll work on the attitude."

Genevieve snorted. "I'll believe that when I see it."

Trent snickered. "I like her. No wonder you worked so hard to keep her on."

I rolled my eyes at them. "I'm injured, you're not supposed to gang up on me."

"But it's so much fun," Genevieve said.

Trent laughed, and I shook my head.

"Thank you both for being here. It means more than you know."

"It's what family and friends do, man. We're not going anywhere. No matter how big of an ass you are."

Genevieve laughed and nodded. "What he said."

22

KARISSA

I HAD ZERO INTEREST IN GOING TO BOOK CLUB. I'D BEEN avoiding everyone for days. Finley called me every hour, but I ignored her calls. When she told me she was going to show up at the condo if I didn't reply so she knew I was alive, I sent her a text that simply said I was fine. Lies, but it got her to leave me alone. Sort of.

Finley was texting me updates on Xavier, letting me know the extent of his injuries, how he was feeling, when he was released from the hospital, everything. I hated it, but I also needed it.

I was paralyzed with fear. Hearing McJenna say he was in the hospital brought me right back to my mom dying. And then Eddie ending up in the hospital less than a week ago. I couldn't handle it. I couldn't lose someone else. I was already in love with him, but we were still separated. We were dating, not married. Not living together. Just dating. If I let him in all the way, if I meshed my life with his, and then something happened, I wouldn't survive it. I couldn't. So I had to back off.

Which brought me back to book club. Ending things

with Xavier meant creating stress for Finley and Trent. Xavier lived with them. He was Trent's best friend in the entire world. Without Xavier and I together, they would have to choose between us. We couldn't be there together. Maybe I couldn't be there at all.

I didn't want to lose my friends, but I knew it would be easier in the end. I'd already lost enough people to death. I wasn't strong enough to do it again.

But again, Finley threatened me. If I didn't show up for book club, she was moving book club to my condo. She was still on the lease so she still had a key, and she would totally do it, too. She would march everyone down the damn street and up the stairs and let them all into the condo and invade me.

I couldn't handle that, so I was on my way to book club. Maybe I could make an excuse and leave early. Or tell them Eddie needed something. Or just leave.

Finley was at the door when I arrived, like she was looking for me. She smiled and hugged me, ushering me inside before I had a chance to say I couldn't stay. "Laura made cake. You have to stay for a piece."

I groaned and admitted I couldn't turn down Laura's cake. It was too good. Which meant I was stuck. Maybe I could sit and sulk and no one would notice.

Ha! Not with my friends.

I'd been there less than five minutes before the questions started. "How's Xavier doing?" Melody asked.

"He's healing," Finley answered for me. "Resting and trying to figure out how to get around with crutches."

"What happened?" Blake asked. Again, she addressed me, but Finley answered.

"He was trying to move the old concession stand, and it tipped over on him. Broke both bones in his lower leg.

Neither were displaced so no surgery, but it's going to take at least three months for him to heal."

"Wow, really? Is he still working?" Sofia asked.

"Yep," Finley said. "He insisted. Trent took him there Thursday after he got out of the hospital, and he worked Friday, too. He plans to work all next week. The theater opens on Thursday."

"Huh. And why are you answering all these questions and Rissa's stuffing her face with cake and pretending she's not here?" Elise asked.

Finley looked at me with one brow raised, letting me decide what I wanted to tell our friends.

I chewed slowly and swallowed. I lowered my plate and wiped my lips, then looked around the room. "I haven't seen Xavier."

"Why not?"

"Did you break up?"

"What happened?"

They looked between Finley and me, waiting to see who would answer first. Finley just shrugged and stayed silent. Throwing me to the damn wolves.

"Karissa, what happened?" Melody asked gently.

I sighed. "I can't lose him."

"So you're pushing him away?" Blake asked.

"It's what you did with Ian," I countered.

"Yeah, and I was stupid. You're way smarter than I am," Blake said.

I shook my head. "No, I'm not. Especially not when it comes to this stuff. I don't know anything about what I'm doing."

"What would your mom say?" Elise asked softly.

"What?"

"What would Georgia say? That's what I ask myself

whenever I don't know what to do. She was always able to break it down to something simple. No matter what we were talking about, she had a way of making everything seem easy."

"This isn't easy," I said.

"Why not?" Elise challenged me. "You love him. He loves you. You don't want to lose him, but you're going to push him away to guarantee you lose him? That makes no sense. You should be holding tight to him so you can enjoy as many moments as you have with him. Just like Georgia did with Eddie. She married him before she died so she had a few months of happiness at the end. She didn't tell him to leave her and live his life."

Elise was right, but I wasn't my mother. I had never been as strong as her.

"I get it," Blake said. "When Ian and I got too close, I pushed back. I couldn't handle loving him, and I couldn't handle him loving me. I didn't want someone coming into my life and making it messy. But looking back, I hate that I missed out on more time with him. Because I was being crazy."

"I don't think I can do it. I don't think I can let someone else in. It hurts too much when they leave. When they die or decide they don't want me or whatever." I wrung my hands together and shook my head. They didn't get it. None of them had lost the one person in their life who understood them. And I'd done it twice. First with Xavier and then with my mom.

"Why do you think he's going to leave?" Finley asked.

"You did," I snapped.

Finley's eyes went wide.

I sighed. "I'm sorry. I shouldn't have said that."

"Obviously, it's how you feel, so you should have. I'm sorry you feel like I abandoned you," Finley said calmly.

"I want you to be happy. I want all of you to be happy. I don't begrudge any of you that."

"But you aren't willing to have it for yourself?" Trinity asked.

I shook my head and stood. "I just... I need to go. I can't be here right now. I'm sorry. I love you guys, but I need to go."

I hurried past them and ignored their protests. I pushed through the front door and turned toward town, knowing they'd expect me to go home. I passed O'Kelley's and went to Catherine Park, then kept walking.

It was quiet, peaceful. I needed the quiet so I could think. My condo no longer felt like mine because I only thought about Xavier when I was there. It used to be my happy place, restful and relaxing. Now, it overwhelmed me because he'd infiltrated it. He'd been in my bed and on my couch and in my kitchen. His smell hung around, like an invisible reminder of what I could have had.

Even my town reminded me of him. I looked across the water and saw MacKellar Estate looming large in the darkness, lit up like a beacon. I couldn't walk along the water without seeing it and wondering what he was doing. How he was doing.

My phone buzzed in my pocket, but I ignored it. I wasn't in the mood for more lectures and well wishes and concern. I needed to get out. Maybe take a break. A true vacation like Finley and I were supposed to take last year. The break we went on where we ended up at Trent's hotel.

I wandered around town for the better part of an hour, ignoring my phone the entire time. When the calls and texts finally stopped, I made my way back home, avoiding the streets my friends lived on so I wouldn't run into anyone.

I walked along the Riverwalk to get to my building, peeking into the foyer before I let myself in the back door and headed up the stairs. I worried someone would be there waiting for me, but the hallway was empty. Inside my condo was just how I'd left it, too. No Finley or anyone else waiting inside to ambush me.

After I washed my face and changed into pajamas, I sat on the couch and read through my texts. They were sweet and kind, but I couldn't deal with them. Not when I felt like a piece of me had been ripped from my body. Ever since I heard those words from McJenna, that Xavier was in the hospital, I felt like I was no longer whole. And I wasn't sure I ever would be again.

THE THEATER WAS OPENING in three days. I needed to finish the app. But I couldn't do it. I was stuck.

Every time I tried to open the project, I couldn't do it. I got up and paced my condo, staring at the computer like it was going to attack me.

I wasted half the day trying to convince myself to work on it while doing the exact opposite. I couldn't keep sitting there. I needed to get out.

It was a shitty day. Rain fell in sheets, dumping onto the sidewalks and making everything soggy and miserable. Of all the days for me to need to get outside and walk, this was the worst of them. My shoes were soaked within two minutes, and my rain jacket was more rain than jacket. Water resistant was clearly not good enough for the torrential downpour we were experiencing.

I ducked into O'Kelley's instead of going to Book Boyfriends Unlimited. I wasn't ready to face Finley yet, and I knew she'd try to get me to talk. Hudson was safer.

"You're getting my floor wet," Hudson growled when the door slammed behind me.

"It needs to be cleaned, anyway."

"Whatever. I clean this floor every day."

"Seriously?"

"Hell yes. It's gross not to. Do you know how many people spill beer?"

"Most of them," I said, taking a seat at the bar. "I need food."

"Drink, too? You drowning your sorrows?"

"I came here so I didn't get a lecture."

"Yeah, well, you're out of luck. But at least my lecture comes with food and a good drink."

I scowled at Hudson. He ignored me and mixed up something purple that had more than one kind of alcohol in it. When he set it in front of me and walked away without a word, I took a chance and sipped it.

"Holy shit," I groaned. I went back for another sip. It was good. Dangerous, but delicious.

I was halfway done with the drink when Hudson came back up front. He delivered food to the few customers at tables, then smirked at me. "How's the drink?"

"I hate that you knew I needed this."

He laughed at that. I still didn't know how he always knew what people needed to drink. He was like my mom in that way, predicting the behavior of others and giving them what they needed before they knew to ask for it.

"Want another one?"

"No. I need to get some work done this afternoon."

"You're not getting any work done. You're sulking and

feeling sorry for yourself because you're too chicken-shit to enjoy what's right in front of you."

"Are you talking about you? Because I don't think we'd work out."

He snickered and shook his head. "I'm talking about love."

I scowled again. "Why are you getting all philosophical on me?"

"Because I care about you, Rissa. I want to see you happy."

"I am happy. This purple drink makes me happy."

He set another one in front of me but didn't let go of it. "Xavier made you happier than the drink."

I snatched the glass from him and brought the straw to my lips. It was effective. I didn't know what he put in it, but between the copious amounts of alcohol and my lack of food, it was going straight to my head.

"Don't fall off the stool. I'm getting your food."

"I didn't order."

He rolled his eyes. "Do you really think I don't know what you like to eat? After all these years?"

He disappeared into the kitchen before I had a chance to ask him what he ordered for me. It didn't really matter because no matter what, I was going to like it. I hadn't had anything from O'Kelley's I didn't like.

I sipped my second drink slightly slower than the first and had a little more than half when Hudson deposited a grilled chicken sandwich and a side of cheese curds in front of me.

"So good," I murmured.

Hudson chuckled and gave me space to eat.

When I was almost finished with my lunch, Hudson leaned against the bar. "Why are you running from this?"

I looked up at him. We'd gotten closer over the last year since Finley got pregnant and Hudson blamed himself for not telling her who Trent was. He was a senior my freshman year of high school, so we didn't know each other until we were adults. I didn't know Hudson before Hillary, but I knew he was different. And I thought he'd understand.

"When Xavier and I were in college, I thought nothing could change things. I was convinced we were going to get married and live here and have a long life together. He chose not to do any of that. I hated him for destroying my plans. Maybe that's the wrong way to say it, but I thought my life was mapped out. I had my man, I knew what I wanted for a career, I knew where I was going to live. Like a three-legged stool. It was set. But he pulled that one leg out, and the whole thing felt off balance since. I love my job and living here, but without that third leg, it wasn't right."

Hudson nodded and crossed his arms over his chest, allowing me to continue.

"I did my best to create a life I could enjoy. I was happy enough. I found a way to create a third leg and balance on my own. Then my mom died, and it felt like that one piece got pulled out again. I was off balance once more. I was just starting to get my balance back when Xavier moved here."

"How does that mess up your balance? I thought he was part of it?"

"He was, but then he wasn't. And having him back wasn't the same. It was complicated. We tried to figure it out. We started to get to know each other. We were building things back up. When he got hurt, it felt like someone kicked the entire stool out from under me."

"I understand that part of it."

"So you understand why I can't go through that again?"

Hudson glared at me for a long moment. I thought he'd get it, but the longer he glared, the less sure I felt.

"My wife died. Talk about kicking the stool. She's not coming back. But if I had a chance to be with her all over again, knowing she would die, I would do it in a heartbeat."

"All that pain? Losing her all over again? Why?"

"Because I had her. Because life sucks when you're alone. Trust me, I know. And I think you do, too. Yeah, it hurt to lose her, and there are times when it still hurts, but I have her memories. I loved her the best way I could until she died. I hate that she's not here, but I will never regret the time we had together. And to be honest, I kind of hate you for having the chance to share your life with someone and not being willing to take it."

"Excuse me?"

"You should jump in with both feet. Be happy, Karissa. Don't hide behind your fears and what ifs. Go out there and live your life. You are never going to escape pain, but creating it now to save yourself from worse pain later means you'll wake up one day and be overwhelmed with regret that you didn't grab life by the balls and hold on for the damn ride."

"What about you?" I demanded.

"What about me?"

"Aren't you going to do that? I know you loved Hillary and no one can ever replace her, but why are you still single?"

"Hillary was my world. Losing her was a kind of pain I never want to experience again. But loving her was the best thing that ever happened to me. I'm single because I'm not sure I'll ever find something like that again. Someone who turns me inside out and upside down and makes it okay. Someone who demands everything I have to give and replaces it with everything inside of her. Someone who knows everything there is to know about me and loves all those dark corners of me, anyway."

"So, you're scared."

"Fuck, yes, I'm scared."

I chuckled.

"But you don't need to be scared. Xavier loves you, and you love him. You've already gotten past the hard part."

"What's the hard part?"

"Figuring out if you want to spend the rest of your life with someone. Once you know the answer to that question, the rest is easy."

"You think this is easy?"

Hudson grinned. "It's only not easy because you're not willing to admit to yourself that I'm right, you're wrong, and Xavier is it for you."

"But what if I lose him?"

"You're going to right now if you don't open your eyes and see that he's here for you."

"He is? Where?" I jumped and spun around.

Hudson laughed. "No more drinks for you. I didn't mean physically. He's here in town. He moved here. He wants you in his life. You're it for him. If he never left the hospital last week, if he died, how would you have felt?"

My heart squeezed painfully. I gasped. Tears sprang to my eyes.

"You have your answer, Rissa. Don't let him go. Hold on tight and love him for as many days as you're given the chance to."

I drew a deep breath and closed my eyes. Dammit. He was right. Which meant I had some major groveling to do.

23

XAVIER

FUCKING CRUTCHES. I HATED FUCKING CRUTCHES. IT'D BEEN A week, and I was losing my fucking mind.

"You need to sit down," Genevieve said, coming up behind me in her tap-tap-tap heels.

Fucking heels. She had two good legs. She could walk like a normal fucking person. Fuck.

"There's too much to do for tonight. I can't sit down."

Genevieve sighed and crossed her arms over her chest. Her belly was just barely starting to round out. Of course, I wasn't such an asshole I was going to tell her that. I knew better than to tell a pregnant woman she was showing, even though every man on the planet thought it was sexy.

"Sit your grumpy ass down now before I kick out your good leg." Genevieve scowled at me and pointed to the chair she brought into the lobby for me.

I grumbled and hobbled my injured ass to the chair. Fucking hell. I hated everything. I just wanted to disappear. But first, I had to make sure the theater was a massive fucking success so every damn time Karissa drove by she had no choice but to think of me. God knew she wasn't thinking of me any other time.

I dropped into the chair and glared at my assistant. If my brain was functioning properly, I would have admitted she was right, but my brain was a jumbled mess of hurt and anger and I didn't give a fucking shit if I got hurt again.

No, that wasn't true. I had lived without Karissa in my life. I didn't like it, but I'd been through it. Last time it was my choice, and this time was hers, but I would survive. And eventually I'd stop snapping at everyone around me and biting off their well-meaning heads for trying to help me.

Except Genevieve. She was done with my shitty attitude and had no problem telling me I was being an asshole.

"I'm going to fire you if you don't stop scowling at me," Genevieve said.

"You don't have the power."

"I'll call Mr. MacKellar in a heartbeat. Tell him he either needs to fire you or I quit. Who do you think he's going to choose?" She raised an eyebrow at me and dared me to answer.

She was right, of course. Trent wasn't putting up with me much, either.

The only one who seemed to want to spend any time around me was McJenna. She didn't go out with her friends after school. She came home on the bus every day and hurried upstairs to my room. She did her homework in my room since she knew I couldn't go up and down the stairs easily. She helped me get my dinner every night and sat next to me at the table, jumping up whenever I said I needed something.

I finally talked her into going to the movies with her friends. She wanted to just hang out with me and not see a movie, but I convinced her to join her friends. I was no fun to be around, anyway.

Genevieve worked while I sat in my chair and sulked. The screens had been delivered and installed on time, as promised. The tables and chairs were all set and ready. The restaurants we'd partnered with were prepared for the extra customers. Even the concession stand was perfect. The old one was trashed after it tried to kill me and failed.

Everything was ready to go except me.

I wanted to greet everyone when they came to the theater for opening night. To be at the door and help them figure out where they needed to go. Instead, I was limited to my chair, and Genevieve said she'd hurt me if I got up and tried to walk around on my crutches while the theater was full of people.

She was right, again, but that didn't mean I had to be happy about it.

Afternoon rolled into evening. Genevieve was nervous, pacing around the theater and triple checking that everything was perfect. She'd trained all the new staff we hired and was checking in with all of them. Many were teenagers, but some were college students and adults. Genevieve knew every single person by name and knew everything about their families. They were all talking and laughing, looking pulled together and ready in their MacKellar Theater uniforms.

"Is it time?" Genevieve asked me, checking the time on her phone.

"It is. I thought Teddy was going to be here."

"He is. He's outside. That's why I asked. He said there are people waiting on the sidewalk."

As much as that news made me happy, I was disappointed. I wanted to be out there. Talking to people and making them feel welcome. Not sitting in a chair and looking like the laziest manager on the planet.

"Let's let them in," I told Genevieve.

She turned to the rest of the employees and clapped her hands. "Okay, everyone, I'm going to open the door. Is everyone ready? I heard there's a crowd outside."

"Ready," they all said together.

Genevieve took a deep breath and squared her shoulders. She turned back to me with a smile that seeped into me and made me feel better about all of this. Mostly.

I stayed to the side while she opened the door. As much as I wanted to walk around, I couldn't risk it, but I did stand up. I kept myself out of the way as our first guests streamed inside and marveled at what we did to the theater.

"Wow, look at that!"

"Oh, this is new."

"That's so cool!"

I smiled at their excitement, trying to feel some of it myself. It was a good day, and even though I'd hoped to be spending it with Karissa, I knew we'd created something I was proud of.

The early showing was in the family theater, so the first groups were families and groups of friends with kids. The excitement carried them from the front door to the concession stand and into the theater. I heard the rumble of joy when they discovered the seating and chose their favorite seats, and again when food was delivered from the local restaurants and families settled in for the start of the movie with dinner and snacks.

We had a short lull between movies when the first one had started and guests for the second one hadn't yet arrived. It was during that time when Genevieve came to get me.

"We have a problem."

"What is it?"

"There's a food delivery here."

"Okay. And?"

"It's not a restaurant I know."

"What are you talking about?"

"It's from a place called Benny's Pizza."

My entire world stopped. "Did you say Benny's Pizza?"

Genevieve nodded. "Do you know it? I've never heard of it."

"It's not local," I said slowly. Benny's Pizza was Karissa's and my favorite place to get takeout in college. We ate from there at least once a week, sometimes more. We always ordered the same thing, so much that the place knew our order without us even asking for it. I hadn't had Benny's since college.

"They have an order. Said it was supposed to be delivered now. Can you come talk to them? Maybe you can figure out what went wrong."

I nodded and followed her, the tapping of her shoes and the thump of my crutches the only sounds in the back hallway. We didn't want restaurants to risk getting caught in the throngs of people out front so we had a delivery drop in the back for them.

Genevieve turned the corner ahead of me and said, "He's right behind me."

It took me a few more seconds to make it to where she was, and when I did, I stopped short at Karissa holding a pizza box and wearing a Benny's uniform.

"What are you doing here?"

She held up the box. "Pizza delivery."

"Is that why you haven't returned any of my calls or texts? You've been delivering pizza?"

"No. I haven't returned your call or texts because I'm a chickenshit and I'm terrified I'm going to lose you."

"You know that makes no sense, right?"

She breathed a laugh and nodded. "I know. I've been told that many times over the last week. I was scared. I'd already lost you once, and I lost my mom, who was my best friend, and Eddie was in the hospital, and I just lost my damn mind."

"Okay. And now?"

"And now, I'm hoping Benny's Pizza will help you to start to forgive me."

"You think that's all it's going to take?"

She shook her head. "I'm sure it's not. But it's a start."

"What else are you planning?" I was enjoying watching her squirm.

She nibbled on her lip. "I created an app for you."

"You did what?" I blurted.

"I know it's for the theater and not you personally, but I created it. And I'll order Benny's anytime you want. And I'll help McJenna with school or making friends. And I'll—"

"Shut up and kiss me?" I asked.

She stopped mid-sentence and looked up at me.

Genevieve, who was watching our entire exchange, squealed with happiness.

"You want me to kiss you?" Karissa asked.

"Fuck yes, I do. I love you."

She jumped at me, tipping me off balance. Thankfully, there was a wall behind me and I caught myself before things ended very, very badly.

"Oh, my God, I'm so sorry," Karissa backed away. Her eyes were wide with fear. She put her hands to her mouth, scanning me as tears brimmed.

"Get over here," I growled at her.

She took a tentative step, then another. When she was close enough that I could reach her, I grabbed her hand and yanked her against me, my back solid on the wall.

"I love you. And I love that you almost killed me trying to kiss me. Maybe we can save that for when I have two good legs?"

Tears slipped down her cheeks. "I never thought I'd hear you say that again."

"What? Two good legs?" I teased her.

She laughed and nodded. "Exactly." She slid her hands up my chest and wrapped them around my neck. "I love you. And I'm so sorry I got scared and tried to run from you."

"Good timing, since there was no way I was going to be able to catch you."

She laughed again and swatted my chest. "Don't joke. I was really scared when McJenna got that call. I didn't know what happened, and I thought I was going to lose you."

I shook my head. "Never again. I love you. I don't want to go anywhere unless it's with you."

She sighed happily. "I like the way that sounds."

"So, did you really bring Benny's Pizza here?"

She laughed and nodded. "I did. I thought it might make you happy. I heard you've been tough to deal with lately."

"You can say that again," Genevieve said.

"Hey, I was wounded and broken and hurt," I defended myself.

"Yeah, and I'm pregnant," Genevieve countered.

"You are?" Karissa asked her.

Genevieve smiled. "I am. Sixteen weeks."

"Congratulations. That's so exciting."

"Thank you. And thank you for giving him another chance. He might not have survived the night without it."

"I wasn't going to do anything like that," I argued.

Genevieve raised an eyebrow at me. "I was."

Karissa laughed out loud. Genevieve waved and walked back down the hall toward the front.

"Now what?" I asked Karissa.

"Now we eat dinner and watch a movie."

"I don't have tickets."

"Good thing I do. Genevieve held some for me."

"She was in on this?"

"Of course she was. I think it's the only reason she put up with you as long as she did. She said you were really miserable."

I nodded. "I was. I couldn't stand the thought of losing you again. If you hadn't done this, I would have had to figure out something to convince you to give me another chance."

"Oh, yeah? What would that have been?"

"Probably nothing as good. You were always the creative one."

"Wait until you see the app."

"Is app code for something because you totally made that sound dirty?"

She chuckled. "No, it's not code. I mean, it is code, but code code, not code... Oh, just forget it. You can have dirty time when you're healed."

"The doctor said I could resume all normal activities."

"All? What about walking and swimming and riding bikes?"

"You're a buzz-kill." I scowled at her.

"I love you too much to risk you getting hurt again. I can think of a few ways we can have some fun that won't injure you further."

"Oh, yeah? Like what?"

"Like you just lay back and I'll do all the work. We can

pretend we're getting to know each other again and be creative with our hands and mouths."

I groaned and licked the edge of her ear. "Can we get creative right now?"

She laughed, a husky, throaty sound. "Not right now. There will be others here soon with food. But later. And tomorrow. And every day for the rest of our lives."

"Are you...? Did you just ask me to marry you?"

She smiled. "Not officially, but I'm done trying to pretend I don't want you in my life for good. I don't know if you're there yet, but—"

"I am. Trust me, I am. I've been looking at houses and I could never decide on anything because I didn't know what would suit you."

"You're looking at houses?" she asked.

I nodded, realizing I missed a step. "I need to stand on my own two feet. Figuratively. Eventually, literally, but doctor's orders prevent that right now. I've relied on Trent for a long time, and now with Finley and George, I know it's time for me and McJenna to be on our own."

"Did he say that?"

I shook my head. "He's always told me we're his family. And I know that. But I also know J is going to college in a few years, and I think Trent and Finley might have more kids, and I don't want to be the weird pseudo-uncle who lives down the hall. I want my own place. Our own place, if you're open to it."

She grinned, and I swore it was the most beautiful thing I'd ever seen in my life. "I'm definitely open to it. We should start looking for a house."

"Really?"

"Yeah. I've been debating giving up my condo. It isn't the same without Fin there. You guys can move in with me if you want, but obviously the stairs are an issue right now. Maybe we can find something by the time you're back on two feet. Stand on your own in more than one way."

"As long as I get to stand on my own with you," I told her. I kissed her cheek as she laughed.

"As long as you're okay with that."

"Absolutely."

She lifted on her toes and kissed me, being careful not to lean too much weight on me. I hated that I couldn't wrap my arms around her and pull her close, but we'd figure it out.

A knock on the outside door had us pulling apart. We let in the delivery driver and thanked him for bringing over all the food.

"My pleasure. This is a great idea. I'm looking forward to coming here with my family this weekend."

"Excellent. Thanks for your support."

He nodded and left.

Karissa turned to me and said, "I'm so proud of you. You've really made this place something special again. And to involve the community and really bring people together is amazing."

"Thank you. I couldn't have done any of it without Genevieve, but I'm so happy to see it all turn out the way it did. And you were right all along. This is a perfect place for us to spend the rest of our lives."

She smirked. "It's about time you started listening to me."

Genevieve came back and picked up the food, using the food cart to take the orders to the front for guests. Karissa and I followed her after another minute and a few more kisses.

Trent talked the other guys who usually went to guys' night into coming to the opening night of the theater. When we walked into the lobby, they were all standing together, some with wives and girlfriends and some without. When they saw us, they all cheered.

"Finally figured things out, huh?" James asked.

"Yes, we did," Karissa answered for us.

"I'm so happy for you," Laura told her.

"Thanks. I didn't know all of you were coming tonight. Isn't this amazing?" Karissa hugged them all, one by one.

They all agreed and pointed things out to each other. It was everything I hoped it would be. A gathering place for locals, date night for couples, and an experience for families.

Seeing it all come together was worth the long hours and broken leg. Even more to be able to share it with Karissa and McJenna.

"Have you seen McJenna?" I asked.

Karissa pointed behind me, and I turned. J was just walking in with Bianca and two other girls. She spotted me and waved, leading her friends toward our group.

"I thought Genevieve said you were going to stay sitting down," J chastised.

"It's my fault," Karissa explained. "I needed to talk to him and got him out of his chair."

"What are you wearing?" McJenna asked. She looked at Karissa's outfit. "Wait, is that Benny's Pizza?"

"How do you know Benny's Pizza?"

"My dad talked about it all the time. Said it's the best pizza in the world. He talked about taking me there, but we haven't been yet. He said it was the most special place ever."

Karissa looked up at me and smiled. "It is. It's where we had our first kiss."

I shifted one crutch to the other side and hooked my arm around her shoulder. I kissed the top of her head.

"Does that mean you two are back together?" McJenna asked.

"We are. For good this time," Karissa said. "You okay with having a step-mom?"

McJenna's grin was as wide as Karissa's. "I think I'd really like that."

J hugged us both.

It took me seventeen years, but I finally had everything I'd ever wanted. I wasn't letting it go. Ever.

EPILOGUE
HUDSON

It'd been a long damn time since I stood up front at a wedding. Never thought I'd do it again. Finley was stunning, like a goddess, with her dark hair tied up in some complicated twist thing and pieces blowing in the breeze off the water. Of course, the most beautiful thing about her was the smile on her face. It was good seeing her so happy.

"I, Finley Jameson, take you, Trent MacKellar, to be my lawfully wedded husband, from this day forward. I vow to love and honor you, for better and worse, in rich and poor, in sickness and health till death do us part. I vow to be honest with you. To always lift you up. To share every part of me with you. To love our son and any more children we have. And to always make time for us."

Trent beamed at her words, his eyes glassy with unshed tears. Man, I remembered that feeling. Knowing I was linking my life to someone who fit every piece of who I was. Hillary never judged me. She never thought less of me. She supported me in everything I chose to do, and I was the same for her.

Seeing Finley and Trent, and so many other friends, do

the same reminded me that love never died, even when the person did. Hillary wasn't around, but my love for her was.

But I knew it was time to move on.

That scared the shit out of me, but after watching Finley risk her heart for Trent and seeing Karissa take a chance on love for Xavier, I had to admit I'd been hiding. I wouldn't let myself care about another woman because I thought it meant I was being unfaithful to Hillary. I'd slept with women since she died, but I'd never let it be more than sex.

Being alone sucked. I missed sharing my life with another person. I didn't have any idea who that person would be, but I was ready to find her.

The ceremony ended, and the wedding party went toward the house. I'd never get used to being at MacKellar Estate. The place was massive, and a little intimidating. But Finley was softening it up and making it look like her home.

"Thank you," Finley said, hugging me close.

"You're welcome. I'm just happy I didn't have to chase his ass down and beat him," I told her.

Finley laughed. Her relationship with Trent didn't have the easiest start, but it turned out damn well in the end.

George gurgled and squealed, my heart pinching tight when I turned and saw him in Anna's arms, reaching for his mom. Finley cooed and went to him, his face brightening when she spoke. Anna handed him over and smiled at them, congratulating Finley.

"I feel like I still asked you to work, and I'm sorry about that."

Anna waved her hand. "He's not work. I've missed having babies. Not that I want more, but he's fun to be around. For a little while."

The two of them laughed. I turned away, feeling creepy for intruding. I'd always wanted kids. Hillary and I were talking about trying when she died. That was one dream that kept tugging at me. One thing that made me consider dating before now. It wouldn't have been fair to the other woman, so I always gloved up and didn't get involved, but I'd always regretted not having kids.

"Another one down," Ian said, handing me a beer.

"Yep. She looks happy."

Ian nodded, watching his sister and his wife with Anna. Blake reached out and offered George his finger, which he promptly shoved into his mouth.

"You ready?" I asked.

Ian shook his head. "Not even a little. But we're getting in as much practice as we can with George."

"You two are going to be pretty damn good parents."

Ian looked at me, gratitude and overwhelming emotion choking him up. "Thanks," he whispered.

I clapped him on the back. "You have nothing to worry about. That's a lucky kid."

"I appreciate it. It's hard to believe we're going to be responsible for someone else's life."

I laughed. "Yeah, but you're ready."

He nodded. "I hope so."

"Finley looks happy," James said as he joined us. "You two didn't steal the show from her."

Ian and I chuckled. "Definitely not," I said.

James looked around the lawn at the people talking and laughing and eating the appetizers. "So, who's next?"

"Nico," I said. "He's ready to propose."

"Yeah?" Ian asked. "I was going to say Xavier. He's looking like a man ready to make it official."

"I think they're both ready," James said with a nod to Karissa and Xavier holding each other as close as his crutches would allow as they swayed to the music. "Colin might be my vote."

"You think she's going to say yes?" Ian asked.

James shrugged. "They've been living together for a while. I don't think Elise is going anywhere, and I have a feeling they're both ready. Then again, they could be married already."

"What do you mean?" I asked.

"I wouldn't put it past them to just go somewhere and get married and tell everyone later," James said. "Colin said they're planning a long weekend away next month. They might come home married."

"That's a really good point," Ian said.

"What about you? Throwing your hat into the ring?" James asked me.

I shrugged. "I've been thinking about it."

Ian and James stumbled backward. "What? No fucking way," Ian said.

"I just said thinking."

"Thinking about what?" Xavier asked. He and Karissa came up behind me without my noticing.

"Hudson said he's thinking about dating," Ian said.

"Good for you," Xavier said.

"Anyone I know?" Karissa asked with a smirk.

"Yeah, who is she? We'll make sure you don't scare her off with your brooding and angry glares," James said.

I flipped him off.

James and Ian laughed, the assholes.

"Fuck you both."

"Ignore them. I'm happy for you," Karissa said.

"I never thought I'd see the day Hudson Grant was ready to date. Hey, you need to get on Karissa's app," James said.

"Then you can impress a woman without her knowing who you are."

"That's how you got Trinity," I told him.

"Exactly. She wouldn't have gone out with me if she knew who I was. Karissa's a genius."

"Yeah, she is," Xavier agreed, hugging her to his side.

I smiled at them. "Yeah, maybe."

"Or you can just pick up someone at O'Kelley's." Ian shrugged.

I shook my head. "Not mixing business with pleasure. That's too complicated."

"App it is," James said.

"Hey, what did you two get Finley and Trent? It's huge," I asked Xavier and Karissa.

They shared a look and smiled. "It's a map of the stars on the night they met," Xavier said.

"Whoa, really?" Ian asked.

Karissa nodded. "He wanted something special for them. Finley loves looking up at the stars and said she thinks them being together was written in the stars, like a romance novel. Xavier found this company online that will print a map of the night sky on any date from any location."

"That's really cool. Definitely unique and totally them," Ian said.

"Fin's going to love it," I added.

"We hope so," Karissa said.

We all talked a few more minutes. James got called away by Trinity, and Ian asked Xavier about the theater. I took advantage and excused myself to grab another drink, needing a minute to clear my head before being pulled back in to wedding duties. I hadn't planned to tell anyone I was thinking about dating, and I definitely didn't plan to have them tell me I only had two options. I didn't like the idea of a dating app, but meeting a woman who came into my bar didn't feel right either.

I tossed my beer bottle into the recycling bin and went to the appetizer table. Just as I reached for the last spaghetti and meatball cup, someone else did, too, our hands bumping when I grabbed it just before they did.

I looked up, intent on apologizing and offering it to the other person, even though I already touched it and was clearly there first, when I saw who it was.

"Of course you were trying to steal the last one," Anna snarled at me.

"So were you," I countered.

"Yeah, for my kid. It's the only thing Matty is willing to eat right now."

I looked behind her to where Matty was sitting with his brother, Joey. Joey was a busboy at O'Kelley's, and Matty did his homework at the bar after school until Anna and Joey finished work. I liked Anna's boys. Not such a big fan of her.

"It looks like he's eating pretty well," I said as Matty shoved a slice of bread in his mouth.

Anna looked over her shoulder and tensed. She turned back to me with a scowl. "Fine. It's for me. Are you happy?"

I shrugged. "Blissfully."

She stared at the spaghetti and meatball cup on my plate, and I swore to God my cock hardened at the look of desire in her eyes. Fucking hell.

"Here," I mumbled. "You can have it." I dumped it on her plate and turned and walked away.

No. Hell fucking no. Of all the damn women, she was not going to be the one I was attracted to. She drove me up the fucking wall.

Maybe you should nail her against one.

Fuck! Nope. I was not going to start thinking of Anna and that *fuck me* look in her eyes. Her son was my employee. She worked for one of my closest friends. And she made me fucking nuts.

Not happening. Not now. Not ever. No matter how much my cock wanted to demand otherwise.

THANK **you** for reading Karissa and Xavier's story! Did you catch all the mentions of them through the other books? She even saw him in His Curvy Craving (at the hotel), but she convinced herself she was wrong. And of course, he was the one that got away. I loved bringing them back together!

The next book in the series is Hudson and Anna's book. The only thing they have in common is how much they irritate each other. Maybe one other thing, but neither of them is willing to admit that. They have no choice but to coexist since her son works for him, but that doesn't mean they have to like each other. They just have to tolerate each other. Between kisses and touches and fights that are oh, so fun to make up after. Start His Curvy Fantasy today!

WANT MORE from Karissa and Xavier? They're buying a house and subscribers get to move in with them! Sign up now to read their bonus epilogue!

AFTER SELF-DOUBTS and embarrassment make her think she needs to change her appearance, curvy girl Sam goes the one place she vowed never to go. A gym. Instead of hating every second, the sexy owner shows her there's not a thing she needs to change to be beautiful in his eyes. Pick up your copy of Fat & Fine now!

ABOUT THE AUTHOR

USA TODAY Bestselling Author Mary E Thompson spent most of her childhood wishing she had a few less curves. She hid in the pages of books because her favorite characters never cared what size her clothes were. Now, neither does Mary, and she writes stories that celebrate women like her. Real women who have curves, chase dreams, and find love, because we should all be happy, no matter our dress size.

Mary spends her non-writing time with her husband and two kids, watching too much TV, cheering for her hometown football team (Go Bills!), and hiding chocolate from her family.

Visit https://MaryEThompson.com/ to sign up for Mary's newsletter, **Romancing the Curves**. Subscribers get free ebooks and other fun stuff, like exclusive, members only content and giveaways, plus are the first to know about new releases and sales!